THE
LEGACY

THE
LEGACY

A THORNTON MYSTERY

C.L. TOLBERT

LEVEL
BEST BOOKS

To all of my supportive friends, readers, and writers. My gang. You know who you are. With much love.

Praise for The Legacy

"Tolbert delivers another beautifully crafted and compelling Emma Thornton Mystery. I couldn't put it down. *The Legacy* delivers the evocative writing, gripping plot, and memorable characters that make her Emma Thornton Mysteries such a great read. Driven by a compelling protagonist determined to find legal justice for the marginalized even if it means putting her own life in danger, *The Legacy* will stay with you long after you reach the last page."—Ellen Byron/ Maria DiRico, Agatha and Lefty Award Winner, *USA Today* Bestseller

"Fearless, relentless, compassionate, and driven by an unyielding sense of justice, law professor Emma Thornton battles mounting evidence in a race to save a mentally ill young man from a presumption of guilt in the gruesome murders of his parents."—Roger Johns, a Georgia Author of the Year and author of the Wallace Hartman Mysteries

"Fearless Law Professor Emma Thompson returns to defend a young man with schizophrenia accused of murdering his mother. Faced with a second murder, an unscrupulous prosecutor, a family with mental health issues, a pusher of pain meds, and a Gitanes-smoking stalker, Emma finds her marriage in jeopardy and her life on the line. Author C. L. Tolbert proves the Big Easy has never been easy, especially for a fighter like Emma whom I would follow anywhere."—Valerie J. Brooks, award-winning author of the Angeline Porter Trilogy

"Unwavering in her conviction, law professor Emma Thornton must navigate a labyrinth of lies and deception to arrive at the truth and vindicate a disturbed young man wrongly accused of murder. Not only a suspenseful story, *The Legacy* represents the triumph of the human spirit to persevere in the face of seemingly insurmountable odds."—Lawrence Kelter, International bestselling author of the Stephanie Chalice Mystery Series

"Memorable and haunting, this absorbing mystery is all the more chilling because it edges close to reality. *The Legacy* features law professor Emma Thornton, an attorney with a cool exterior and a heart that beats for lost causes and lost souls. This time, Emma puts herself in harm's way as she fights to prove her 21-year-old client innocent of his mother's murder. Author C.L. Tolbert delivers a masterful narrative of the way our legal system can fail people with special needs and the lengths one woman will go to find justice. *The Legacy* will have you turning pages well into the night."—Mally Becker, Agatha Award-nominated author of *The Counterfeit Wife*

Chapter One

March 19, 1997

Sally Wilcox wiped her hands on the dishcloth and folded it neatly before placing it on the kitchen counter. It had been a long day at the shop. Two funerals down, and they had already started preparing for a weekend wedding. She loved working with flowers, but the job triggered her sciatica. She could hardly stand by the end of the day. She was glad to be home.

She hobbled to the TV room and sat down on the couch, the pain in her body immediately eased by the down-filled cushions. She bumped into the table next to the couch and knocked over her favorite photograph of her kids, Jeremy and Becky. She placed the frame back on the table and stared at it for several seconds. She missed them so much.

The cat curled into a circle on Sally's lap as she propped her legs up on a fluffy ottoman. Comforted by her surroundings, she dozed off almost immediately.

Three hours later, she was awakened by the sound of static from her television. Channel Six had signed off for the night, and refrains from the national anthem had just begun. An American flag fluttered across the television screen. It was just past midnight. She moved the cat from her lap, turned off the television and all the downstairs lights, and began making her way up the stairs toward her bedroom.

She stopped when she heard something that sounded like a restrained step. The cat's ears twitched in the direction of the noise. Could someone, a stealthy burglar or worse, be creeping around the house? She almost laughed out loud, amused by her own foolishness. She was such a worrier. Of course, it had to be Charlie the parrot ruffling his feathers. She couldn't remember if she draped the cloth over his seven-foot-tall cage.

Still, she waited and listened, not moving for several seconds. Then she froze as she heard a thump. She glanced out of a nearby window and could see trees blowing in the wind. Thinking that a branch must have bumped against the roof, she stood on the stairs for a few more seconds. Just to be sure. Hearing nothing, and convinced everything was okay, she continued up the stairs. Six a.m. came early.

In her bedroom, she changed into her favorite nightgown, the silk one that felt like butter on her skin, cleaned her face, and flossed and brushed her teeth. No matter how exhausted she was, she always completed her nightly routine. Her mother had insisted on it when she was young and still at home, pointing to an aunt's ravaged face as an example of what could happen if she didn't comply. The practice had become her only indulgence.

The cat had already curled up on top of the coverlet when Sally pulled back the sheets. Then she heard another sound. A muffled bump.

She grabbed a robe and stepped into the upstairs hallway. The staircase and the light switch were only a few feet from her bedroom door. She found the switch and flipped the toggle up, but nothing happened.

"What the..." she whispered.

The cat rubbed up against Sally's legs, and she jumped.

Then she heard another sound and glanced out of the window at the end of the hall. The trees were still blowing fiercely. She tip-toed down the first two steps and peered over the banister, unable to see anything in the dark. She continued down the staircase, stopping every few feet to listen.

When she was at the second step from the bottom, she stopped.

"Hello? Is anyone there?" Her voice quavered.

"Youuu Whooo!" Charlie was awake now.

She still couldn't see anything but didn't hear any unexpected sounds in the house. She shook her head, embarrassed by her overreaction. The sounds had to be from Charlie, or maybe it was the wind in the trees. But just to be safe, she fled to the kitchen, feeling her way in the dark, and grabbed a knife from the block on the counter. Then she stopped, making certain all was well, and turned to retrace her steps back to her bedroom.

Seconds later, she felt a sharp punch in her stomach. She swung the knife she clutched in her hand, wildly stabbing into space until she felt resistance. She'd nicked something. She turned, and raised her hand, stabbing blindly, then felt another punch in her stomach and one in her chest. Then another and another. A warm liquid flowed down her legs. Her hand flew to a spot on her chest where she felt piercing pain and she realized that blood was pouring from her body. Something had happened. Someone was in front of her. She could sense their presence. Hear their breathing. She'd been stabbed.

Her robe was wet, and blood was beginning to drip onto the floor. She felt dizzy. Her legs were on fire, as if a thousand needles had been jabbed into her shins. Then her legs started to shake. She collapsed, falling to the ground on her knees.

Then a swift rush of air. She wasn't certain what it was until it was too late. She saw the knife this time. And a dark figure.

Charlie squawked, "Youu whooo!"

The last thing she felt was a crushing pain in her chest. Her heart, already broken, had stopped.

Chapter Two

As she was on her way to lunch, Assistant Professor Emma Thornton dropped by the law clinic's administrative office at St. Stanislaus Law School to check her mail. She rarely received anything of any significance unless it was her monthly direct deposit slip, or the law school's weekly calendar. But she checked her mailbox every day out of habit.

Today, Emma's cubby had a yellow sticky note placed on top of her name.

Call Katherine Green, Legal Aid

Emma grabbed the note and walked back to her office. Lunch could wait until she spoke to Katherine. It must be important. She never called.

Emma had met Katherine Green a few years ago at the continuing legal education class Katherine taught every year. The course was for lawyers who were interested in *pro bono* work for kids with mental illness or other special needs. Emma had been a special education teacher before she became an attorney and was interested, but needed a refresher on some of the newer laws.

Katherine's voice, when she answered the phone, was lower and more somber than usual, betraying her concern.

"There's a special matter I'd like you to consider taking on. Jeremy Wilcox, one of my clients, has been arrested." She paused for a moment and sighed. "For killing his mother. The officer I spoke to said it was a pretty gruesome scene. I can't represent him because Legal Aid only handles civil matters. I don't want the judge to randomly assign a Public Defender to him. He needs a good attorney, but selfishly, I'd like his attorney to be someone I could work with, too. Someone I know and trust."

"Thanks for thinking of me. I'm flattered." Emma paused. "What evidence did the police have on Jeremy?"

"There was no weapon at the scene of the crime, but there was a lot of blood and bloody prints from the toe of a tennis shoe. The police say the prints matched a pair of Jeremy's Converse All Stars. I have the preliminary homicide report to give you. I can fax it. Also, the police found an old tennis ball at the scene. Jeremy had developed an unusual attachment to a grubby old tennis ball that he's carried with him wherever he goes for a couple of years. He never lets it out of his sight."

"That could have been planted."

"Yeah. I agree. But his fingerprints were also at the scene. It doesn't look good for him."

"What about the shoes? Was there blood on Jeremy's shoes?"

"I don't know if they've done testing on the shoes. I haven't seen any of that, yet."

"I'm guessing since you're involved, Jeremy has special needs?"

"Yep. He's twenty-one now. When he was seventeen, he was diagnosed with paranoid schizophrenia. He has sporadic hallucinations. He'll carry on conversations with people who aren't there.

"Just so you know, he can be volatile, especially if he doesn't take his medication. Sometimes he lashes out when he gets upset. His outbursts could be related to his occasional use of opiates." She shrugged. "And he drinks too much sometimes, too. I think the opiates problem started when he raided his dad's bathroom cabinet. But, usually, he's a quiet and mild-mannered young man."

Emma jotted down notes.

"I don't think Jeremy would do something like this. And he's not much of a planner. I think the crime was premeditated, and I suspect he's been set up. But I don't have any facts to back that up." Katherine paused. "From what I understand, you're great at developing the underlying facts of a case."

"Your flattery is showing, friend. But that's okay. I'd love to help if I can. But why do you think the murder was premeditated?"

"The fuse to the downstairs lights was switched off before Mrs. Wilcox was attacked. Someone knew where the fuse box was. Or maybe that's not such a hard thing to figure out. But I think Jeremy is more reactive, or impulsive. I can't see him plotting out a murder, especially his mother's murder."

"You mentioned something about outbursts. How often do they happen?"

"I don't know, really. I don't spend long stretches of time with him, but usually, he seems just fine. He's a smart guy, so he can carry out an intelligent conversation. But then there are days when you notice that his face is expressionless. He won't laugh at jokes, or he might not notice people when they walk into the room. On another day, he might giggle at inappropriate times.

"I was with him in an elevator once while he carried on a complete conversation with someone. But, besides me, he was the only person there. And he wasn't talking to me." Katherine sighed. "Also, he wanders. His medical records are full of notes about him absconding from the hospital. Sometimes he'll wander away from his home, or he'll sneak out of Charity Hospital. He's always found by the police, or by his dad. A few times, he was found uptown. That's miles away from his home on the West Bank. And that means he's crossed a bridge. On foot. Probably the Huey P. Long. So, he's lucky to be alive.

"He's never threatened me, but I understand from others that a few people at Charity Hospital, patients and staff, have felt intimidated by him."

"How often does this happen?"

"I couldn't tell you. I think the episodes come on gradually, so you don't really realize it at first. But I'd feel better if you'd talk to his doctor about that. I'd say he had a couple, maybe more, episodes a year. But I don't really know. I've had clients with schizophrenia before, and some of them were rigid planners. You know, planning every moment of their routine. I think that might help them cope, or maintain their schedule of meds. But not Jeremy. At least not from what I've seen. I've never heard him talk about his future, and I don't think he makes plans with others. But, again, I don't see him that often.

"I do have a suggestion when you're working with him. If I suspect Jeremy of sliding into another episode, I try to ground him. It was something suggested to me by one of his ED teachers."

"What do you mean by grounding?"

"You just remind him where he is. Try to reorient him. If he seems to drift away, or if he won't make eye contact, say something like, 'Jeremy, it's Friday, March…' whatever, you know. Give him the date. Tell him where he is, like, 'you are at Orleans Parish Central Lockup.' And then tell him what you want to do. 'I'm your attorney, and I want to talk to you.'"

Emma nodded. "That's great information. Thanks. But even though you say Jeremy isn't a 'planner,' he was arrested for a murder that was planned, pre-meditated. And when there's pre-meditation, it might be hard to prove that the killer didn't know the difference between right and wrong at the time of the killing, which is the core of the insanity defense." Emma paused. "But I'm getting ahead of myself. I haven't even met Jeremy."

"True. But what you're saying is right. Especially if the murderer made an effort to cover his tracks. Also, the bloody shoe print was of the tip of one shoe only, so it looks like the killer was trying to avoid the pools of blood."

"I'm not sure what I think about it since there are so many unanswered questions, but I'd be willing to meet Jeremy. Does he have a guardian?"

"Yes, his father."

"Then I'd need his okay before I could represent him."

"I can arrange a meeting with the two of you."

Emma pursed her lips. "I can't imagine how awful the dad must be feeling. His wife dead. His son charged with the murder."

Katherine cleared her throat. "I'm not so sure about that. Mrs. Wilcox lived by herself. She left the family home years ago."

Emma's eyes widened. "Why did she leave?"

"I've never known."

"How did you get involved with them?"

"I'm Jeremy's educational advocate. I've been involved with him and his family since he was about nine. His mother finally gave up and pulled him out of school when he was ten to homeschool him. He went back to school after she left, and it's been a struggle to find appropriate placement for him.

The school system never met his needs until this recent placement in an emotional disorder, ED, classroom. And then this happened."

"He was still in school?"

"Yes, until his arrest. Since he has a disability, he can stay in school through his twenty-first year."

"So, he was doing better in the smaller classroom."

"I think he was okay, but he was better off when he was homeschooled. Mrs. Wilcox pulled him out of school because she lost faith in the system, but homeschooling takes dedication, especially if you've got a problem kid."

"What would make a mother who was so involved in her child's life walk away from that child and the entire family?"

Katherine inhaled sharply. "We can talk more candidly about this if Jeremy's dad okays your representation. But I can tell you that Jeremy's records reflect that there was a lot of tension between the doctors and Mrs. Wilcox. She didn't think Jeremy needed some of the medication the doctors had prescribed. And Jeremy fought taking it. Mr. Wilcox didn't seem to have an opinion about Jeremy's care one way or the other." Emma could hear pages rustling. "I suspect he didn't understand what was going on with Jeremy. I know Mrs. Wilcox tried to establish some rules and boundaries, but the dad didn't believe they were necessary."

"And now the dad has all the responsibility," Emma said.

"That's right. Did I tell you there's a sister? I don't know anything about her." Katherine made a "tsk" sound. "After Mrs. Wilcox left, Jeremy continued to have flares of aggressive behavior and temper tantrums. I'm not sure what triggered them. Occasionally, he and his father would even get into fights."

"Fights?"

"Yes. And every time that happened, Mr. Wilcox would have Jeremy hospitalized."

"When you say hospital, are you referring to Charity?"

"Yes, after he was seventeen, his dad would call 911 and have the ambulance drop him off at the psych ward at Charity, on the third floor."

"Poor guy."

"Yeah. Before she left, Mrs. Wilcox had always handled everything. All medical and mental health appointments. Everything. I'm guessing it's been all a little too much for Mr. Wilcox."

"Do you know if Jeremy had a special tutor when he was home-schooled?"

"In addition to his mom? I don't know. I do know he's very good at math and that he loves to draw. His mom knew drawing calmed him down, so she got him to draw his feelings. She worked really hard with him. Mrs. Wilcox always believed in Jeremy and in his intelligence and thought she could do a better job with him than his teachers did. It's sad that she left them."

"Okay. I'll meet with the dad, see if he'll give me his permission to represent Jeremy."

"I'd really appreciate it, Emma."

"And I'll meet with Jeremy, too."

"Sure. But don't expect much when you meet him. He isn't always responsive. Especially after sudden changes. He'd been doing a little better lately, but now, I expect he'll be confused and withdrawn. Especially since he's confined."

"I have one more question. You said Jeremy occasionally wandered as far as the uptown area. That's got to be at least ten miles from the West Bank. Maybe more. Where did his mother live?"

"She lived on Arabella Street."

"And that's uptown. Do you think Jeremy was trying to find his mother's house when he walked there?"

"I have no idea. But it's certainly a possibility."

Chapter Three

Emma glanced at her sleeping husband and stumbled out of bed. She liked the morning hours before everyone else in the house woke up. She flipped on the switch of the coffee maker and walked out to the balcony, where she peered out over the railings. People were already milling about on St. Charles. She never wanted to live anywhere else. But they'd outgrown their apartment. The boys were growing up. They each needed their own space.

She nearly tripped over boxes piled by the front door. She hated moving. She hated messes, and she hated spending money. But she didn't have a choice.

The dogs, Maddie and Lulu, woke up and ticked their way downstairs from the twin's bedroom. They were bewildered by the boxes and the mess too. Emma put their leashes on and walked them out the front door for their morning constitutional.

The smell of coffee had filled the stairway by the time she walked back up the stairs with the dogs. She unhooked their leashes and poured herself a cup, then pulled the flour off of the shelf. She'd promised Billy and Bobby, her twin fourteen-year-old–soon to be fifteen-year-old-twins, that she'd make them pancakes, their favorite breakfast, as a celebration for some recent good grades.

They all loved pancakes. Ren too. Ren, her husband of only five months, had the weekend off, which was rare since he was a detective with the New Orleans Police Department. The boys were in between sports seasons, so there were no practices or games that day, which made Emma the only person with plans. She was beginning to regret her decision to see Jeremy Wilcox's father, Todd, at his home in Bridge City. She'd much prefer staying home this lazy day. For one thing, if she didn't have plans, she'd be free to snuggle back in bed with Ren. That was on her list of favorite things to do on the weekends, especially when the boys hadn't awakened.

She was enjoying being married. Ren was a stabilizing influence in her life and in the boys'. He was eternally loving—patient where she was impetuous, thoughtful where she was rash. They were complete opposites, except for one thing. They both put family first. She knew how unusual it was that Ren put her boys before himself, even though he wasn't their father. But he did. Day after day, month after month. He was consistent and true. She was lucky, and she knew it.

She began measuring out ingredients. Making pancakes was therapeutic for her. Meting out the flour, baking powder, salt, and sugar and swirling it together with the other ingredients was kinetic and soothing. Her pancakes were more like little crepes, thin, light, and always perfectly round. She knew the aromas floating from the kitchen would soon tempt everyone out of their beds.

As she flipped the last pancake, she heard the thunderous sound of the boys descending the spiral staircase from the third floor. Ren wasn't far behind.

"What's cooking?" Bobby skidded into the kitchen. Billy scuffed into the kitchen a few seconds later.

"You two put the silverware and plates on the table." She watched as they slammed drawers and opened cabinets for the next few minutes, then laid out the tableware. Everything was akimbo, but that was fine. She smiled as they filled glasses with orange juice. Bobby's blonde hair was jutting out at odd angles, and Billy was still groggy, his eyes only half open. But they managed to pull everything together.

Ren shuffled into the kitchen and grabbed a cup of coffee, leaning over to plant a kiss on Emma's cheek.

"Want to grab some napkins?" Emma nodded toward the napkin holder on the counter.

11

Ren grabbed a handful of paper towels as they all sat down.

"Well, good morning, everyone," Emma passed the brimming plate to Ren. "There's plenty."

The boys mumbled a greeting.

"What do you guys have on your agenda? I've got a meeting this afternoon."

"On a Saturday?" Ren frowned. "A new case?"

Emma nodded. "I don't have it yet. But I'm running by to see if I can get the retainer signed. I shouldn't be long. Do you have anything planned?"

"Nah. You're good. I don't really know what I'm doing today. What about you guys?"

Billy and Bobby shook their heads. "Nope. We don't have any plans," Bobby said. "So, how about some driving practice?" Both boys turned their heads, looking at Ren and then back to Emma with hope that bordered desperation. Every chance they had, Billy and Bobby lassoed Ren into letting them drive his truck in the local A&P grocery store parking lot. Ren sat in the passenger's seat, patiently instructing while the boys drove in and out, around and around the lot. The twins never tired of it, and Ren remained calm when they drove over curbs, or came too close to oncoming cars. Emma was not. Embarrassed by her full-throated scream when Bobby nearly ran over a pedestrian, she'd vowed never to get in the car with the twins, at least until they had their licenses. And that would be a while. Louisiana didn't give permits to anyone under sixteen. Still, she didn't think it hurt to let them practice. Just as long as Ren handled it.

"That's entirely up to Ren." Emma stood up and started clearing the table. She motioned for the boys to help.

"We might be able to work in a little practice today." Ren smiled as Billy and Bobby punched the air in celebration. "Don't worry about us. We're good."

Ren followed Emma to their bedroom while the boys finished cleaning up the breakfast clutter. She opened her closet door and pulled out a pair of slacks and a shirt.

"Think your client's guilty in this one?"

"For one thing, I have no client yet. As for his guilt? I have no clue."

* * *

Emma did all she could to avoid the Huey P. Long Bridge. It crossed the Mississippi River and connected New Orleans to Bridge City on the West Bank. She'd only crossed the bridge a handful of times since she moved to the city. It scared her. Built in 1932, it was one hundred and fifty feet tall, rusty, and too narrow for wider modern trucks. It shook each time a car passed over the span. Railroad tracks were set in between the two traffic lanes, and when a train crossed over the bridge, the entire structure shuddered as if hit by an earthquake.

Emma saw an extra-wide truck get stuck at the bridge's highest point once—her worst nightmare coming to life before her eyes. She'd found every chance she could to avoid the bridge since then and feared it would collapse someday, throwing drivers and pedestrians into the river. To fight the ravages of time, the state employed a painting company full-time just to keep the rust under control. It took them a year to cover the bridge with silver paint, and once finished, the painters would turn around and start the process all over again.

Even though she did all she could to avoid the Huey P. Long Bridge, she was required to attend several hearings on the West Bank over the years and had become familiar with the handful of good restaurants close to the courthouse. One of them, Lucy's, was famous for baked macaroni and cheese with a marinara sauce they called "red gravy." Dinners there were served cafeteria style, with lunch lines and trays, and lunch ladies lined up in a row serving up the comfort food from steaming stainless steel pans. She had a feeling she'd find her way back there after her meeting with Mr. Wilcox. A reward for her trip and a great take-out dinner for Ren and the boys.

The West Bank is what New Orleanians refer to as "across the river." Since the river twisted and turned, the communities 'across the river' weren't always on the west bank, but over the years, the name stuck. West Bank communities like Chalmette, Bridge City, and Algiers Point, to name a few, were the industrialized, working-class neighborhoods of New Orleans. Home to several refineries, manufacturing plants, and shipyards, the West

Bank was a vital part of the New Orleans economic structure. A suburb of its illustrious sister city, it was sometimes called the 'Queens' of New Orleans, an affordable but proud community.

Chapter Four

Emma rapped on the door of a quaint West Bank bungalow. The sturdy house, constructed of cypress a hundred years ago, was in need of a paint job. Sections of several boards were bare, the silver-colored wood entirely exposed. But because it was cypress, it wouldn't rot, even if it was never painted again. And it was too hard for termites to bother with. An old bungalow, especially one made of cypress, was a treasure. She knocked on the frame of the screen door.

The door creaked open and a man scowled behind the screen. He wasn't that much taller than she was and was slightly built. Although he didn't seem athletic, he looked like the sort of man who'd be fast on his feet if he had to be. His hair was close cropped. Nothing about him seemed unnecessary. Even his smile was an infrequent, rare flash.

"You must be Ms. Thornton. Come on in." He held the screen door open for her.

The room was cave-like, dark. Colorless drapes were drawn and the television was on in the living room. A drab brown sofa was placed in front of the TV with two matching chairs, each flanking the coffee table. A tiny trashcan sitting next to the sofa caught beer cans and pop tops.

Emma noticed that the floors were constructed from barge boards – thick, wide, rough-hewn lumber taken from the bottom of barges that carried cargo down the Mississippi River during the nineteenth century. Since the barges couldn't be sent back up the river, they were disassembled in New Orleans and sold as cheap lumber. The boards made beautiful flooring, but Mr. Wilcox's were dusty and littered with piles of dirty clothes. Emma

15

could hear the washing machine churning in the background.

Mr. Wilcox motioned with his hand toward the couch. Emma sat down and pulled her notebook and a retainer agreement from her briefcase. He sat down in the chair opposite Emma.

"I'm so sorry about the death of your ex-wife, Mr. Wilcox. It must have been shocking. I know you must be upset, especially by Jeremy's arrest."

Mr. Wilcox blinked slowly and nodded. He seemed to be chewing something.

"You can call me Todd." He paused and sighed. "Yeah. It's been a shock." He pointed to a pack of gum in his pocket. "Tryin' to quit smokin'. Want some?"

Emma shook her head. "No. I did the same thing when I quit. I know it's tough." Even though he was dressed in khakis and a work shirt, Todd reminded her of a cowboy from a cigarette commercial. He was quiet, terse, a man of few words. Except for an occasional squint, his face was expressionless. She could tell he was uncomfortable.

Todd nodded, his facial expression still unchanged. "And Sally was my wife, not ex-wife."

"Oh. I'm sorry. I thought she moved away from the family several years ago."

He nodded. "That's right. But we never got around to gettin' a divorce." He sniffed.

Emma scribbled down Todd's statement. She pressed her lips together. Sally and Todd were an unusual pair. Most couples would divorce if one partner walked out.

"I'm here today because Katherine Green asked me if I might be interested in taking Jeremy's case. I think you'd asked her to show up for the bail hearing. Did she explain that her agency, Legal Aid, doesn't take on criminal cases?"

"Yeah. But she got me appointed guardian of Jeremy, too."

"Right. So, before I could represent Jeremy, I'd need your approval." She placed a retainer agreement on the coffee table. Todd pulled it closer, but only glanced at the document.

"Is there a charge?"

"No. I might run the case through my clinic, though. I have a law clinic at St. Stanislaus law school that serves the homeless. But you wouldn't be charged for anything."

Todd picked up the agreement and read it, pointing to each line as he read. He nodded. "Yeah. This looks okay. But Jeremy isn't homeless."

"He'll be approved for the clinic. You don't need to worry about that."

Emma handed Todd a pen, and he carefully scratched out his signature.

"I'd like a copy of the guardianship papers if you have them. I need to see what your appointment was based on."

"It was based on the fact that I'm Jeremy's father."

Emma noticed a flush appearing on his cheeks. He was quick to anger. "I'm sure you're correct. But since Jeremy's an adult, the guardianship was probably based on Jeremy's diagnosis, or his doctor's opinion that he wasn't competent to care for himself. That's why I wanted to see the papers. I'll need a copy, too."

Todd frowned. "I don't think those doctors were right when they diagnosed Jeremy with schizophrenia, but I'll admit that he don't do so good around other people. He thinks people are pickin' on him when they're not. Even me. We've gotten into a couple of tussles. He might smoke pot sometimes or pop pills so he don't get so bothered. He drinks too much sometimes, and when he does, he usually pops off at the mouth. I don't tolerate that." He crossed his arms across his chest and shrugged. "But I don't have no problem getting those papers for you. I'll get them before you leave."

"Okay, I have a couple more housekeeping issues before we talk about Jeremy."

She laid out two medical release forms in front of Todd. "I'll need Jeremy's psychiatric records, including the records from his admissions to the hospital." She moved one page toward Todd, who glanced over the form and signed it.

"I've also got a release that would allow me to take a look at Sally's medical and psychiatric records. You can sign it since you were married at the time of her death."

Todd raised his eyebrows. "Sally's?"

"Yes. You're her next of kin, unless she appointed someone else. Her records could be important."

He shrugged. "Okay." He scribbled his signature at the bottom of the form.

"What makes you think Jeremy smokes pot, or drinks beer, and that he might do other drugs?"

"I can tell when he's high. I'd say he smokes pot a few times a week. And I think he might take painkillers, too, 'cause I had some, and now they're almost gone. And I only took a couple. Jeremy's a lot more-quick tempered than he used to be, and sometimes his eyes are red. That's one of the reasons I keep his disability money. I don't want him buying pot."

Emma nodded as she took notes, interested to hear what he had to say about keeping Jeremy's money. But this was a man who got into fistfights with his mentally ill son. Todd was fractious and difficult to work with. She didn't think he was mature enough to parent anyone, but especially not a disabled child.

"Have you ever seen him smoke pot or take painkillers?"

"No. But one time, I talked to his doctor at Charity about it. He said he'd talk to Jeremy. But I never heard anything else about it." He looked out of the window at a passing car.

Todd seemed disconnected from everything—his conversation with Emma, his relationship with Sally and their children, Jeremy's illness, absolutely everything in his life, except his anger. He was very connected to his anger.

"If it isn't too difficult for you, I'd like to go over what you recall about the day of your wife's death and about Jeremy's relationship with his mother. I'd also like to know about your other children."

Todd dropped his chin once. Emma assumed that was an okay.

"Where was Jeremy on the day of the murder? Was he at your house, or was he at the hospital?"

"He was here."

"Do you know what time Jeremy went to sleep that night?"

Todd shook his head. "I really don't know anything about what Jeremy did that night. I don't see how going through all of this is going to help with anything."

"It could. I'd like you to try to answer everything, to the best of your ability. If you don't know the answer to something, that's fine."

"Okay. I always went to bed before Jeremy. Usually around nine. Jeremy takes his medicine at night, and that makes him sleepy. If he took it that night, he'd have gone to bed by about ten o'clock. And he usually sleeps 'til morning." He shrugged. "But if he skipped his meds, like he does sometimes, he could have stayed up late, or even all night. I've had to go look for him a couple of times."

"You don't supervise him when he takes his medicine?"

"No. He's twenty-one. He has to learn some responsibility." Todd leaned back on the couch.

Emma scribbled in her notebook as Todd spoke. She couldn't imagine how a mother could leave a child, but leaving a child with a man like Todd was unthinkable. Especially a child with problems like Jeremy's.

"But he skips his medicine sometimes, doesn't he? I heard you two have even gotten into fights when he's off his medication. Is that true?"

"You shouldn't be makin' a big deal out of that. But I guess the answer is yes, a few times. I always have him picked up and taken to Charity when that happens. I'm not going to put up with that stuff from him."

Emma sighed, hoping Todd didn't notice her frustration. He was either incapable of understanding Jeremy's diagnosis, or he didn't care. Emma suspected the latter.

"Did you hear the door open, or see Jeremy leave the house the night Sally was killed?"

"No. But that don't mean he didn't leave. I'm a sound sleeper. Always have been." His facial expression was still unchanged.

"Was he there, in his room the next morning, when you left to go to work?"

"Yeah, I checked up on him. He was awake, but he was in his room."

"Were you with Jeremy when the police arrested him?"

"Yeah."

"Did you tell them about his diagnosis?"

He nodded. "I told them he had some mental problems. But I got the feeling they knew that already."

"Did they speak directly to Jeremy?"

"Yeah. They asked me if it was okay, and then they asked him a bunch of questions. Mostly they wanted to know what you wanted to know – what was he doing the night his mother was killed. But his medicine kind of slows him down. When he spoke to the cops, he didn't really remember where he was or what he did that night."

"Did the cops take any evidence with them when they spoke to Jeremy? Shoes, or anything else?"

"Yeah. They took his Converse All Stars. They were looking at the toe of one of the shoes."

"Did you see anything on the shoes? Anything on the soles or the tip of the shoes?"

He shook his head. "Nah. They looked clean to me."

"Anything else?"

"They showed him an old tennis ball and asked him if it was his. He grabbed it and shoved it in his pocket. He was always carrying an old tennis ball, like it was his good luck charm. He thought the ball they showed him was his."

"Did it look like the one he carried?"

"I guess. It was pretty scuffed up, and his was too."

"How often did Jeremy and his mother see each other during this past year?"

"I don't know. Not too much. Sally didn't have no regular schedule for seeing him." He hesitated. "They never told me nothing about it really."

"How did he get over to his mom's to see her?"

"I don't know. His driver's license is suspended, but he can take buses. He prefers walking, though. He walks most places."

"You never drove him to see his mom?"

"No. I never did."

The more Emma listened to Todd, the more she understood why Sally

20

would want to get away from him. He had no compassion, no empathy. It was if he was empty. Soulless.

"I understand that Jeremy was about twelve when Sally left the family home. How was he after she left?"

"He was real upset. So was Becky."

"Becky is Jeremy's sister?"

"Yeah. Younger, by two years." He paused. "I think Jeremy blamed himself for his mom's leaving."

"Why would he do that?"

"Because he always caused a lot of problems. Acted out a lot. He yelled at her and at other people, too. He'd been doing that since he was about ten."

"He had a temper?"

"It wasn't just a bad temper. Sometimes he'd explode. You know, really lose control. Before Sally took him out of public school, he'd grab anything close by and throw it right at someone, or he'd start chasing kids down the block or down the hallway at school. The smallest thing would set him off. It scared Becky.

"That's when Sally pulled him out of school and started teaching him at home. She said he seemed a lot better there. Calmer. Sally said he could concentrate more on his work without other kids around. But he still had problems."

"What sort of problems?"

"Things would set him off. Like not being able to work math problems—easy ones—stuff he could do when he was little. And he'd stay awake all night sometimes. Sally said she'd catch him up in his room in the middle of the night. And he didn't want to take baths anymore. I didn't think that was so bad. Kids don't like baths, but Sally worried about that. She took him to a therapist."

"How did that go?"

"She said the guy talked to her more than he talked to Jeremy. Then Sally started seeing him too."

"Do you remember if the doctor gave Jeremy a diagnosis at that time?"

"When he was ten? I don't know. I think he said something like he was showing signs of having problems. Like depression or something." He touched his temple. "But the thing that got to Sally is that the doctor said it was her fault. That really upset her."

"Her fault? Why?"

"I don't know. I never was too clear about that. Something about her being too protective, maybe? And I kind of agree with that."

"I see. Do you have that doctor's name?"

"Nah." He hung his head for a moment. "Maybe Rayford? That might be it."

"Did Jeremy continue to go to the therapist?"

"Maybe for a little while. Then Sally stopped taking him. She didn't think it helped."

"How old was Jeremy when Sally stopped taking him to the therapist?"

"I think it was about the time she left. He was twelve then. She said she didn't want to hurt Jeremy, or Rebecca, and she didn't think she should be in their lives anymore." He shook his head. "But that wasn't right. Sally would lose her temper sometimes, but I think the doctor was off base. It was real bad around here when she left."

"But you never took Jeremy to the therapist, is that right?"

"Yeah." He nodded. "Except for when I called 911 and had him picked up." He paused. "But it still ain't too good at our house. Jeremy had always been close to his mom, kind of a momma's boy. He liked to read books. Stay inside. But after she left, he wouldn't come out of his room for days. Even for dinner."

"Did Sally explain what she meant when she said that she had to leave before she hurt Jeremy and Rebecca?"

"No. I didn't understand that. This whole thing's been a surprise to all of us. I never thought she'd do something like this." He shook his head. "All I know is I got home from the refinery one morning, and she wasn't there. The kids were with a neighbor, Mrs. Delacroix. Ethyl."

"Did Mrs. Delacroix know why Sally left?"

"No. She didn't know nothing about what Sally was doin'. Said Sally just wanted her to watch them a little."

"Is Ethyl still living next door?"

"Yeah. She's still there. Old, but she gets around."

"Sally didn't talk to you before she left, or tell you anything about how she felt?"

"Not really. But we didn't get much time to talk. I worked the night shift, which messed up the time we had together. My shift was from ten o'clock at night until six o'clock the next morning. I got home when everyone else was waking up, and I was so tired I always went straight to bed. At that time of the morning, she was getting the kids up, and fixing them breakfast. So, we never talked. I slept all day, then woke up around six o'clock in the evening for dinner. The only time we had to talk was right before I left for work, but usually, at that time, she was getting the kids' dinner and then getting them to bed. It went on like that for years. But I always thought we'd stick together, for the kids if nothin' else."

"After she left, did Jeremy go back to school?"

Todd nodded. "Yeah. He did. He's been in a special class."

"And Becky goes to the same school?"

"She does. But she don't live with us."

"Why not?"

"After her mom left, a friend's family invited her to live with them. The Shepherds. I couldn't take care of the girl and Jeremy. It was just too much."

Poor Becky. Emma's heart ached for her.

"Do you know why Sally didn't take Rebecca with her?"

Todd shook his head. "Just what I said before. We never talked much, really."

"Have the Shepherds had problems with Rebecca?"

"If they have, they haven't told me about it."

"I don't mean to be rude, but is there a reason why Sally and you didn't divorce?"

He leaned over, elbows propped on his knees, and stared at the floor for a few seconds.

"I don't know." He shrugged. "Gettin' a divorce costs a lot of money. Sally's dad left her some money when he died, and she paid off this house. She did that so Jeremy would always have a place to live. It was easier to stay married, but separated. She had her place. And Jeremy and I have this one."

Emma raised her eyebrows as she took notes. She understood why Sally would want to make certain that Jeremy always had a place to live. But Jeremy needed much more than a house. In fact, paying off the house seemed a little short-sighted. Wouldn't Jeremy still need a caregiver? And what about Becky? Wouldn't she resent her mother for pouring all of her time and now all of her money into the care of Jeremy?

Emma glanced up from her notes. "Do you know anyone who would have wanted Sally dead?"

Todd shook his head. "She might not have been very popular around here for leaving her kids, but I don't know anyone, including anyone in her family, who'd want her dead."

Emma watched Todd's face as he answered her last question. It was empty. His eyes, still expressionless.

One fact stood out in the midst of everything Todd had said that day. He and Sally were still married, and Todd stood to benefit from Sally's death.

"After Sally paid off the house, do you know if she still had any of her father's money left?"

Todd sat back in his chair, squinting at Emma. "I don't know why you're asking somethin' like that. I don't think it's none of your business."

"I'm representing your son for the murder of your wife. Everything about Sally and the family, including finances are relevant, Mr. Wilcox."

He sighed. "I think she had a little. Maybe a couple hundred thousand."

Emma left Todd's house that afternoon feeling as if she could breathe easier. She'd made progress. Todd had a motive for murder, after all. And unless Becky was unusually altruistic, she did too.

Chapter Five

Emma unwrapped the tin foil which covered the top of the baked macaroni and cheese, then unwrapped the marinara sauce and breathed in deeply. It smelled like heaven to her. She popped the macaroni in the oven to keep warm and poured the sauce in a small pan to keep it simmering on top of the stove. She started washing lettuce to prepare a salad. The guys would love this. She was certain none of them had been to Lucy's, and she didn't know of any other place that offered such a combination of foods.

She expected Ren, Billy, and Bobby to walk in the door any moment, Ren exhausted and the boys excited from a day of driving lessons. The boys would spend all their time at the A&P parking lot driving in circles if they could. Driving was a rite of passage, but she'd never seen anyone as keen to drive as the twins.

She heard car doors slam outside. Then footsteps tromping up the stairs. Keys rattled, and the front door flew open.

"What's that smell? Pizza?" Bobby ran into the kitchen, his face flushed with excitement, his blonde hair ruffled from driving with the windows down.

"It's better than pizza. Lots better." Emma beamed.

Bobby opened the oven. Billy was right behind him. "Mac and cheese?" Bobby rolled his eyes at Billy.

"You put this on top." Emma lifted the lid of the small pot containing the marinara sauce.

"Ewww. Gross." Bobby grabbed his stomach.

"It's good. Real good. You need to try it, at least. You might like it."

"No way." Bobby shook his head.

"I will," Billy said, his face solemn. He scooped up a tiny portion into a small bowl and ladled marinara on top. He took a bite.

"Not bad. I think I like it. I could eat this for dinner."

"Not me. Unless you leave off the red sauce." Bobby wrinkled up his nose.

"Okay, well, it's this or nothing tonight. Unless you can find some leftovers in the fridge. And you're on your own there. Like my mom used to say, 'I'm not a short-order cook.'"

Ren walked into the kitchen. "Did I just hear you quoting your mom?"

Emma tried not to smile. "It applied to the situation perfectly."

"There's a life lesson in there somewhere."

"Okay, okay. Boys, please set the table for dinner. I'll be back after I change clothes."

Bobby and Billy grabbed flat wear and plates from the kitchen and brought them, clattering and clanging into the dining room, where they sat them out on the table.

Emma and Ren left the boys to their job. In the bedroom, she sat on the bed and kicked off her shoes.

"I got that new case today."

"Good for you. Will you run it through the clinic?"

"Probably. I'll have to speak to the Dean. The client isn't really homeless, but he runs away a lot. He ends up at Charity sometimes for acting out, and he runs away from there, too. It sounds like he runs away every chance he gets."

"So, he's occasionally homeless."

Emma shrugged.

"And by hospital, do you mean Charity, third floor?"

"Yes." She glanced at Ren, nodding. "The psychiatric wing."

"And this is the guy accused of killing his mother?" Ren untied his shoes and took them off. He leaned back against the headboard.

"That's right. The mom lived about ten miles away from the kid's house. That's a lot of walking, especially at night. But some evidence that points to him was found at the scene."

"How do you feel about the case?" Ren reached out and grabbed her hand.

"I'm not sure. I haven't started my investigation yet, and I haven't read the preliminary reports. But I'm afraid I'm not going to do a good job in this case. There are so many things I don't know."

"Like what?" Ren turned on his side, facing Emma.

"Well, for one thing, I'm not sure where he is, physically, in the jail. Do they have a psych floor at the Orleans Parish jail? A special place for prisoners with known psychiatric problems?"

"They do, but that doesn't mean he's there. You should ask. Prisoners with mental health issues can get lost in the shuffle."

"Right. He shouldn't share a regular cell with another inmate. That could blow up pretty fast." Emma paused. "You're sure the case hasn't been assigned to you?"

"I'm certain."

"Have you ever had a case with a mentally ill defendant?"

"No. Sounds like it complicates things."

Emma nodded.

"But if he's mentally ill, you've got a perfect defense to the crime, right?" Ren studied Emma's face.

"It's not that simple. If the court finds that he could distinguish right from wrong at the time of the murder, he'll be prosecuted." She sighed. "And I don't know the answer to that right now."

"How can you even begin to figure it out?"

"I don't have much information yet, but there are a few facts that suggest an effort was made to be clandestine that night."

Ren squinted. "Interesting. So, the murderer must have known that what he was doing was wrong."

"Right. Remember Jeffrey Dahmer? The guy who cannibalized his victims? His lawyers tried to plead the insanity defense at his trial. He'd been diagnosed with borderline personality disorder as well as schizotypal personality disorder. But because he developed plans for the murders, had some self-control, and hid his victims' bodies, he showed he was aware that what he was doing was wrong. The courts found him criminally responsible for those murders."

"Guess I hadn't thought about that before."

Emma nodded. "If the jury finds that there's any evidence that my new client planned his mother's murder, they could easily find that he's competent and criminally responsible too, no matter what his diagnosis is. Just like Dahmer."

"When are you going to meet your new client?"

"I don't have class Monday morning. I thought I'd run by the jail then."

Chapter Six

Monday morning, Emma stopped by the criminal court building and filed a motion to enroll as counsel of record. The jail, where she was meeting Jeremy, was right around the corner.

Very few places in the city of New Orleans had the power to negatively affect her mood, but the jail was one of them. There were so many hopeless cases behind its walls; so many people there had been lost for years because of foolish mistakes or flawed evidence.

She faced the front of the ten-story, poured concrete building, and squared her shoulders. It looked like a giant bunker, but she wasn't intimidated, even though she didn't know what to expect. Not from Jeremy, or the prison administration, or even the police reports. She'd represented dozens of mentally ill clients at the law clinic, but this case was different. Matricide was different.

Emma placed her purse and cell phone on the conveyor belt for inspection and walked through the X-ray machine. Deputies nodded her through the line. She approached an officer sitting behind a large desk in front of the elevator and showed him her bar card.

"I have an appointment to see Jeremy Wilcox. But I don't know what floor he's on."

The officer looked at his directory.

"He's on the second floor. You can go on up. Just identify yourself and show them your bar card when you get there."

"Is the second floor the area designated for inmates with mental illnesses?"

The officer shook his head. "No. Psych floor's on three."

"Who would I need to speak to about getting my client moved there?"

"You'd have to speak to the Sheriff. He's the one who runs the jail for the Parish. Or maybe you could call the judge assigned to your case. But I don't know anything else about that."

Emma nodded and clenched her teeth, her jaw muscles tightening. How could this have happened? Todd told them about Jeremy's diagnosis when he was arrested. She was certain Katherine had at the bail hearing. But she didn't know if anyone explained to the judge that Jeremy didn't do well in social situations and that sharing a cell with another inmate was a bad idea. Especially if that inmate teased him or picked at him. She sighed. She had a feeling Jeremy wasn't going to do well in jail and made a mental note to call the Sheriff about moving him.

Emma took the elevator to the second floor and followed a guard to an isolated room. It was small, no more than about ten feet square. Although intended for privileged conversations between attorneys and their clients, the room was open, surrounded by bars instead of walls. One small metal table stood in the center of the room with two metal folding chairs.

Emma could see down the hall and, within seconds, caught sight of a tall, thin young man with dark hair approaching, followed closely by a guard. She could hear the sound of shuffling feet and clanking chains. The young man's head was down; he was mumbling. His wrists and ankles were chained. He scuffled, then paused every few feet, muttering to himself. When he stopped walking, his chatter continued. The officer prodded him forward with his flashlight, then motioned for him to stop so he could unlock his handcuffs, and ankle chains.

Jeremy entered the small room where Emma sat waiting, and stopped again, still keeping his head down. He didn't look well. Purple shadows encircled his eyes. His skin was pallid; his lips were tightly drawn against his teeth. He was so thin his shoulder blades protruded from his shirt.

Emma felt so badly for him. Even though he was twenty-one, he looked much younger, not much older than her boys. His world was collapsing, and it was obvious that he didn't know why. His face was pinched, desperate. Keeping his head down, he glanced furtively around the small cell.

The officer announced, 'Jeremy Wilcox,' and gestured toward the other chair in the room.

Emma stood. "Please have a seat here, Jeremy."

He hesitated. The guard prodded him again, and Jeremy spun around, glaring. The guard moved his hand to the taser on his belt. Jeremy turned back around and shuffled toward the chair. When he looked up, Emma could see that he had a bruise on his cheek.

Emma lowered her voice and leaned in. "My name is Emma Thornton. I'm your lawyer. I'm here to help you and to talk to you about why you're here."

He shrugged.

"Where you can, please use spoken words."

Jeremy stared at Emma. His gaze was unsettling. Emma took a deep breath in and counted to three. She was nervous, unsure of the questions she'd prepared. He was so young and so vulnerable. When she was planning her session with Jeremy, she considered not asking him about his mother's death. She was afraid she'd upset him and only make things worse. But she decided to proceed. Although her main goal was to establish a baseline of trust with him, she also needed to see what he remembered about the night Sally was killed and what he remembered about his arrest. But it was a big risk to take.

"How did you get that bruise on your cheek?"

Jeremy shrugged. "I don't remember."

"Do you know why you're here?" She spoke softly.

"They think I've done something. Something bad." He squinted his eyes as he spoke and crossed his arms. His voice was deeper than Emma thought it would be.

"Do you know what the police officers think you did?"

He shrugged. "I don't know. They talked to me about my mom. I remember that. But I was upset. I don't remember much."

"Do you remember them telling you that your mother had died?"

His face froze. His hands began to shake.

"They think you may have hurt your mother, so I need to ask you some

31

questions about the night she died."

He slammed his hand down on the table, stood up, and began pacing the room, back and forth across the small space, breathing heavily. The guard spun around, his hand on his taser again.

Emma froze, immobilized by a rush of adrenaline. Then she held her hand up. "It's okay." She waved her hand toward Jeremy. "Why don't you come sit down again. We can talk better if you're sitting down."

He stopped pacing, then shuffled back to his seat. Emma nearly collapsed with relief.

"Have you been taking your medicine since you've been here at the jail?"

"Medicine?" Jeremy shook his head.

"Yes, pills. Have you been taking your pills since you've been here?"

"No. I don't have any pills."

Emma sighed, her breath shaky. Her heart pounding. No wonder he was confused. "Can you understand that the police believe you hurt your mother badly and that she died?"

Jeremy's chest began to heave.

"My mom is dead?"

"Yes, Jeremy. And I'm here to help you. I represent you. You said you remembered talking to the police. Do you remember anything about what they said to you?"

He shook his head. His face was flushed. "No. Except they wanted to know where I was sometime last week. I told them I couldn't remember."

"Do you remember now? That was five nights ago. March 19."

Jeremy leaned his head back and squinted. Then he leaned over and put his head in his hands, and shook his head. "March 19? I don't know. I don't remember March 19."

Emma nodded as she took notes.

"My mom is dead?"

"She is, Jeremy. I'm so sorry."

He shoved his chair back and ran to the bars at the side of the room and began shaking them and banging his head, screaming heart-wrenching, full-throated screams. "Mom! Mom!" His head started bleeding almost immediately. Emma, horrified, ran to his side. This was her fault. She shouldn't have mentioned his mother at this first meeting. It was too much for him.

She tried to make eye contact with Jeremy again, but couldn't. "I'm so sorry, Jeremy. I didn't mean to upset you."

The guard turned and ran toward Jeremy, calling for help.

When Emma saw the guard check his taser, she stepped forward and yelled, "No!"

But the guard grabbed Jeremy's left arm, pulling it behind his back, and quickly clamped hand cuffs on that wrist. Jeremy swung around and punched the guard with his other fist, then tried to pull away. By that time, another guard, responding to the call for help, came barreling around the corner and grabbed Jeremy as he lunged for the door.

Emma screamed, 'Stop!' as the second guard pulled out his taser. But it was too late. Jeremy's attempted run ended with 50,000 volts of electricity. Emma stared as his body twitched. For a moment, she was afraid she was going to throw up. Unable to speak for a moment, she felt tears well in her eyes. But she blinked them away and cleared her throat.

"Get a medic, now." She grabbed her notebook and hastily wrote down both of the guards' names.

* * *

Emma climbed into her car and rested her head on the back of the seat. *Holy shit.* She took a deep breath. She could still see Jeremy sprawled across the cell floor, twitching from the electricity moving through his body. She'd never be able to forget it or forgive herself. She closed her eyes. Her blunder could have cost Jeremy his life.

After she was certain that Jeremy had stabilized, she called Sheriff Neely. She wasn't surprised that he wasn't available, but she left a message that should scare him, or at least cause him some concern. His office was clearly negligent when they placed Jeremy on a floor with the general prison population. Any harm which came to Jeremy would be on their hands.

Before she left, she stopped by the medical office at the jail and informed them of Jeremy's circumstances and need for daily medication. Todd had promised to drop off his medicine.

Still, the afternoon had been a disaster, and it was her fault. Jeremy was unmedicated and in the middle of an episode. She should have known that he wasn't able to respond to questions. Especially to questions about his mother and her death. Jeremy needed an advocate who cared about more than his defense. He needed a lawyer who could anticipate what he would need. That is what Katherine Green had expected of her, but she failed. She failed badly.

She leaned her head on her steering wheel. Poor, poor Jeremy. She had so much to learn.

Chapter Seven

Emma pulled up to a modern townhouse on Prytania, the address Todd had given her for the office of Dr. Douglas Rayford. She'd called the day before to set up an appointment, but discovered that he'd retired. So, she scheduled a time to speak to the man who had taken over his practice instead. Dr. James Washington. She hoped the records were still accessible.

The townhouse didn't seem to belong on Prytania Street. Lined with some of the most elegant Victorian and Georgian homes and gardens in New Orleans, Prytania was one of her favorite streets in the city. Except for the commercial, medical office section.

Dr. Washington's office was located only a few feet from Tabor Medical Center, one of the highest-rated hospitals in the city. The intersection next to the hospital entrance was a blur of activity, with doctors and nurses crossing the street holding to-go lunches in one hand while they checked their beepers with the other. Ambulances flew down the street at odd intervals all day and night, creating a frenetic energy that was unusual in uptown New Orleans.

The interior of the office was cold, indifferent. The paint on the walls was chipped and dingy. The chairs, which were lined up in a row along the back wall, looked hard and uncomfortable, as if someone didn't want the patients or anyone else to get too comfortable. The front desk window slid open.

"Name?"

"Emma Thornton. I have a 1:00 appointment to see Dr. Washington. I also have a couple of releases for medical records I need the doctor to review."

Emma handed the clerk the releases. "One is for Jeremy Wilcox's records. He was a patient of Dr. Rayford's. I also have a release for his mother's records. Her name was Sally Wilcox. She was a patient of Dr. Rayford's, too."

"I don't know which records are here and which ones are off-site. But I'll check. I remember both patients." The female voice was coming from a tiny woman dressed in scrubs. Why scrubs in a psychologist's office? "And I'll let Dr. Washington know you're here."

Emma sat back down, only to be called immediately by a tall young man dressed in slim gray slacks and a blue button-down. His shirt sleeves were rolled up.

"I'm Dr. Washington. Come on back."

He escorted her to a comfortable-looking back office furnished with a dark leather couch and chair. College diplomas hung on the wall, and the shelves were lined with books. Oddly, there was nothing personal on the walls or shelves, not family photos, artwork, or decoration.

"When did you take over Dr. Rayford's practice?"

"I guess I've been here about three months. I'd just finished my residency when I got a call from Dr. Rayford." He paused. "Good timing." He smiled.

"How long ago did Dr. Rayford retire?"

"About the same time I came on. He'd been waiting to find someone he liked to take over. I'm glad he liked me." He smiled.

Emma couldn't help staring. He had to have worn braces. No teeth could be that perfect. And he was at ease. Comfortable with who he was. Unusual for someone so young.

"I represent a former patient of Dr. Rayford's, Jeremy Wilcox. I gave your assistant a couple of releases for his records today. I'd like to pick them up as soon as possible." She hesitated. "And, like I said on the phone, I'd like to ask you a few questions."

Dr. Washington looked at his notes. "I don't know how I could help you. I don't know anything about Jeremy. Could you remind me why Jeremy needs legal representation?"

"He's been charged with the murder of his mother."

He raised his eyebrows. "Oh! So, their relationship would be very important to his case." He squinted. "I remember seeing something in the paper about a young man being arrested for killing his mother. But I didn't realize at the time that he had a mental health issue. If these patients don't understand the arrest process, it can be difficult, even traumatic for them." He paused. "Didn't you say Jeremy was diagnosed with paranoid schizophrenia?"

Emma nodded. "That's right. When he was seventeen. But Dr. Rayford stopped seeing Jeremy when he was twelve."

"I'm still confused why you want to speak to me. I've never seen Jeremy, or his file, so I can't give you my opinion on anything related to his case. Are you interested in using me as an expert in the case?"

Emma nodded. "I am. I'd like to hire an expert, but I don't have the funding for one. That puts me in an awkward situation, because I'd like to ask you a couple questions."

"So, you're asking me whether I'm willing to help you with a few questions, free of charge?"

Emma grinned. "That's about it."

Dr. Washington paused, then nodded. "Okay. I can take a few minutes today. And if you'd like to talk to me in the future, all I ask is that you set up a time during lunch. I can't afford to take time away from my patients, since most of them actually pay me." He smiled.

Emma returned his smile. "Thanks. I promise not to take up too much of your time." She skimmed her notes. "Jeremy's mother left the family home, including her husband and both of her children when Jeremy was twelve. I was curious about whether the shock of his mother's abandonment could have caused schizophrenia?"

Dr. Washington shrugged. "It could have been a factor, but every situation is different. And we don't attribute schizophrenia to any one cause. Having a family history of schizophrenia is a known risk factor. And some environmental factors may make a person more likely to develop the condition. If someone is genetically prone to schizophrenia, a stressful emotional life could trigger an episode.

"But I think you told me that five years had passed between the time Jeremy's mother left and his official diagnosis. So, his mother's leaving probably didn't play much of a role in his first episode. But I don't know enough about him or his case to give you an opinion that would hold up in court."

Emma nodded, writing as quickly as she could. Dr. Washington spoke in a clipped New England accent instead of the slower southern drawl she was accustomed to. It was difficult to keep up with him.

Emma checked her notes. "That's fine. I won't use your statement in court. I was just trying to understand Jeremy's situation. And I'll probably need help interpreting Jeremy's psychiatric records, too, the records from Dr. Rayford and Charity Hospital, especially. And I've also asked for his mother's records. Looks like she was also a patient of Dr. Rayford's."

"I'd be happy to help. Just call and let my assistant know that you'd like to meet and what you'd like to discuss. She's in charge of my calendar, not me. And I'd like some time to prepare for our discussion, too, so if you can, please arrange for the meeting at least a couple of days in advance."

"That's so kind of you." Emma paused and glanced at Dr. Washington. "I have one more question."

Dr. Washington nodded.

"Can you tell me whether a diagnosis of paranoid schizophrenia could affect memory? For instance, if a person in the middle of an episode was arrested, is it possible he may not recall the events of the arrest, or what led up to the arrest?"

Dr. Washington nodded. "That's entirely possible. People usually associate hallucinations or delusions with paranoid schizophrenia, but psychotic episodes can cause memory loss, too. Most of the medications treat the hallucinations and delusions, but not the memory loss."

"That's good to know. Thanks so much for all of your help today."

Someone knocked on Dr. Washington's door.

"Come in."

The tiny lady in scrubs opened the door and handed Emma a stack of Xeroxed papers nearly a foot thick.

"That's all we have." She stepped out of the room as quickly as she came.

"That was fast!"

Dr. Washington grinned. "We have a really fast Xerox machine, but it's mostly Clare. She's a gem. Grumpy almost all of the time, but great. No one works like that anymore. She worked for Dr. Rayford for years. She should be able to help you if you have any questions about him. But I have one more for you."

"Okay."

"Do you think Jeremy's innocent?"

"I couldn't answer that question if I actually knew, or had an opinion. But I don't. I don't have much information yet. I think he'd be the perfect candidate to set up for a crime like murder. But there's still a lot of work to be done."

Chapter Eight

Emma hurried back to the law school, speeding down St. Charles much faster than she should have. She wanted to review Sally's medical records, hoping they'd give her some insight before she spoke to her class about the case.

Once she was in her office, Emma separated Sally's medical records from Jeremy's, discovering that Sally's medical records were only a little over an inch thick, much less voluminous than her son's. But her scant reports contained valuable information.

In 1984, desperately worried about Jeremy's problems at school, Sally began developing migraine headaches, stomach troubles, and various aches and pains. Dr. Rayford described Sally's condition as 'psychogenic pain' and 'chronic pain syndrome without obvious pathology.' Opioids and anti-anxiety medicines were prescribed both for her pain and to calm her down. Dr. Rayford had noted a 'low incidence of addictive behavior' associated with opioids and recommended that Sally's oxycodone dosage be increased.

Sally couldn't sleep at night. Her concerns about Jeremy looped through her head in a continual spiral. She was a worrier. The more she worried, the sicker she became. Each time she complained of stomach cramps, or pain anywhere in her body, Dr. Rayford referred her to her primary care physician for an increase in her oxycodone dosage. She found herself falling asleep in the middle of the day, and when she was awake, she was nauseated. She feared her children would be taken from her by the state. As her problems became more overwhelming, she started losing weight. A tall woman at five-foot-nine inches, her weight dropped below one hundred ten pounds.

Dr. Rayford tried relaxation therapy. He and Sally practiced deep breathing, meditation, and biofeedback. But nothing worked to relieve Sally's anxiety and pain. Noting her continued weight loss, he suggested that she see a psychiatrist for electro-shock therapy, which Sally refused. He was concerned that her depression and anxiety were intransigent and ultimately untreatable. Dr. Rayford's notes mentioned something he called treatment-refractory depression. He had no hope for her recovery.

Dr. Rayford didn't see the obvious, but Emma did. Emma knew what it was like to worry about a child who was angry and depressed and who didn't seem to fit in. Sally couldn't get better unless Jeremy did. And if he couldn't, she wouldn't either. They were forever linked. Dr. Rayford noted days when Jeremy was happy and had even enjoyed himself for brief periods. On those days, Sally was effervescent. But when Jeremy was angry and upset, Sally was inconsolable, filled with angst. It seemed as if there was no room in Sally's life for anyone or anything beyond Jeremy. But none of this gave Emma insight into why Sally left.

Then she noticed a hand-written notation by Dr. Rayford in the margins of one of the typed office reports. She couldn't read the entire entry. Part of the message said, 'She said she wanted ....' The report was dated August 2, 1988. About a month before Sally left her family.

She picked up Dr. Rayford's hand-written notes and began flipping through the pages. Several contained notations in the margins.

On October 2, 1984, Dr. Rayford wrote: 'discussed relaxation techniques with Sally.' In the margin of that page he also wrote, 'Sally not comfortable with neck massage—will try again later.'

There were several entries throughout the years where Dr. Rayford offered to give Sally massages. Emma wasn't certain why Sally kept going back. Then she noticed Sally's telephone number in the margins of several pages. Under the phone number were hash marks. Four small lines and one line diagonally crossing the other four. Dr. Rayford was keeping a tally of something. Telephone calls? Telephone calls to Sally Wilcox, or was Sally calling him?

She needed to ask Clare a few questions, but she wasn't sure of the best approach. Clare was a steely woman. Tiny but fierce, she wore her 'keeper of the records' crown with pride. And she wasn't the sort to be easily fooled.

Emma's afternoon class was still hours away. She grabbed her keys and set out to Dr. Washington's office for the second time that day.

* * *

Emma stepped into Dr. Washington's clinic, clutching the releases Todd had signed. She could see Clare working in the file area toward the back of the room and approached the receptionist.

"I have a couple of questions for Clare."

The receptionist waved Clare over. Emma smiled as sweetly as she could. But Clare stared at Emma, squinting. She didn't like to be stopped when she was in the middle of a project.

"Have a seat. I'll be there in a minute."

Several minutes later, Clare plopped down next to Emma.

"I have a few questions about Sally Wilcox."

"I've only got a couple of minutes. Then I have to get back."

Emma nodded. "Do you remember whether you ever saw Dr. Rayford and Mrs. Wilcox leave the office together?"

The furrows in Clare's forehead deepened. "I'm not sure why you're interested in what Mrs. Wilcox did on her own time. Or Dr. Rayford, for that matter."

Dr. Washington was right. Clare was tough.

"Jeremy's been arrested for killing his mother. I need to know as much about Sally as possible. Right now, anything could be relevant. If something was going on between Dr. Rayford and Sally, I'd like to know about it."

Clare nodded. "I'm still not sure how this is going to help you, but okay. Dr. Rayford may have been interested in Mrs. Wilcox, but I don't think she was interested in him, at least not in that way."

"What makes you think that?"

"Well, for one thing, I'd get the bills, including the phone bill, and could see how many times he called her a week. This was up until recently." She paused. "Or, up until her death. Some weeks he called her every day. Usually, his calls weren't answered. But when she did pick up, the phone call didn't last very long."

Emma was stunned.

"Did Dr. Rayford regularly call his patients, or have telephonic sessions with his patients?"

Clare shook her head. "No."

"Isn't Dr. Rayford married?"

"Yes. But," she made a thin line with her lips, "that doesn't matter to some people."

"I'm sure." Emma hesitated, glancing at Clare. She was willing to bet that Clare was as disgusted by Dr. Rayford's behavior as she was. "Would it be possible to get a copy of those phone bills?"

Clare hesitated. "I'd have to go back years. Some of those files have been taken out of the office and put into storage."

"Could you give me copies of whatever you can put your hands on now? If I need to, I can subpoena all of the phone records later."

Clare nodded. "I can do that."

"Did Sally ever come to see Dr. Rayford without Jeremy?"

"If I remember things correctly, both Sally and Jeremy would see Dr. Rayford on the same day. I don't think she deviated from that schedule. I know she didn't like to leave Jeremy at home alone."

"How long did you work for Dr. Rayford?"

"I worked for him about twenty-two – twenty-three years."

"So, you know a lot about him."

Clare nodded. "That's true."

"Do you see him very often these days?"

"I see him every once in a while. He lives across the street."

"Can you tell me about any of Dr. Rayford's habits or quirks?"

"Habits? He smokes. It's sort of a habit and a quirk. He smokes those French cigarettes. Gitanes. They're a little longer than the usual smoke. I think that's why he likes them. He gets them from a guy in the Quarter.

They're hard to get because they have to be ordered from France. There's no distributor for them in the United States."

"Well, that's fancy. Aren't those cigarettes black?"

"That's right. And Dr. Rayford likes fancy. That's another quirk. Have you ever seen his car?"

"No. What's he drive?"

"A Ferrari 456 GT."

Chapter Nine

Emma pulled into the driveway of a stately home on Prytania. Dr. Rayford's residence. A bright white, Greek revival, with a fancy-looking silver-colored car in the driveway. Clare had given her Dr. Rayford's contact information and said she'd let him know Emma would be calling.

As soon as she left Dr. Washington's office and sat down in her car, Emma called Dr. Rayford. She was shocked when he agreed to see her that same day.

Emma knocked on an elegant mahogany door and after hearing steps, peered through foggy leaded-glass windows. A graying, mustached man appeared and opened the door. He wore John Lennon glasses and held a black cigarette in his hand. Blowing cigarette smoke toward the ceiling, he motioned for her to step inside.

Emma showed him the medical releases for both Jeremy and Sally, and gripped their medical records in her other hand.

"I'd like to ask you a few questions about your former patients, Jeremy and Sally Wilcox."

"That's fine. Clare may have told you, today is the only day I can talk to you for the next six weeks. I'm about to take the trip of a lifetime. We're flying to Paris and then traveling on the Orient Express all the way to Istanbul." He ushered her into the house with another wave of his hand.

"Lucky you. I'd love to do that someday. Are you an Agatha Christie fan?" Emma walked into a marble-floored foyer. Grand mahogany stairs led to the second floor.

"No, but my wife is." He motioned toward another hallway. "We'll be chatting in the library." He turned to the left and led Emma down a corridor that opened to a wooden paneled room lined with books. He smiled. "I call this the library, but it's actually my office." He sat down behind a large, nineteenth-century walnut desk. An entire collection of Jung's works was displayed on the bookshelves behind him.

First, the trip on the Orient Express, and now this amazing library. The man led a perfect life.

"My wife has wanted to take this trip since she read *Murder on the Orient Express* when she was thirteen." He chuckled and waved her toward one of the chairs across from his desk.

"Well, I'm jealous." Emma paused and pulled out her notepad. "Thanks for agreeing to see me today." She put the releases and records on the chair next to her.

"I'm yours for the next thirty minutes, so shoot."

"Also, I have to ask this, are you a witness for the prosecution? I'll need to stop if you are."

"No. I'm not." He cleared his throat.

"Do you remember when you first met Jeremy? It was in October of 1984."

"Yes. Well, I remember the meeting, but not the date. It's hard to remember specifics, but I think Mrs. Wilcox said that she brought Jeremy in at that time because he'd changed so much over the past year. He'd been outgoing and friendly, but had become more introverted and withdrawn. He even stopped talking to friends at school. And his grades dropped."

Emma nodded. There was something in Dr. Rayford's eyes, a coldness, or disinterest. He wasn't likable.

"Right. I read that Jeremy became more introverted and stopped playing sports. And even though he was sleeping more, he was easily agitated. He lashed out at friends and at teachers, too."

"I don't recall everything Mrs. Wilcox said that day, but that sounds right."

"After that meeting, you diagnosed Jeremy with a major depressive episode. Do you remember that?"

He nodded. "I do."

"Why depression?"

"Because he had all the symptoms of childhood depression. That's how they act. They're cranky and angry. They withdraw socially. There might be changes in appetite or sleep, and sometimes they have vocal outbursts. I think he had trouble concentrating too. He displayed almost every behavior associated with childhood depression."

Emma flipped through Jeremy's medical records until she found a report written in 1986, when Jeremy was ten. "Here's a report that talks about Jeremy becoming upset in the classroom. He even tried to hit his teacher when he couldn't work a math problem in front of the class. After that, Jeremy's mother removed him from the public school system and began home-schooling him. His diagnosis was unchanged."

"That's right. I didn't change his diagnosis because he was still exhibiting behaviors which were in line with depression in a child, especially anger."

Emma flipped through the office notes. She couldn't find any notes about Dr. Rayford's treatment of Jeremy. "You continued to see Jeremy throughout the next two years and didn't note major changes in his behavior until October of 1988, when he was twelve. How did you help Jeremy with his depression issues?"

"Well, we would talk about problems he was having."

"I don't want to put words in your mouth, but did you give Jeremy guidance in how to cope with his depression?"

"Of course. I'd have him talk about his feelings, and I validated them. And I talked to him about coping skills."

Emma nodded. "Looks like he was quieter, even withdrawn, during that October 1988 visit. He didn't make eye contact, and he didn't respond to any of your questions. His mother said that he was angry about something at home and picked her up and rammed her against a wall."

"Right. I remember that. When I asked Jeremy why he was upset, he retreated even more, staring straight ahead. He didn't blink for long periods of time."

"Did you consider another diagnosis besides depression at that time?"

"No. His symptoms were still more in line with depression than anything else."

Emma checked her notes. "I have several reports which show that you also accepted Sally as a patient. Isn't that a conflict?"

"No. Nothing's wrong with seeing both Sally and Jeremy. For one thing, their interests were aligned, and, for another, there was a natural flow to it. I started speaking to Sally following every session with Jeremy right from the beginning. She agreed it would be a good idea."

"So, it was your idea?"

"It was." He nodded.

"Did Sally have mental health issues?"

"Of course. She was a very anxious person, and with her family history, she should have been seen every week. But she and Jeremy only came to see me every other week. Sometimes once a month."

"What family history?"

"Her father had been diagnosed with schizophrenia."

"How do you know that?"

"Sally reported it. We ask patients to fill out a questionnaire about their family history."

"But you never treated her father?"

Dr. Rayford shook his head.

"I see. I also noticed that you diagnosed Sally with anxiety, depression, a pain syndrome and recommended medication to treat all conditions. Do you know whether her primary care doctor actually prescribed the medications you suggested?"

"She did. Dr. Andrews and I have an excellent working relationship."

"Did you see any improvement in Sally's depression and anxiety levels during the time she was your patient?"

"She seemed to hold her mental health issues at bay. Or she hid them. She functioned on a pretty high level. But she also developed psychogenic illnesses. She was the sort of person who kept her personal issues private."

Emma quickly wrote down Dr. Rayford's comments. She thought the statement about Sally 'holding back' could be important and drew a star next to it.

"It's been about nine years since you've seen Jeremy. Was there anything special about him? Something different that made him stand out in your memory? You must have seen dozens of patients a day, yet you remember Jeremy and things he did in detail."

Dr. Rayford cleared his throat again. He poured a glass of water from a carafe on his desk. "I guess it was Sally. She was a dangerously beautiful woman, and she was worried about her son. I felt sorry for her. These things are difficult to cope with, especially with her background. She didn't understand why Jeremy was thriving one day, then would retreat from everyone and every activity that meant anything to him the next." He shrugged. "You don't see many young people exhibiting signs of severe depression. He was incredibly reactive, and even though I didn't tell her this, I always thought he would be a dangerous adult. Things like that stay with you."

"What do you mean by 'dangerous adult'?"

"I was afraid he'd have even more problems controlling his temper as he aged."

"Is it possible that Mrs. Wilcox's beauty affected your diagnosis of Jeremy?" Emma watched as the veins began to stand out on Dr. Rayford's forehead. "Let me rephrase that." Emma smiled. "Could you have been overly sympathetic with Mrs. Wilcox? And could your empathy for her have caused you to downplay some of Jeremy's symptoms?"

Dr. Rayford cleared his throat. "Of course not. It's true that she was beautiful, but, as far as I know, that didn't affect anything, especially Jeremy's diagnosis. My encounters with Jeremy were as they should have been—insightful, professional." He chose another cigarette from the pack and lit it, waving the match in the air to extinguish the flame.

Emma noticed a bright red flush on Dr. Rayford's face as she shuffled through the reports. She'd hit a nerve. "I have a report which includes a statement that mothers can induce schizophrenia. What did you mean by that? You stopped seeing Jeremy when he was twelve, and he wasn't diagnosed with schizophrenia until he was seventeen."

"It was just a warning. Sally was closer to Jeremy than anyone. She wanted to shelter him from all harm, and that's understandable, especially for a mom with a special needs kid. But the 'schizophrenogenic mother' is overly protective, and so was Sally. She tried to control everything for him and even tried to keep him from the normal conflicts that occur in most elementary classrooms. Sometimes that's what the child needs. But usually, it's better to learn coping skills through trial and error."

Emma paused. The 'schizophrenogenic mother?' She'd never heard the term. Dr. Rayford's report must have shaken Sally Wilcox to the core.

"Did you explain what a schizophrenogenic mother is to Mrs. Wilcox that day?"

"I believe I did. I put it in the report, and she got a copy of that."

"No. You didn't define it in the report. What makes the schizophrenogenic mother different from any other mother?"

"Mainly, like I said, she's overly protective, but she's subtly rejecting too. It causes confusion in her children."

Emma caught herself before she scoffed. That was hogwash. "What sort of rejection are you speaking of? It seems that Mrs. Wilcox was extremely involved in Jeremy's life."

"She could be cold. I never saw her hug Jeremy, and she was often rude, as only beautiful women can be."

What the hell did that mean? Emma paused a moment to collect her thoughts and stave off her temper. She couldn't afford to offend him. But it seemed obvious that Dr. Rayford had a problem with attractive women.

"I don't understand that statement. Are you saying Mrs. Wilcox was rude to you?"

"She could be."

"She wasn't unkind to Jeremy, was she?"

"No. I never saw anything like that. She only wanted the best for Jeremy." Emma shook her head. He wasn't making sense.

"So, you're saying she was kind but rejecting? I don't understand how that's possible."

"I was just giving Mrs. Wilcox a warning. She needed to understand what could happen to Jeremy and that her behavior could be the root of his behavior."

"Did anything happen between you and Mrs. Wilcox that made her treat you rudely?"

Dr. Rayford's face twitched before he smiled. "No. Nothing that I can think of."

"I see." Emma frowned as she transcribed Dr. Rayford's comment word for word. She bit the inside of her lip to avoid blurting out something offensive. "Let's move on. Was Sally upset when you told her about your schizophrenogenic mother theory?"

"She might have been."

"I have one more question before I go. In several places throughout Sally's records, there are hand-written notes mentioning that you offered her neck massages during her sessions. Is massage typically offered by psychologists to their patients?"

"Psychologists often suggest relaxation techniques, and massage is one of them."

"Did you learn about massage as a relaxation technique when you were in school? Was massage a part of the curriculum?"

He looked at his watch. "I'm afraid that was one question too many, Mrs. Thornton. I'm so sorry that our time is up, but I really must go. I hope I've been able to help."

Emma squinted at the bright sunlight as she walked out of Dr. Rayford's home. Sally Wilcox left her family shortly after that last appointment. The appointment where Dr. Rayford warned her about mothers inducing schizophrenia in their children. Could he have influenced her decision to leave?

As Emma opened her car door, she was startled by a sound behind her.

She turned around and saw Dr. Rayford stepping out of a side door to the house and walking to his car. He waved.

"Got to run an errand!"

Emma watched in her rear-view mirror as Dr. Rayford's silver car followed her down the driveway and trailed her from Prytania Avenue all the way to the law school.

* * *

Emma turned into the law school parking lot, checking to make certain that Dr. Rayford didn't follow her into the lot. Something seemed off with that man. He gave her the creeps.

It was almost one thirty. Hoping Dr. Washington was still on his lunch break, she picked up the phone to call him and was connected immediately.

"So sorry to bother you, especially after talking to you only a couple of hours ago. Do you have the time to answer a quick question?"

"Sure. I don't have a patient for another fifteen minutes. What's up?"

"I saw a report in Sally's file that said something about mothers inducing schizophrenia in their kids. I met with Dr. Rayford a few minutes ago, and he explained what he meant, but I'd like to hear what you have to say about it."

"I think you're talking about an antiquated theory that was debunked in the 1970s. If someone is still pulling out the 'schizophrenogenic mother,' argument, they need to go back to school. No one believes that theory is valid."

"Why do you think Dr. Rayford referred to such an outdated theory?"

"That's a better question for Dr. Rayford. But I've had an opportunity to review about half of his files which are still active, including several where the patient has been diagnosed with schizophrenia. I noticed that, even though standards of care may have changed, Dr. Rayford still tended to use older theories and concepts in his advice and diagnoses. I saw a couple of other references to the 'schizophrenogenic mother' in his files, too."

"Have you ever applied that theory to any of your patients?"

"No, never. But then I graduated about thirty years after Dr. Rayford. Let me assure you, even though we really don't understand everything about schizophrenia, we do know that protective mothers don't cause it."

* * *

Emma hung up the phone and flipped through the few medical records from

Charity that Katherine Green had given her. Dr. Albert Johnson of Charity Hospital had diagnosed Jeremy with paranoid schizophrenia only four years ago, in 1993. Emma skimmed the reports.

Jeremy was having hallucinations and was speaking to imaginary people when his father brought him to Charity Hospital. He was diagnosed that same day. The doctor noted that Jeremy had been seen "…talking to a wall." When he was asked who he was talking to, Jeremy said, 'Freddy Kruger,' who, Jeremy said, had given him a special tennis ball that had powers to keep him safe. Freddy also told him that he was surrounded by evil people. People who wanted to hurt him. Jeremy believed it was necessary to keep his tennis ball with him at all times.

Emma counted seven hospitalizations since the day of his diagnosis. Most were initiated by Jeremy's father following a fight, stating to the 911 operator that Jeremy was 'a danger to himself and others.' The magic words for commitment. And Emma couldn't find any records showing that Todd had taken Jeremy to regular, monthly therapy sessions.

Sally had been protective of Jeremy, but she was also the one who took him to psychotherapy appointments. She was the one who schooled him and worked with him. There was no indication from any of Jeremy's records that she ever yelled at him, or fought with him, like his father did.

Dr. Rayford used an outdated, disproven theory to warn Sally against her own protective instincts. Why? Did Sally reject him in some way? Were his comments a deliberate attempt to undermine her confidence, or did he actually believe mothers could induce schizophrenia?

Even though Dr. Rayford's comments may have played a part in her departure, Emma had a sense that something else was going on when Sally left. Something that frightened her enough to make her leave the children she obviously loved.

Chapter Ten

Emma grabbed her notepad and a pen. Class would start in about ten minutes. She had just enough time to try Sheriff Neely again, hoping to avoid the need to file the motion to transfer.

This time the sheriff picked up.

"Sheriff Neely, this is Emma Thornton. I left a few messages for you earlier about a client of mine, Jeremy Wilcox."

"Yes, Ms. Thornton. I got your messages." His words sounded muffled, but she'd heard that sound before. She knew what it was. He was chewing tobacco. "I understand what you need, but we don't have any room on the tenth floor right now. It's only got a hundred and fifty-seven beds, and they're all filled." He paused. Emma could hear him spit into something. Sounded like a tin can. She thought she was going to get ill. "And there's a long waiting list to get in. I'm hamstrung, you know? I'd transfer Jeremy if I could, but I can't."

"What about transferring him to Charity, to the third floor?"

"I can't do that. But the judge assigned to the case should be able to help you with it." He hesitated, sighing. "But there's something else. Last night Jeremy was involved in a fight with another inmate, and they were both placed in solitary confinement."

"Oh no. Was Jeremy hurt?"

"I don't think so, but I'll have to get back with you on that. No one has reported an injury, yet. But sometimes those reports are delayed."

"Delayed? You don't even know if anyone was hurt? How could you put someone with a known mental health issue and a possible injury in solitary confinement? Isolation could make his condition worse. And what if he needs medical care for an injury? This is a blatant disregard for my client's well-being, Sheriff."

"I'm sure he's okay. They wouldn't have put him in solitary if he'd been in bad shape."

Emma could hear the sheriff breathing heavily into the phone. Was he nervous?

"What do you mean when you say 'bad shape?'"

"You know, serious. I don't think he has a serious injury."

"But you don't really know, do you?" She paused. "Look, Jeremy's dad left his medicine with the jail doctors. But when I saw him, he said no one had given it to him yet. I am asking you one more time to make certain he gets it and takes it. Your failure to administer a prescribed medicine is not only negligence; it's a violation of his constitutional rights. If he doesn't get a dose tonight, I'll have no choice but to report this to the Department of Corrections."

"He'll get his medicine. I'll see to it."

"I'm driving out to the jail today to check on him. If visitations are limited for inmates in solitary confinement, I'll need you to make an exception for Jeremy. I must see him, especially now, after the fight."

"I'll do that. But you're going to have to ask the judge for the transfer."

* * *

Emma walked into her classroom and stood at the podium glancing out over the group. Several students stopped what they were doing, staring back at Emma as if they weren't certain why she was there. Today was a Tuesday, one of the days she reserved throughout the week to review cases with her students. She didn't lecture during these sessions and never stood at the front of the class. Students were seated around a large set of tables that had been placed in a "U" shape to promote easy access and discussion. Typically, Emma would walk around checking on student progress, updating her 'to-do' list for each case, and planning weekly goals. She also introduced new cases during these sessions.

The room became quiet as the students settled into their seats.

"A new client has been approved for the Homeless Clinic, Jeremy Wilcox. Jeremy isn't technically homeless, although he's been known to run away from home and from Charity Hospital, where he has spent some time on the third floor. His home life, when he is at home, is unstable. Jeremy has no checking account, no money, and no one seems to care. Except his attorney, Katherine Green, and us, of course." Emma checked her notes. "Who knows the significance of the third floor at Charity?"

One person raised her hand. Angela Burris.

"What's that, Angela?"

"That's the psych floor. Charity's the state-owned hospital here in the city, and the third floor is where people are involuntarily committed if they're found to be a danger to themselves or others. Most of the patients have serious mental illnesses, and they get some attempted suicide cases there too."

Emma nodded and explained Jeremy's diagnosis and charges to the class. "He's been accused of killing his mother. I'll need some help coordinating interviews, conducting research, and preparing pre-trial motions. We don't have a trial date yet.

"I know it's the middle of the semester, and most of you have a full slate, but, right now, I need one of you to volunteer to work on this case."

The classroom was filled with whispers. Several students flipped open their calendars and checked dates. Angela raised her hand.

"How old is he?"

"He's twenty-one. That's one of the few things I do know, but there is much more I don't. One of the first things we'll need to do is file a motion to transfer Jeremy to a safer setting. He's been housed with the general population at the jail, and that won't work. We'll also need to file a motion to dismiss for lack of competency. This is different from a hearing on the defendant's sanity or whether he could distinguish between right and wrong. Does anyone know what this is?"

Angela Burris raised her hand. "It's when you ask the court to rule on whether the defendant understands the proceedings and the charges filed against him and if he can assist in the preparation of his defense. If he can't do that, the court would find him incompetent to stand trial."

Angela had a master's degree in psychology and had worked as a therapist at a family therapy clinic for years. Emma had hoped to spark her interest in this case.

"That's right." Emma paused and glanced around the classroom. "He wouldn't receive a 'not guilty' finding at a competency hearing. It doesn't matter what his mental state would have been at the time of the murder for a ruling on competency. What matters is whether he understands the situation he's in and can help his attorneys."

Emma looked at Angela. "But wouldn't it be hard to prove incompetency if a person only has periodic episodes of psychosis? He could be incompetent at one phase of the trial, and completely coherent the next day."

Angela nodded. "Yeah. That could be a complication, and I can see the DA raising that as an issue."

Tom Bolton raised his hand. "Does that mean the defendant could have an episode because he forgot to take his medicine, but then, once he's hospitalized and his meds are stabilized, he'd be okay? He could stand trial?"

Emma nodded. "That's a possibility, and that's why this issue could be a difficult one to win."

She looked out over the class. "If we lose the competency issue, we'll look at filing a criminal insanity defense. You all know what that is from criminal law." Several students nodded. "We'll take a look at that later if we need to."

"But there is one thing that stands out from the facts we have which could weaken the insanity defense in this case. The murder took place at night, and the fuse was turned off. Why is that a problem for the defense?"

Tom Bolton raised his hand. "It looks like the murder was planned."

"I agree. Does that mean the murderer knew the difference between right and wrong?"

Tom shrugged. "I think it means he didn't want to get caught."

"Right. Let's take it further. If the defendant doesn't want to get caught, doesn't that mean he knew what he was doing was wrong?"

Tom nodded. "Yeah. I can see that."

"The woman who referred the case to me has represented Jeremy in a few civil matters. She doesn't believe he's capable of planning a murder. She says he's disorganized, volatile, and impulsive. But, I'm not so sure she's right about that.

"Like I told you, he regularly escapes from Charity Hospital even though the doors on the third floor are always locked. No one has figured out how he does it, and he hasn't told anyone. His escapes are planned. And he keeps everything about them secret. So, it looks like he is capable of planning and pulling off something he knows he isn't supposed to do." Emma glanced around the classroom.

"If we do go to trial, and if the jury finds that Jeremy meets the legal definition of insanity at the time of the murder, he'll be placed in a state hospital. He could stay there for years and years. Sometimes mentally ill defendants spend longer in a state hospital than they would have spent serving time in prison for the underlying crime.

She sighed. "Of course, if the jury finds he's mentally competent to stand trial, and they also find that he doesn't meet the legal definition of insanity, he'd be sentenced as any other criminal defendant. He'd be subject to bullying throughout his term, and mental health care would be tenuous at best."

Someone toward the back of the class piped up. "So, if he doesn't get off, he's screwed."

Emma watched the class as the twitter of laughter subsided.

"Just know that every step in this case is important. Every motion, every fact we dig up, every defense. A person's life is at stake. It's serious business."

The noise level in the classroom dropped to zero.

Emma paused and glanced around the classroom. "Does anyone have time in their schedule to work with me on Jeremy's case?"

Angela raised her hand, as well as two other students.

"I'm glad to see so many of you are interested. Tom, how many cases are on your list right now?"

Tom pulled his case list out of his backpack. "Looks like I've got three active cases."

"That's a pretty big load for clinic. Mandy, what about you?"

"I've got two. One's a juvenile case, and the other a robbery case in criminal court. We have a hearing on my motion to suppress evidence in the criminal case this week."

"Angela?"

"I just settled a case, which leaves me with one active case. A constructive eviction on a Section 8 apartment complex that's about to be condemned. The place is toxic. But I can take on one more. I'd really like to work on Jeremy's case."

"Okay. It makes the most sense to assign it to you. You've got more time than anyone else, and you've got the perfect background. You can teach us all a thing or two about Jeremy's mental health issues."

Angela nodded. "Just so you know, I wouldn't be surprised to find out that Jeremy actually killed his mother."

"We'll see. We have a lot to learn. If you've got the time today, drop by my office after class."

* * *

Emma was preparing a 'to-do' list for Jeremy's case when she heard a rap at her door.

"Come in."

Angela walked into Emma's office carrying a yellow legal pad. A little older than most of the students enrolled in law school, Angela was poised and confident. Her work with families who had loved ones with mental illnesses gave her a perspective no one else in the class had, including Emma. She guessed Angela was probably around thirty-five. Emma glanced at Angela's long, black pencil skirt. With her dark hair slicked back into a bun, anyone would have thought she was in the fashion industry, or a ballerina.

"I'm so glad you volunteered to work on Jeremy's case. You're just what we need." Emma smiled.

Angela laughed. "Thanks. I really wanted to work on it."

"Good. We'll need to get in all of Jeremy's medical records from Charity and Children's Hospital and should contact each of his doctors so we can prepare the two motions. I've already got a head start on that." She nodded toward the stack of medical records. "The sooner we file the two motions, the better. When do you think you can have them prepared?"

"I'll try for the end of the day, and if I don't finish today, tomorrow for sure."

"We'll need to get an affidavit from Dr. Johnson, who diagnosed Jeremy, so it will take a little longer than that. Work on the motions, and I'll work on the affidavits. We'll need to file everything within fifteen days. We shouldn't have a problem with that.

"I didn't mention in today's session that Jeremy has been placed in solitary confinement at the jail. He got in a fight with another inmate. I need to get over there and check out what happened."

Angela nodded. "I agree. He could easily decompensate."

"Also, before I forget about it, I'd like to speak to some of the mother's friends and family members, too. I need to know more about her. I think a good place to start would be the flower shop she worked at, Garden District Flowers. Sometime this week, please get in touch with the owner and set up a time for us to come by." Emma paused. "Do you have any questions?"

"Could you give me your schedule so I can set up times for you to meet with everyone?"

"Good idea. I'd like you to come along for a couple of interviews too." Emma jotted down her schedule and handed it to Angela.

Angela nodded. "I'll start right away."

"But first, I'm off to Central Lock Up. Want to come?"

Chapter Eleven

Emma was growing more and more anxious as she waited for Angela at the entrance to Central Lock Up. She forgot to tell her to bring her student ID. The jail wouldn't allow her to accompany Emma to the interview room without it. And it was getting late. She wanted to be home no later than six o'clock.

Emma closed her eyes and took a deep breath. She didn't know what to expect. If the sheriff did what he promised, she'd be allowed to speak to Jeremy, even though Jeremy was in solitary confinement. But, if she got that far, she was afraid of what she might find. Even though Todd had dropped off Jeremy's medicine, Emma didn't know if the nurses had begun dispensing it. Isolation could have ramped up his anxiety or triggered an episode. And she didn't even know the extent of his injury.

She saw Angela approaching and watched her walk up the steps.

Angela waved her student ID in the air. "I didn't forget!"

"Good. But just so you know, since Jeremy's in solitary, I'm not sure we'll both be able to see him. They may only allow me in. We're just going to have to wing it."

Once Emma and Angela were through the screening process, Emma approached an officer sitting at the information desk.

"I would like to see my client, Jeremy Wilcox." Emma hesitated. "He's in solitary confinement."

"Then you can't see him."

"I've spoken to Sheriff Neely. He said even though he's in solitary, I'd be able to see him today. Jeremy shouldn't be there in the first place. He

61

belongs on the tenth floor." She paused. "I insist on seeing him now. Right now."

"Hang on for a minute."

The officer walked over to a deputy sheriff standing by the elevator. Emma couldn't hear, but watched their facial expressions change as they spoke. The officer from the information desk walked over to Emma and Angela.

He nodded toward the deputy by the elevator. "That's my supervisor. He said that the sheriff called and said you'd be coming. They'll get the inmate out, but it will take a while. They'll bring him up to you on the second floor. He'll take you up. But," he hesitated as he looked back toward his supervisor. "Did you know your client, Jeremy Wilcox, stabbed an inmate in the canteen the other day?"

Emma's eyes widened. "I heard Jeremy had been in a fight. I didn't know anyone had been stabbed."

The officer nodded. "Something happened he didn't like, and he picked up his fork and jabbed it into a guy's hand. It went all the way through. That's why he's been isolated."

"That doesn't sound like Jeremy. I don't think he's ever hurt anyone before."

The officer squinted his eyes at Emma. "Isn't he in for murder?" He shook his head and nodded toward the deputy sheriff. "Go on up, but be careful."

* * *

Emma and Angela waited nearly thirty minutes in the cold, ice-box-like room reserved for attorney-client meetings.

Emma rolled her eyes. "I always forget to bring a sweater. I may not be able to function here much longer. I'm frozen."

Then they heard the tell-tale shuffling and clanking sound made by a prisoner walking with shackles. Jeremy and the guard approached the barred door to the room, then stopped so the prison guard could remove Jeremy's handcuffs and shackles. Scuffing his feet along the cement floor, Jeremy made his way to the table where Emma and Angela were sitting.

Emma was shocked at his appearance. The dark circles under his eyes were far deeper than they were only a few days ago. His nose was swollen, and his lip was cut. Perspiring, his nose running, he was obviously not feeling well.

"Jeremy, this is Angela Burris. She's working on your case with me. We're here to check up on you. See how you are feeling. I also wanted to make certain you were not hurt. Let's start there. I heard you were in a fight recently. Can you tell me about that?"

Jeremy shrugged. "A guy stuck his foot out and tripped me. My food went everywhere. That guy was out after me from the first day I got here. He won't be doing that again." He raised his knee and rubbed it. His hands were shaky. "But I wasn't in a fight."

"I heard you stuck him with a fork."

"Not a fork." He wiped his nose with the back of his hand. "It was my sword. He was laughing. He thought he was so funny. But his hand was lying on the table, just waiting for me to do something. So, I stabbed it. Blood went everywhere, and I could see the bones in his hand."

"Jeremy, I know you know that stabbing that guy in the hand wasn't okay. Why did you do it?"

"Because I have Conan's sword. It gives power to those who use it and frees all users from guilt. No one can harm me when I'm using that sword." He glanced up at Emma. "And he stopped laughing. That was the best thing."

"Can you show the sword to me?"

"They took it. But I'll get it back."

Emma wrote down Jeremy's response in her notepad. "Okay. Let's change the subject for a minute. I asked that Sheriff Neely start giving you your medication. Do you remember if you received any pills today?"

"I don't think so. I don't remember taking any medicine."

"Do you know why the sheriff placed you in solitary confinement?"

Jeremy shrugged. "He wanted my sword. He's afraid I'll get it back, so he stuck me in that small cell."

"Are you okay in there, or do you feel bad?"

"I'm not alone. I have people to talk to. But I don't like this place. Not any of it."

This was the first time Emma had heard Jeremy mention the imaginary people he spoke to. This is what happened when he didn't take his medicine.

"Who are you speaking to, Jeremy? Are they here with you now?"

"No one's here right now. They're back at the other place. That little room."

"You don't look as if you feel very well. Is there anything you need, besides your medication?"

"I need some Oxy and some money. Can you help? My dad keeps all my money. I have to fight him for it, and sometimes when he's asleep, I take it out of his wallet."

"What money does your dad keep? Your social security money?"

He nodded. "Yeah. My disability money. My dad says he pays for groceries with it. But he hardly ever buys groceries. He just buys beer."

"Where do you usually get Oxy from, when you're not in here?"

"I have a friend who gives it to me. She usually comes over once a month. Sometimes I meet her in the city."

"The same place every time?"

He shook his head. "No. Different places."

"But you're not taking Oxy now, is that correct?"

He nodded.

"What's your friend's name?"

Jeremy shrugged.

"How do you get in touch with her?"

"She gets in touch with me."

Emma ran her hand through her hair. "Okay. We're going to try to get you placed on a different floor, a better one for you. But it could take a while." She paused. "You may have to stay in the small room a little longer, unless the sheriff agrees to move you sooner."

Emma couldn't tell whether Jeremy understood what she'd said. "First, we'll have to file some documents, and then we'll have to go to court. There will be a hearing, and you'll be there for that. No one will ask you any questions. You will just be there to listen." Emma glanced at Jeremy. "Do you want to ask me anything?"

Jeremy shook his head.

She nodded toward Angela. "Do you have anything you'd like to ask Jeremy?"

"Yes." She shuffled through her notes. "Jeremy, if a nurse or doctor comes to your cell and hands you a pill to take, what will you do?"

He shrugged.

"It's important that you take the pill. It will make you feel a lot better."

"Those pills don't make me feel better. That's a lie. They make me twitch and do weird things with my tongue."

"Would you do me a personal favor?" Angela smiled. "I'd like it if you'd take the medicine. It's good for you, and we all care about you. We all want you to feel better."

Jeremy's cheeks flushed. Then he giggled.

He was still giggling when Emma and Angela walked out of the room.

* * *

After the disaster of her first meeting with Jeremy, Emma was pleased she managed to speak to him again without causing another breakdown. Small steps. But he still wasn't taking his medicine, despite his father's and her efforts. He was unstable, and he'd stay that way until he started his meds again. She was afraid for him.

Chapter Twelve

The green stucco building on St. Charles was one of Emma's favorites. She glanced at the sign attached to a pole in the front. *Garden District Flowers*. Even though the building hadn't been painted in years, an air of grace and elegance radiated from the place. Large bundles of fresh-cut flowers thrown into antique crystal and blown glass vases crowded the front room. It looked like a fairyland forest. The store was also known for its Easter displays, enticing children from miles away. They'd crowd around the large front window, eager to see live baby bunnies hopping around giant pastel-decorated Easter eggs. Emma loved the shop and often bought flowers there.

The bell tinkled as Emma pushed the door open. Angela followed and stepped into the shop.

"Can I help you?" A young girl emerged from the back. She had pollen on her clothes and a few tiny leaves in her hair. Emma could see the workroom and a huge table in the back covered with flowers, scraps of greenery, and petals. The owner, an octogenarian with dyed black hair and stacks of diamond rings on each of her fingers, sat in the back office, punching numbers on her adding machine and smoking Salems from a long black cigarette holder. Garden District Flowers was a family business and had been on the corner of St. Charles and Second Street for nearly a century.

"My associate and I represent Jeremy Wilcox. We have an appointment to speak to Beatrice Belmont this morning. Is she here?"

The girl nodded. "She's in the back. I'll go get her."

As she turned to walk back to the work area, a woman stepped up to the counter. She was dressed in a flowing skirt and a blue jean shirt with sleeves rolled up to her elbows. Layers of bracelets stacked on her arms gave her an exotic look. She pushed back her long blonde hair, twisting it into a ponytail, then secured it with a clip.

"I heard you walk in but wanted to wash my hands before we met. Thanks, Dawn." Beatrice nodded toward the girl, then introduced herself. "Please call me Bea. I thought you'd like to talk somewhere more private." She gestured for them to follow her and led them up the back stairs to a large space on the second floor. "We used to rent this space to a bridal store, but they didn't renew their lease. We've been using it for storage, but it's a perfect place to talk." She waved her hand toward a couple of metal chairs next to a large folding table. Emma and Angela scooted the chairs into position and sat down.

Emma recalled driving by the shop and seeing the elegant display of bridal gowns on the second floor. She glanced out of the empty picture window. Wind blew the limbs of the two massive oak trees which flanked the building. She could almost feel the branches sway.

"I feel as if I'm in a huge treehouse." Emma smiled and scooted her chair closer to the table. She pulled out her notepad. "I understand you've known Sally Wilcox for years."

"I've known her all my life. We went to the same schools, had the same friends. I guess she was my best friend." She blotted her eyes.

"I'm very sorry for your loss."

Bea nodded. "It was a shock. She'd been working here at the shop for nine years. I saw her every day. But she and I always talked a lot, at least once a week. I knew she was going to leave Todd, and once she finally did, I told her about the opening here. She loved working with flowers."

"But Sally walked away from more than Todd, didn't she?"

Bea pulled at a ravel on her sleeve. "You're right. She did." She paused. "She also left her kids."

"Do you know why?"

She shook her head. "I'm not sure. There were problems at home. Some were with Todd, I do know that. And there were problems with Jeremy, too." She paused and looked out of the window. "She'd been having bad nightmares on and off for at least a year before she left."

"What sort of nightmares? Are you suggesting that Sally left her family because of nightmares?"

"I don't know. But they frightened her."

"I'd like to get back to that. But, what about her daughter, Rebecca?"

"Poor little Becky. Sally was always involved with something urgent - either with Jeremy's school or trying to make Todd happy. Becky was in the background, not by choice, and Sally just let her stay there. Not because Sally didn't love her. She loved her so much. But Becky didn't seem to need her as much as Todd and Jeremy."

"Did Sally blame herself for Jeremy's problems?"

"I think she did."

"Did you both grow up on the West Bank?"

"No. We grew up here in the city, uptown. Her family lived on Robert Street. We lived a couple of streets over, on Upperline."

"What was Sally's maiden name?"

"LeFleur. They're an old New Orleans family."

Emma hadn't lived in New Orleans very long, but she knew what that meant. The LeFleurs 'belonged.' Even if a person was a little eccentric, or downright odd, their pedigree would give them automatic inclusion in New Orleans' society. It was a unique club, and its membership couldn't be purchased.

"Did you go to school together?"

She nodded. "Yes. We both attended St. Ursula Academy from kindergarten through our senior year in high school."

"Did Sally attend college?"

"She did. We both started at St. Stanislaus. It had a good art program, which I liked since I wanted to be an art therapist, or work in an art gallery. Sally was thinking of social work, or teaching. I know she took some psychology classes. Then we met a couple of boys, and that ended our college careers. She got married, and I took off with my boyfriend to backpack across Europe." She smiled. "I think I had more fun."

Emma smiled. "How long were you at St. Stanislaus?"

"It was about two and a half or three years. I didn't finish my junior year. But Sally did. She dropped out right after fourth year started." She paused. "She was pregnant. With Jeremy. She was a very serious student, not like me at all. So, it was sad when she dropped out."

"Did you meet Todd during that time?"

"Yeah. I actually dated him first. When Todd and I broke up, they started going out. She asked me if I minded." She shrugged. "How should I have answered that? Seems to me she should have known it would have, at least a little. But I said 'no.'"

That was interesting. Emma scribbled down Bea's comment and circled it. Was she still carrying a grudge after all those years?

"Was Todd a student, too?"

"No. We both met him at a sorority party. He'd been invited there by an old high school sweetheart."

"Did you and Sally do things together after she got married?"

"Not really. She was so busy. But she called when she needed someone to talk to. So, like I said, I knew about her decision to leave, but I didn't question it or give her any advice. I just wanted her to know I was there for her. Sometimes a person has to come to conclusions their own way, and when they do, their choice isn't any of your business to judge. And I never judged Sally for leaving her family."

"Did you know Sally's mom and dad? Did you ever go over to her house when you two were younger?"

Bea nodded. "I did."

"What can you tell me about them? Did she have brothers and sisters?"

"There were three kids, in addition to the mom and dad. Sally was the oldest. Then there was her brother Brad and sister Holly. Her dad's deceased, but her mom's still living." She paused.

"Does anything stand out in your mind as unusual about the family?"

"I don't know what you mean by unusual. Her dad was a little strange. He was a CPA, I think, but he worked out of the family home. He seemed to stay to himself. The kids were told not to bother him, so I never saw him much. Everyone else in the family seemed good."

"Why did you say that Sally's dad was a little strange?"

"Sometimes Mrs. LaFleur, Sally's mom, would ask one of us to bring something to eat or drink to his office. We were all a little afraid of him, so when Sally was asked to help deliver her dad's lunch, she'd take me with her, if I was there. Sometimes when we knocked, he didn't answer. A few times, we walked in anyway and found him talking to himself. It was weird. He was staring straight ahead and talking as if there were someone in the room standing right in front of him." She paused. "And he left the family when Sally was twelve."

Emma was shocked that Sally's dad had left their family, just like she'd left hers.

"Oh. That must have been upsetting for everyone."

"Yeah. It was."

"Do you remember whether Mr. LeFleur acknowledged you and Sally that day you two walked in and found him talking to himself?"

"No, but we didn't give him much time to respond. We ran in, put the plate on his desk, and took off."

"When did Mr. LeFleur die?"

"It was a few years ago. I don't remember the exact date. He was living in a small uptown apartment at the time. You know, one of those mansions they split into several living spaces? He'd been there a few days when they found him. He worked at home still. I think he was found by one of his clients.

"But since he'd abandoned the family, Sally didn't keep up with him. She learned about her dad's death from one of her siblings. Pretty sure it was Holly."

How could a woman with that family history, a woman who had taken education and psychology classes and thought about teaching and helping others, have abandoned her own children?

"It's surprising that Sally also left her family since she knows, firsthand, how painful that could be. Jeremy was twelve when she left, the age she was when her dad left." Emma frowned.

Beatrice nodded. "I don't know. It's sad. Sally was insecure, always afraid someone she loved would leave. Mr. LaFleur left the family mentally before he left physically. He was withdrawn and just wasn't ever there for anyone. When Jeremy started having some of the same problems her father did, I don't think she could take it. I think that could have been one of the reasons she left."

"And she didn't divorce Todd. I guess her father and mother never divorced either?"

"That's right."

Emma raised her eyebrows as she scribbled on her notepad. Sally repeated some hurtful family history.

"Do you think she abandoned Jeremy before he became worse?"

"I don't know. Maybe. She was devastated when her dad left. I think that was why she started her own family at such an early age. That stabilized her until Jeremy started changing from a loving seven-year-old to a troubled eight-year-old. When he began to withdraw, so did she."

"Where does Sally's mother live?"

"She's in the same nursing home as my mother. But she's on the memory care wing. They're pretty sure she has dementia."

"Do you know anyone who would be able to give me some information about the family or how I might get in touch with Sally's mom and her siblings?"

"Not really. And Mrs. LaFleur doesn't recognize my mom now and they were neighbors their entire life. I don't think she'll have any of the information you need." She clasped her hands.

"But I can ask around to see if any of the old neighbors have kept up with either Brad or Holly." Beatrice paused. "There's something else about Sally's dad you should know. Mrs. LeFleur heard someone walking around in the house one night when Sally was a young girl. I guess about ten or eleven. Mrs. LaFleur followed the noise until she got to Brad's room, where the door was ajar. She walked in, and there was Mr. LaFleur, a knife in his hand, hovering over Brad, who was still sleeping."

Emma gasped. "Oh, my God."

"I always wondered if he left the family to protect the kids."

"I can't imagine." Emma shook her head as she began to gather her belongings.

"There's one more thing you should probably know about."

Emma looked up. "What's that?"

"Sally had been complaining for years about a guy who kept pestering her. She said she went to the police about it, but since he hadn't threatened her, there was nothing they could do. So, she said she was going to speak to her lawyer."

"Do you have the name of the lawyer?"

"I think his name is Roger Lewis."

* * *

After checking for on-coming traffic, Emma pulled away from the curb next to the flower shop and onto St. Charles Avenue. She needed to make an immediate left turn and put on her blinker. She glanced at her rear-view mirror again to make certain there were no on-coming cars, then sat up with a start. She could see, two cars back, a silver vehicle which looked very much like Dr. Rayford's. But that was impossible. He was in Paris.

Chapter Thirteen

Emma was up and dressed before the boys and Ren awakened. She wanted to review her notes for the hearing. She and Angela were going before Judge Quigley at nine o'clock. Angela had done a good job on the motions they'd filed. The motion to have Jeremy moved to the tenth floor of the jail, or to the third floor at Charity Hospital should be granted. Dr. Johnson's affidavit in support of the motion was solid, spelling out the dangers of leaving Jeremy on any of the floors with the main prison population.

But the second argument, the motion to dismiss based on Jeremy's competency to stand trial, wasn't a clear winner. Angela's reasoning in the brief was sound, but the judge could easily rule either way. Even she believed that Jeremy would be able to understand the legal proceedings when he took his medicine. But he didn't always take it. And unmedicated, he was a different person – withdrawn, delusional, and hallucinating. Dr. Johnson raised an additional issue that could impact the judge's decision. He stated that people with paranoid schizophrenia could have a relapse even when medicated. It was less likely to happen. But it could. There was no way to tell how many episodes Jeremy may have in a given year, even if he took his medication every day.

Emma flipped through her notes for the hearing as her family began to wake up. She heard the boys scrambling around upstairs and Ren hopping in the shower. They should all be down soon. She placed her notes in her briefcase and closed the latch. It was time to go.

As Emma was putting on her jacket, she heard the thunderous sound of the twins descending the metal spiral staircase. They were dressed for school, but their faces were still puffy with sleepiness, their hair sticking out at odd angles. She still thought of them as her babies, but they were growing up. She glanced at Billy. The more sensitive of the two, Billy hadn't been doing as well lately. He didn't shrug off jabs from the kids at school like Bobby. He cared too much about what others thought of him. She reached out and combed Billy's hair with her fingers, trying to smooth down one of his cowlicks. He shook her off.

"Did you two finish your homework last night?"

"Yeah," Bobby said.

"Billy, what about you?"

He shrugged.

"Did you do everything you needed to do, or not, Billy? What about that math homework you told me about?"

Bobby opened the cabinet door and shuffled through its contents, looking for breakfast foods. He found a granola bar and began unwrapping it as he turned to walk out of the room.

"Bobby, hold the bus for your brother. He'll be down in a minute." Emma frowned at Billy. "What's up? I'm guessing you didn't do your math homework. Is that right?"

Billy nodded.

"Why not?"

He shrugged again.

Emma put her hand on his arm. "A shrug doesn't work as an answer. What's going on with you?"

"Nothing." He paused. "I don't know."

"I have to be in court in less than an hour, and I need to go. And you need to catch your bus. I think we need to continue this discussion tonight. You don't have basketball or anything. So, we'll have plenty of time to talk." She gave him a hug. "Try to have a good day. I love you."

Billy nodded. Emma gave him one more hug.

She grabbed her briefcase and purse, shouted 'goodbye' to a still-showering Ren, and headed down the stairs just in time to see the bus doors close.

* * *

Emma arrived at the criminal court building with a few minutes to spare. She had time to check Jeremy's file in the clerk's office to see whether the DA had filed any last-minute responses or motions. The DA's office knew how to secure an advantage, often strolling into the courtroom right before the time of the hearing and handing defense counsel a brand-new, last-minute argument or a newly filed motion. She didn't know how they got away with it. But they did.

She walked briskly down the criminal court's halls, impressed, as always, by the grandeur of the art deco building. Its twenty-foot-tall arched hallways were lined with carved marble and crowned by coffered ceilings, which did nothing to absorb sound. Every step, every page of paper that rustled, and every word whispered was amplified and echoed throughout the passageway. It was not a good place for secrets.

She adjusted her face as she neared the court clerk's office and tried to change her attitude. She shouldn't anticipate trouble. But she didn't want to be naïve either.

"I'd like to check out Jeremy Wilcox's file." She smiled as she handed the clerk the case number.

"Judge Quigley's already got it. Just sent his clerk down for it."

Crap. Emma took the elevator up to the second floor, courtroom B. She knew the judge's secretary and clerk, Julio. Maybe one of them would let her see the file.

She relaxed when she saw that Judge Quigley's secretary, Hilda Switzer, was in her office. Hilda knew everything. Emma noticed that the doors to the judge's chambers were shut.

"Hi, Ms. Thornton. What can I do for you today?"

Emma explained that she needed to see the case file.

"I'd love to help you out, but the clerk was correct. The judge has the file. He and Julio are going over it in preparation for the hearing. And I know Judge Quigley wouldn't want to be disturbed right now. I'm so sorry." She paused. "Trying to cut the DA off at the pass?"

"Well, I was trying to prepare for another of the DA's last-minute efforts. Of course, the briefs they file on the day of the hearing are always stronger than what they file on time. But I'm not bitter or anything."

Mrs. Switzer chuckled as Emma walked out of the door.

* * *

Emma walked into courtroom B, relieved to see that Angela was there, seated in the benches behind the defendant's table. Emma nodded at Angela and walked up to the court reporter to see the docket sheet. Jeremy's case was the second on the list.

Emma glanced at the group of inmates, all seated in the area normally reserved for the jury, dressed in their orange jumpsuits. Prison guards stood nearby. She saw Jeremy, his hands folded in his lap, his head down. He didn't glance up when people walked into the courtroom. But he didn't seem shaky or jittery either.

Emma asked one of the guards if he'd allow Jeremy to sit with her during his hearing. The guard promised to walk Jeremy over when their case came up.

She searched the courtroom for Jeremy's father and sat down on the bench next to Angela. "I don't see Todd Wilcox, and he told me he'd be here. The judge could have questions about his affidavit, so I told him to come." Emma turned and scanned the courtroom again.

"He's still got a few minutes." Angela checked her watch.

Emma nodded. "Right. I couldn't get the court's file either. Let's hope the DA isn't up to his usual tactics."

The room was filled with a booming voice. "All rise." The bailiff pushed open a heavy wooden door. Everyone stood while Judge Quigley followed the bailiff into the courtroom and sat down at his bench. The mahogany paneling and dim hanging lights added to the solemnity of the occasion. Even the row of prisoners sitting at the front of the courtroom was quiet and still.

Emma looked around the room for an Assistant District Attorney, but didn't see anyone she recognized. Emma had been in front of Judge Quigley a couple of times and had found him fair, usually, but he could be unpredictable. He'd been on the bench for twenty years and usually produced well-reasoned opinions. He'd grown up living with his parents in the penthouse suite of a large hotel in New Orleans and, as a child, rode his bicycle around and around the top of the building since the streets weren't safe. Emma often wondered how he could be a judge after growing up in such a privileged environment. How could he know how people really live?

The first motion scheduled for the day was granted without argument, and at nine o'clock on the dot, the court reporter called Jeremy's case. Emma and Angela made their way toward the defendant's table. The guard walked Jeremy over, gesturing for him to sit down in the chair next to Emma. Jeremy obliged, but kept his head down, not making eye contact with anyone. Emma searched his face. His eyes were hollowed, underscored by deep, dark circles. It was obvious that he hadn't combed or washed his hair in weeks.

Emma turned when she heard the back door to the courtroom swing open and slam shut. The ADA, Stephanie Manor, briskly walked in. This could only mean trouble.

Chapter Fourteen

Stephanie Manor was a problem. Emma knew her from other cases. Stephanie's expensive haircut and five-hundred-dollar shoes couldn't hide the fact that she pushed every case she had as far as she could, ethically. Lying was second nature to her. She had no conscience, so she didn't play fair. Driven by a Machiavellian desire to win, she manipulated every situation to her advantage and would do anything for a favorable verdict.

The DA, Francis Giardino, was getting old. Everyone knew Stephanie was gunning for the job. She flirted with TV cameramen and reporters and, as a result, was on camera for one reason or the other at least once a week. People had started to take notice.

Stephanie's showy entrance into the courtroom was timed perfectly. Pushing the door open with the sort of flourish that made everyone sit up, she had the entire courtroom's attention. They would hang on her every word. And so would Judge Quigley.

The judge checked his watch and looked down his nose at Emma. "We have two issues filed on behalf of defendant Jeremy Wilcox scheduled for hearing today." He flipped through the paperwork on his desk. "Let's start with the motion to transfer. Counsel, are you prepared to proceed?"

"We are, your honor." When Emma stood, she noticed Todd Wilcox walk through the back door to the courtroom and softly close it behind him. He tip-toed to a bench in the back.

Emma outlined the facts supporting the motion to transfer for the court. "In conclusion, the decision to place Jeremy on one of the floors designated for the general inmate population was a serious error and resulted in substantial injury to Jeremy and another inmate." Emma glanced at her notes. "Dr. Johnson, his treating psychiatrist from Charity, verified Jeremy's diagnosis. And Jeremy's father, Todd Wilcox, told his arresting officers about his diagnosis. Both Dr. Johnson's and Mr. Wilcox's affidavits are attached to our motion.

"Jeremy should have been placed on the tenth floor of the jail, which is the floor designated for mentally ill inmates. Since his arrest, none of the jail doctors or nurses have made an effort to distribute the medicine brought to the jail by Jeremy's father. No one has checked on Jeremy's mental status. According to Jeremy, he hasn't taken any of his medications since his arrest.

"I've also attached the jail's roster of visitors who registered to see Jeremy between March 20 and April 2 as an exhibit to the motion. None of the doctors or nurses who provide care to prisoners are on the roster. The one doctor who came to visit Jeremy was Dr. Albert Johnson, who saw Jeremy on March 25. As you can see in Dr. Johnson's affidavit, Jeremy told him that he was not taking and had not been given his medication.

"Dr. Johnson also explained that the failure to take medication can lead to an exacerbation of symptoms, and an increase in the number of episodes. He was concerned that any therapeutic progress Jeremy may have made in the four years since his diagnosis may have been undermined by his failing to take prescribed medication.

Emma glanced at Jeremy to see if he was paying attention. Still staring at a fixed point on his lap, Jeremy didn't show any signs of listening or understanding what was going on in the courtroom. "A schizophrenic episode could easily lead to behaviors that aren't tolerated in jail. And, as I explained earlier, this happened on the evening of March 23, not long after he was incarcerated.

"When an inmate acts out, he's usually put in isolation. Jeremy was put into isolation on March 24. Periods of isolation would be difficult for anyone, but to a person diagnosed with schizophrenia, the results can be deadly. Self-harm is strongly associated with solitary confinement, especially when it is coupled with a serious mental illness.

"If the arresting officers had properly identified the defendant as mentally ill when they charged him, we believe he would have been placed on the tenth floor, and he would have avoided the altercation of March 23 and the ensuing solitary confinement which began March 24. We ask that the court grant our motion to transfer defendant Jeremy Wilcox to the tenth floor of the jail, or alternatively, to the third floor of Charity Hospital."

Judge Quigley cleared his throat. "I've read both briefs thoroughly. Ms. Manor, are you still objecting to this motion? Just so you know, I'm leaning toward the transfer. From what I understand, there are ample nurses on the tenth floor, at least enough to disperse medicine to the inmates. It seems to be the safest place for someone with schizophrenia."

Stephanie Manor stood. "Your honor, we oppose the motion. We do not believe defendant Wilcox currently has or ever had schizophrenia. The only proof offered by the defendants are the affidavits of Mr. Todd Wilcox, the defendant's father, and Dr. Johnson, a treating physician attempting to defend his erroneous diagnosis. It is our position that the defendant is using a misdiagnosis of schizophrenia as a convenient defense and that Jeremy Wilcox is a malingerer. He's feigning a mental illness to avoid responsibility for his crime.

The ADA checked her notes. "Jeremy Wilcox is also a drug addict. We have affidavits from fellow inmates that lay out how Jeremy approached them asking for 'Oxy.'

"At this time, Jeremy is where he belongs, in solitary confinement. On March 23, he stabbed a man in the hand with a fork. The fork was jabbed with such force it went all the way through this man's hand. Jeremy Wilcox is a violent criminal. He shouldn't be allowed to hide behind the contrived illusion of mental illness, especially when his primary problem is drug addiction."

Emma rose from her seat. Stunned by Stephanie's argument, she was convinced the ADA was desperate, or she wouldn't have tried it.

"Your honor, there is no evidence in support of the state's argument, and the defendant's diagnosis is well documented. I request that any and all references to malingering and drug addiction be struck from the record."

Judge Quigley nodded and looked over his glasses at Stephanie. "I don't see an affidavit or any other evidence in support of the state's position, Ms. Manor, including the affidavits from the other inmates."

"I can explain if I can go forward."

The judge lowered his chin in a quick nod. "Proceed."

"For one thing, it's clear from Dr. Johnson's affidavit that he's only seen the defendant a handful of times. He made a diagnosis of schizophrenia based on Jeremy's statements and answers to questions. No psychological battery was completed. It's our understanding that for years, prior to seeing Dr. Johnson, Jeremy's diagnosis was simple depression. Simple depression is not one of the conditions which would require hospitalization or a transfer to a mental health facility. We have attached an affidavit to our reply brief from Dr. Douglas Rayford, Jeremy's psychologist for years, especially during the critical years of his youth." She paused and handed Emma a copy of Dr. Rayford's affidavit. "And we're still working on the inmate affidavits."

Emma glanced at Dr. Rayford's affidavit. She knew Stephanie was going to try something. It was dated yesterday, but Stephanie didn't send her a copy. Also, Dr. Rayford should have been out of the country at the time the affidavit was signed. Something wasn't right. She dug her fingernails into her palms in an attempt to keep her temper under control. Anger only made things worse.

"Your honor, I also object to the prosecutor's last-minute attempt to submit Dr. Rayford's affidavit. Even though it's dated April 2, I didn't receive a copy from the ADA. So, I haven't had a chance to read it. All briefs and supporting affidavits were due three days ago.

"Dr. Rayford's diagnosis of major, not simple, depression was made when the defendant was eight years old. He stopped seeing Jeremy when he was twelve. Finally, Dr. Rayford told me he was leaving March 26 to go to Europe and planned to stay six weeks. If he left eight days ago, as he said he would, he couldn't have signed the affidavit on April 2. I request that the court strike the affidavit from the record."

Stephanie stood. "For one thing, the defendant's attorney should get her facts straight. Dr. Rayford is in town. I suggest she give him a call and see for herself. Also, Dr. Rayford's affidavit explains that schizophrenia is often misdiagnosed, especially with patients in their late teens or early twenties. He explained that 'hearing voices' is often a sign of anxiety, not schizophrenia, especially in younger adults like the defendant. A proper diagnosis takes hours, and the defendant's records reflect that no treating psychiatrist or psychologist has spent that sort of time with him except for Dr. Rayford. Dr. Rayford also explains that the defendant has exaggerated his symptoms and was pretending to be mentally ill, which would make him a malingerer. Dr. Rayford is an essential witness to the state. His affidavit should not be struck."

The judge raised one hand, as if he were giving up. "I'm going to allow it. Ms. Thornton, you obviously knew about this doctor and what he might say. You won't be prejudiced by this late filing." He nodded. "And the missing inmates' affidavits don't really address anything before the court today. You may proceed, ADA Manor."

"It's clear that the defendant has manipulated the system and Dr. Johnson to achieve what he wanted, a diagnosis of schizophrenia. With such a diagnosis, he could kill his mother and not serve time. Dr. Johnson's affidavit was based on scant information, is not reliable, and should be struck.

"Also, Todd Wilcox's affidavit was prejudiced in Jeremy's favor and should be struck. He should not be allowed to testify on behalf of his son, either through affidavit, or via live testimony. Any parent would do anything to protect their child.

"We ask the court to strike both of the defendant's affidavits and to deny defendant's Motion to Transfer."

Emma stood again. "I have made my position clear and ask, again, that Dr. Rayford's affidavit and any reference to malingering be struck."

Emma glanced at the judge. He was paying attention. "Also, Dr. Johnson is a board-certified psychiatrist and diagnosed schizophrenia in Jeremy by following the guidelines of the DSM IV, the official manual of the American Psychiatric Association. Psychological testing is not required for this diagnosis. Mr. Wilcox, Jeremy's father, is the only person who can give the factual testimony contained in his affidavit. The ADA's arguments have no merit."

Judge Quigley frowned. "I agree that Dr. Johnson's affidavit supports a diagnosis of schizophrenia. So, I'll sign an order transferring Jeremy, for a period of fifteen days, to the tenth floor of the jail, or alternatively, to the third floor of Charity Hospital, if there is no room at the jail's psych ward.

"The defendant is ordered to undergo psychological and psychiatric testing while an inpatient at either of the facilities. The testing is to determine the defendant's current psychiatric and psychological status, as well as whether or not he is a malingerer, as the ADA has implied. So that issue will be resolved.

"And another thing. I am not going to rule on the competency issue until the defendant undergoes the testing I just ordered. I'll postpone the motion on competency until his testing is complete. Ms. Thornton, prepare the order for the transfer."

Judge Quigley banged his gavel on the bench and walked out of the courtroom.

* * *

Emma slung her briefcase in the back of the car and fell into the driver's seat, throwing her head against the seat's neck support.

"Crap!" She yelled as loud as she could. Screaming made her feel better. She banged the steering wheel. That made her feel even better yet. She closed her eyes and sighed.

Stephanie Manor was infuriating. Emma could feel a headache coming on as she started her engine. But she shouldn't allow Stephanie to get to her. Especially since they won the motion to transfer. Even though the transfer was only for fifteen days, it was a good first step.

Judge Quigley didn't buy Stephanie's antics. Plus, he could see what was going on with Jeremy. It was an effort for him to hold things together enough to sit on the bench in the courtroom. That probably influenced the judge to rule in Jeremy's favor more than anything else. All in all, it was a pretty good day in the courtroom. She could only hope that Jeremy's upcoming testing would go as well.

A silver car sped through the court parking lot and pulled out into the heavy traffic of Tulane Avenue. Emma peered over her steering wheel. Was that Dr. Rayford? Maybe he was still in town after all. She made a note to call him when she got back to her office.

Chapter Fifteen

A ngela was waiting outside Emma's door when she got to her office. She checked her watch.

"You made it here in good time."

"I saved time by driving Camp Street. I was going to give you another five minutes." Angela laughed.

Emma unlocked her door. "I sat in the car at the jail lot for a while before I started the engine. I was running over the hearing in my head." She sighed. "And, before I forget. I think I saw Dr. Rayford's silver car in the court's parking lot. Don't let me forget to call him today."

"It's weird how he keeps showing up."

"It is." Emma flipped on the lights. "I'm upset with myself for failing to anticipate Stephanie's malingering argument. Although, now that I've thought about it, it makes sense that she'd question Jeremy's diagnosis. It plays into her plan for the case. But I don't see how I could have anticipated Dr. Rayford's affidavit. That was right out of left field."

Emma threw everything she was carrying on the credenza behind her desk and gestured for Angela to have a seat.

She pulled out her chair and sat down. "I'd like for you to find a psychologist who could administer the MFAST to Jeremy. That's the test that's designed to ferret out malingering. We need a psychiatrist to take a look at Jeremy for an evaluation, too."

"I'll get on that today."

"I have a list of potential candidates." Emma reached in her desk and pulled out a printed list of names.

Angela nodded and glanced at the list.

"You get the doctors organized and arrange for Jeremy's testing, and I'll see if I can find his sister. Maybe she can throw a little light on Jeremy's and his mother's relationship."

* * *

Emma was looking forward to meeting the Shepherds, the family who so generously welcomed Becky Wilcox into their lives. She stepped out of her car and looked around. Elegant, well-constructed homes lined the street. Although they lived only a couple of blocks from Todd Wilcox's more modest home, the Shepherd's residence, and all the houses on their street could have been featured on a cover of *House Beautiful.* The lawns were manicured, and garages were filled with German-manufactured SUVs and Land Rovers. It looked like Becky had won the jackpot when it came to friends.

A dog barked when Emma knocked on the massive front door. She could hear the lock sliding back. A perfectly put-together middle-aged woman opened the door. She extended her hand.

"You must be Professor Thornton." She flashed brilliantly white teeth. "I'm Catherine Shepherd. Please come in. Rufus, sit down and behave." The dog wagged his tail at Emma and sat down next to his mistress. Dressed in a pink voile flower print blouse with poofy long sleeves, slim-fitting pink slacks, and tiny pink shoes with kitten heels, Catherine Shepherd was flawless.

"Thanks for allowing me to come by this evening. I hope I'm not interrupting anything."

"Not at all. I haven't even started dinner. Becky is waiting for you in the sunroom." She gestured toward a room at the back of the house with sliding glass doors.

Emma followed Mrs. Shepherd through the family room, impressed by the large windows which let in so much light and the beachy décor. It was the sort of place anyone could be happy.

Emma stepped into the sunroom and smiled as she gazed at a female version of Jeremy. Becky had the same shock of thick, dark hair. She was tall and lanky like her brother, and wearing blue jeans and a white tee shirt, she could easily be mistaken for him. But that's where the similarity ended.

Becky flashed a toothy grin at Emma as she shook her hand, making Emma realize that she'd never seen Jeremy's smile. And she'd never seen his eyes shine like Becky's, either. It was remarkable to see how two people could be so alike, yet so very different.

"You look a lot like Jeremy."

Becky nodded. "That's what people say."

"I'm so sorry about your mother. Thank you for agreeing to speak with me. If it becomes too much for you, let me know, and we can stop. I can come by another time."

"It's okay. I told Catherine I didn't have any problems speaking with you. She should have told you that."

"Okay, I'm glad."

Becky seemed relaxed, unbothered by Emma's presence or by the round of questions she was about to endure.

"When did you learn of your mother's death?"

"The morning it happened. My dad called and spoke to Catherine. Catherine is the one who told me about it."

"Did the police question you that day?"

"Yeah. They came here that morning and wanted to know where I was around midnight." She paused and glanced up at Emma. "I was right here with Annabeth. The police asked me a few more questions but not very many. Annabeth and I have shared a bedroom since I moved here nine years ago."

"What other questions did the police ask you that night?"

"They wanted to know if I knew anyone who had anything against my mom, or who would want to hurt her."

"What did you say?"

"I couldn't think of anyone. I mean, she left us and everything, but I still loved her. It's always hard to tell what Jeremy is thinking. But I know he loved her, and I don't think that changed after she left."

"What was your relationship with your brother like?"

"We didn't have much of one." She shrugged. "I was gone all of the time, even before I started living with the Shepherds. I mean, we didn't talk."

"Do you know anything about Jeremy taking drugs?"

"Drugs? No. But then, Jeremy was only twelve when I moved here."

"Was your dad upset when your mother left?"

Becky hesitated, then shook her head. "I don't know. He doesn't talk much, so it's hard to tell what he's thinking, just like Jeremy. And he has a bad temper. Sometimes he and Jeremy would get into fights. Rolling around on the floor fights. But I've never seen him hit my mom."

"When was the last time you saw your dad?'

"I usually try to see him a couple of times a year. I think the last time I saw him was at Christmas. Catherine wants me to keep in touch with him because she thinks it's good for me. But I know that if I didn't reach out to him, he'd never call or anything else. So, why would I want to see him? I really don't think about him that much." She leaned over, putting her elbows on her knees. "When I do think about him, I guess I have to admit that he's hurt my feelings. But I've gotten used to it."

"How did your dad hurt your feelings?"

"He didn't even try to have me stay with him after my mom left. I probably would have wanted to stay with the Shepherds anyway, but it would have been nice to have had a choice."

Emma noticed that Becky's cheeks were flushed. "Do you like living here with the Shepherds?"

Becky shrugged. "They have a pretty normal life, but I don't have much to compare it to. They were nice to invite me to stay. No one else did. And I was always over at their house anyway. I ate dinner over there almost every night since kindergarten. That's when Annabeth and I became friends. Sometimes I'd even help with chores. So, when Mom left, Catherine came to our house and talked to my dad. She told him I was like family to them, and she wanted me to live at their house. And he said 'okay.'"

Emma's heart ached for Becky. Her life had been so tragic. She didn't have a stable family life even before Sally left. And why did she eat at the Shepherd's house every night? Didn't Sally cook?

"That brings me to my next question. Did either of your mom's siblings, that would be your Aunt Holly, or your Uncle Brad, ask you to come and live with them?"

"No. I've only seen them a few times in my life, like for Christmas and stuff. So, I don't really know them."

"Did you ever hear your mom speak about her brother or sister?"

She shook her head. "Not really. I mean, I knew about them. But mom never really talked about them."

"Does this place seem like home to you now?"

Becky shrugged. "When I first got here, I was pretty upset. It seemed like no one cared. My mom didn't want to have anyone around, but my dad didn't want to have *me* around. But after a while, I got used to being here." She looked up at Emma. "It's quiet. No one shouts at anyone. I like that. And sometimes I get to go on vacations with them."

"Sometimes?"

"Right. Well, someone has to stay home to take care of the animals."

"And that someone is always you?"

"Right. But I get to go when they're going to a pet-friendly place."

"Did you ever visit your mom after she moved to the house on Arabella?"

"No, and she didn't visit me here either."

"Did you ever talk with your mom on the phone?"

Becky shook her head.

"Do you know if your mom ever saw Jeremy after she left?"

"I wouldn't know." She crossed her arms across her chest.

Emma could sense a growing hostility in Becky's responses and a defensiveness.

"What sort of relationship did Jeremy have with your mom?"

"I'm not the best person to ask. In that house, everyone lived their own separate lives, except for Jeremy and Mom. It seemed like Mom would have done anything for Jeremy. And Jeremy was only happy if she was around. After she started home-schooling him, they were together all day, every day. She helped him with his homework and made him the food he wanted. He only liked fried chicken, hamburgers, and pancakes. And he liked ketchup

89

on everything. Even pancakes. I couldn't eat at the same time he did. And that's probably why I was gone so much. Jeremy needed a lot. He never had friends and didn't really do much of anything except draw. He loved drawing. But Mom was Jeremy's world."

Emma scribbled down notes, trying to follow Becky's story. She was an insightful young woman, especially since she was only nineteen. But underneath that calm exterior, Emma suspected there was a great deal of anger. And for good reason.

"Do you know why your mom left?"

She shook her head. "Not really, but I could guess."

"And what's that?"

"I figured she was tired of taking care of people who couldn't appreciate what she was doing."

"And by people, you mean Jeremy and your dad?"

She nodded. "But she never said anything to me, and I don't think she said anything to anyone else. She just walked out one day and didn't come back."

* * *

Catherine Shepherd was seated in the den, Rufus curled up at her feet, waiting for Emma. Perched in her white wing-backed chair, she looked like a grown-up version of 'Little Miss Tuffet,' all she needed was some curds and whey.

"How did it go?" Catherine smiled brightly.

"I think it went well. She didn't seem upset by my questions. That's what I was worried about."

"Becky's a strong girl. She does well in school, too. We think she's a good influence on Annabeth. We're doing what we can to help her with a scholarship to St. Stanislaus. Don's on the board there, so our kids can attend for free. Since Becky isn't actually one of our children, we're not sure if the school will approve the scholarship. But we hope they will. She could continue to live here. If she doesn't go to St. Stanislaus, I don't see how she could afford an education."

"Is Annabeth going to the same school next fall?"

"No. Annabeth got accepted to Sarah Lawrence. We were thrilled, but I think she chose it just to be able to live close to New York City."

"That would be fun." Emma paused. "I have a question for you, too, if you don't mind."

"I thought you might." She smiled sweetly.

One of Emma's grandmother's favorite sayings popped into Emma's head. "Butter wouldn't have melted in her mouth." Emma had no reason to distrust Catherine, but she couldn't help it. No one was that cheery.

"Becky has other family members who could have taken her in after her mother left. There's an Aunt Holly, and an Uncle Brad, her mother's siblings. They're the only family members I know of. Do you know if they were contacted when Sally left, or did they show any interest in keeping either Becky or Jeremy?"

"I really don't know. I'm not one for gossip, but I think Becky's family life had been unhappy for a long time. But she's like family to us. Asking her to stay here seemed like the natural thing to do."

"Becky and Annabeth must get along very well."

"They're like sisters, sometimes they fuss. But they're both good girls."

"And Becky said she was here at midnight on the night of the murder. Can you verify that?"

"If it happened at midnight, I'd already been asleep a couple of hours. So, I can't really say where she was, but she's not one to wander. If she said she was here, then she was."

"Did the police talk to you the day they spoke to Rebecca?"

"They did. They asked questions about what Becky was doing the night her mother was killed. I told them the same thing I told you."

Emma handed Catherine her card. "I'd appreciate it if you'd call me if you can think of anything else, or if you have any questions, or see any unusual activity. Also, do you have the contact information for Rebecca's aunt and uncle?"

"I do. I asked Todd for their phone numbers, just in case. I've never had a reason to call them, though." She smiled. "Let me go upstairs and get it for you."

Emma looked around the room as Catherine climbed the stairs to the second floor. The tables and shelves were filled with photographs of Annabeth from various stages of her life. There were photographs of Annabeth in a ballet costume, Annabeth in a cheerleader costume, Annabeth on vacation. But there were no photos of Becky. Not anywhere.

Catherine walked back into the room and handed the contact information to Emma.

Emma glanced at the folded sheet of paper. "Oh, they live close to my house. Maybe I'll run by someday soon."

Catherine smiled brightly and walked Emma to the door.

Chapter Sixteen

Exhausted after more than twelve hours of work, the day wasn't over. Emma still had to cook dinner. She exhaled loudly. The hours she'd put in that day were complicated and draining. Nothing about Jeremy's case was going to be easy. Stephanie Manor would see to that.

She didn't know what to think about Becky's living arrangements. On the surface, it seemed as if she'd been welcomed into the home of a warm and loving family. Catherine and her daughter Annabeth seemed perfect, with their smooth skin and meticulous clothes. Catherine had even said Becky was 'like family.' But was she? If Becky was as important to the Shepherds as another family member, why wasn't there at least one photo of her on a shelf, or on the mantle? Why did they have Rebecca stay at home to take care of the family pets while the rest of the family went on vacations? Couldn't the financially comfortable Shepherds have hired a pet sitter? What else was Rebecca expected to do?

* * *

Emma pulled up to her apartment and parked. She hated cooking while they were in the middle of a move. It was so chaotic. Half of her kitchen utensils were already in boxes. She'd scrounged through packed boxes looking for the perfect pan, or the cheese grater, or a measuring cup more times than she could count. She'd had it. But the move was a month off. She had to find some patience, for her family's sake and hers too.

As Emma walked up the stairs, she could smell something cooking—

93

something delicious. Ren's pot roast with potatoes and carrots? She almost wept. The man always knew when she was at a breaking point. This wasn't the first time he'd jumped in to help just at the right time. Exhausted, physically and emotionally, in moments like this she could understand how Sally walked out. But Sally didn't have Ren—a man who always seemed to know when she needed a hand.

She threw down her purse and briefcase, said hello to Maddie and Lulu, who were dancing around her knees for attention. She walked into the kitchen to give Ren a hug. The dogs trailed behind, their noses quivering from the nearly palpable aromas.

"There's nothing like the smell of your pot roast. Talk about perfect timing." She kissed his cheek. "A lot went on today. Thanks for making dinner." She hugged him again.

Ren gathered Emma in his arms. "We should go sit down. I need to tell you something." He kissed the top of her head.

Emma froze, unable to move as she watched Ren open the oven to check on the roast. He slammed the door shut and took her hand, leading her into the living room. Emma's heart was pounding.

She sat down next to Ren on the couch. "What's going on? This seems so ominous." Her voice quavered.

"I got a call from the guidance counselor at the boys' school today."

Emma closed her eyes. She couldn't bear to look at Ren, afraid of what she might see in his face.

"She couldn't reach you. I think you must have been in court. And I'm the next name on their list."

Emma opened her eyes. "Please cut to the chase. Is everything okay?" Her eyes started to water. "I had my phone turned off for the hearing. I think it's still off." She paused. "Is this about Billy?"

"Everything's okay. I didn't mean to scare you. And, yes. This is about Billy. Looks like he may have played hooky today." He paused, watching for her reaction. "He didn't show up for any of his classes. But," He reached out and squeezed Emma's arm. "He's home now. He showed up a few minutes after the guidance counselor's call. About four thirty, I think. I told her that

94

I wasn't sure where he was. That you schedule the boys' doctor and dental visits and that I didn't know anything about it. And I told her that neither one of you was home."

"What did she say about that?"

"She just said okay, and to have Billy bring a letter from you tomorrow explaining his absence."

Emma frowned. Her face felt flushed.

Ren spoke slowly. "I wasn't sure what to do. I thought you'd want to talk to him about it and see what he was up to today." He paused, searching her face. "But we can handle this. The school year's just beginning, and I don't want to see him start off on the wrong foot any more than you do."

"I don't know what I can say about a kid just not showing up for school. I can't provide an excuse for that unless I lie."

"Let's talk to him first. We can find out what he was up to and go from there." Ren's face was beet red. "I'm sorry if I overstepped."

"You didn't. And I think you're right. I shouldn't jump to conclusions. I knew something was wrong this morning, but he wouldn't say what it was. I had to be at the courthouse by eight, so I told him to get on the bus and that we'd talk tonight." She paused. "The bus doors were just closing when I left. I don't know whether he was on it or not." Her voice sounded strained.

"Don't blame yourself for this."

"If I hadn't been rushing off to court, it probably wouldn't have happened."

"It's okay, Emma. You had to go. That's understandable."

"But it makes me feel awful. I hate it when I can't be there for my kids."

"Let's talk to Billy. You're assuming a lot." He squeezed her hand and stood up. "I'll go get him."

A few minutes later, Ren and Billy sat down next to Emma.

She cleared her throat. "Do you have anything to tell us about your day, Billy?" She tried not to sound upset.

He shrugged. "Not really." He clasped his hands and stared at the floor.

"Ren got a call from your school this afternoon. Seems you played hooky today. They were calling to find out if you were sick."

Billy clamped his mouth shut, his chin jutting out ever so slightly.

Emma sighed. "Something's going on. I know it is, and you admitted as much this morning. Why did you play hooky?"

Billy squinted his eyes and avoided making direct eye contact with his mother.

"How can I help you if you don't tell me what's going on?"

Billy, who was sitting in a chair across from Emma, leaned over, getting closer to his mother.

"Some kids have been picking on me. One guy shoved me into a locker. I can't go back to school without punching these guys. I mean, I'm going to slam them if they say or do anything to me again. And I don't care if I get punched back. If I do that, I'll get suspended. I didn't think you'd want me to get in a fight, or get suspended. So, I didn't go to school." His face was red. Emma could tell he was about to cry.

"Who are these guys?"

"Just a couple of big jerks who think it's funny to pick on people smaller than they are. And they're really big, so everyone's smaller than they are."

"Did you know them from middle school?"

"No. I'd never seen them before this year."

Emma looked at Ren. She'd never encountered anything like this. Neither of the twins had ever gotten into a fight before, and even though she'd run into some mean girls when she was in school, she had no personal experiences with being picked on like that—or with fighting. She could see that Billy's pride had been hurt, and he was ready to do something about it. And she wasn't sure what the best course was.

"I can imagine how you feel. It would be difficult to deal with." She paused. "But please think about what you did. No one knew where you were for an entire day. Something could have happened to you, and no adult in your life would have known what to do, or how to help you. Keeping in touch with me and with Ren is for your own good, not ours." She paused. "Where did you go, by the way?"

Billy's shoulders dropped. He sighed. "I just hung out. I went by Just Perkin' and then walked over to the guitar shop on the corner of Louisiana. I was there most of the day."

"I guess you had a good old time."

Billy shrugged.

"Ren and I will talk. Something has to be done about this. I don't know what yet. I think we need to report that those kids are bullying smaller kids. We'll figure that out and will let you know."

Billy clenched his fists. "But, Mom, you can't tell the school anything. That'll only make things worse on me, and maybe on everyone else. I don't see any way out of it unless I fight back. I mean, I can't skip school forever."

"I can't condone fighting or violence of any kind. What do you think, Ren? I still think the best thing to do would be to report the bullying."

Ren cleared his throat. "I understand how you feel more than you know. That happened to me when I was in my last year of middle school. My dad died, and instead of being nice to me, a bunch of guys decided to pick on me on the way home from school. They made my life a living hell until, one day, I stood my ground. After that, they left me alone. Of course, I didn't fight them at school. After that, one of the guys said he didn't know my dad had died and apologized for starting the fight. Later, he became one of my best friends." He paused. "So, even though I think your mom is right, I think you should decide what you need to do."

Emma glared at Ren.

"Mom. I really can't face those guys if you call the school about them. I need to take care of this in my own way."

"And what would that be, Billy?"

"I need to meet them somewhere else. Off-campus, like Ren. And I need to fight back."

Emma was frightened for him. And worried. He could get badly hurt.

Billy smiled for the first time that day. "I feel pretty good about this."

* * *

Ren and Emma put the last dish into the dishwasher and wiped off the counters. Ren tossed his dish towel on the edge of the sink and grabbed Emma's hand.

"Let's talk about this. I think you may have overreacted to the news about Billy."

They sat down on the balcony's worn wicker chairs. It was dark already, and lights twinkled along St. Charles as traffic sped by. A light breeze fluttered the leaves of the potted plants scattered next to the railings. She hated the thought of leaving this place, especially the balcony. The new house had a nice front porch, but it wasn't the same thing.

Emma sighed. "I don't think so. What I told him was true. No fourteen-year-old should roam the streets of New Orleans without a responsible adult knowing where he is. It's dangerous. And I don't think bullies should be able to get away with threatening and picking on other kids."

"I think Billy wants to take care of the bully. You've got to understand that."

"I know. I do, but I don't want him to get hurt. He isn't that big. And if that kid's as big as Billy says he is, he could get badly injured." She sighed.

Ren scooted his chair closer to Emma. "You always figure out how to handle things. I've never seen you in a situation you couldn't deal with."

"I'm not so sure about that. I'm also upset because I didn't help Billy today. I had to run off to court, and that's got to feel like another form of abandonment to a kid. And I'm upset because he wasn't where he was supposed to be, and I didn't know. It's just scary."

"I know. It is." Ren squeezed her hand. "Is that all you're worried about?"

"Of course not. Mainly I'm upset because I don't know what to do. I've either got to call the school and bring down the wrath of the bully in an even bigger way, or give in to Billy's request that I not say anything, which means he might get badly hurt. What a choice."

"I know, it's tough." He paused. "Is that it? Is anything else bothering you?"

"Yeah." She scooted her chair away from the balcony and propped her feet up on the railing. "When I got to the court house I discovered that the DA assigned to Jeremy's case is Stephanie Manor, one of the most difficult attorneys in the city to deal with. Everything I touched today went wrong."

"What makes Stephanie Manor so awful?"

"She manipulates everything so that she's in a position of advantage. And she lies. So, you can't trust her. Some lawyers always tell the truth. You know you can believe what they're saying because it's been proven again and again that they're honest. But there are others you can never trust. Stephanie falls into that category. She's slick, but she does everything she can to gain attention. Worse than that, if you send her a document by mail, she'll never admit that she received it. She avoids or refuses service of process, but will then stand up in court and swear that she'd never been served in the first place. She does this, on top of the fact that she never files anything on time and gets away with it. Jeremy's case is bad enough without adding her tricks to the situation."

"You can't afford to allow this woman to do that to you, Emma. You've got to beat her at her own game. Anticipate her moves. If she says she's not receiving your documents, stop mailing things to her. Contact a deputy sheriff and personally serve her with anything you file with the court. That way, she can't deny it. The deputy won't charge you anything but a small fee for gas, and you'll have his affidavit of service. That's all you'll ever need. I did that all the time when I was in Jonesburg."

He glanced at Emma. She wasn't looking at him. She was staring at something across the street.

"You can do it, Emma. She's as much of a bully as the kids who pick on Billy. Her tactics might not be ethical, but you can outthink her, especially if that's the only trick she's got up her sleeve."

"Well, she's very pretty and uses that to her advantage, too. But there's nothing that can be done about that."

He paused. "It's interesting that you and Billy are both dealing with bullies. We need to find a better way to help Billy deal with his. You don't need to worry about that either. Just relax. Get some good sleep tonight, and start fresh tomorrow. Everything will be better in the morning."

Chapter Seventeen

Emma woke up early to compose a letter to Billy's guidance counselor. Struggling with what to say, she'd decided on a brief factual statement until she realized, as soon as she pulled out a clean sheet of paper, that honesty was what Billy asked her to avoid. She put the paper away. This had to be handled in person.

The smell of bacon frying soon brought them all, including the dogs, into the kitchen. She sat down with them at the table to drink her coffee while they tore into eggs and bacon with grits. The dogs circled the table, mouths salivating, until she made them sit, giving them both a piece of bacon. She never cooked breakfast on weekdays, and loved seeing how much they enjoyed it.

Thirty minutes later, the boys were ready, their backpacks on their back.

"Please be careful. I don't want you to get hurt today, or any other day." She hugged both boys, and they were off. She watched them catch their bus, then called and made an appointment with Mrs. Clifford, the guidance counselor at the boy's school.

* * *

Thomas Jefferson High School was a public high school in New Orleans for the intellectually gifted. Built on a college campus, it was a sleek modern structure, offering the best teachers the state had to offer. No cost had been spared when it came to the school's furnishings and equipment. It was difficult to get in, and Billy and Bobby were lucky to have been accepted.

The State of Louisiana and the city of New Orleans had poured millions into the construction of the school, but reserved far less in support of the public schools struggling to meet the needs of the general population, or those in need of special education. Emma was elated her boys were able to attend, but she felt guilty when she entered the shiny new building. She couldn't help comparing it to other public schools she'd seen in the city, with boarded-up windows and shabby grounds.

She was shown to Mrs. Clifford's office by a young girl wearing a badge that said, "Office Assistant." The girl knocked on the door, and they were asked to enter.

Emma introduced herself.

"I'm so glad to meet you, Ms. Thornton. I've enjoyed getting to know your boys. They're good kids."

"I'm glad you think so." Emma smiled and sat down in the chair in front of Mrs. Clifford's desk.

"I'm guessing that you want to speak to me in person because there's no simple way of telling me where Billy was yesterday."

"Is it that obvious?"

"Yes. Look, I know that Billy's been picked on by a group of boys, one boy in particular."

"That's right. But Billy didn't want me to tell you or anyone else about that. He thinks he needs to take care of this problem by himself."

The counselor nodded. "I know. Billy and I have had this discussion."

"You have?"

"Yes. Billy's the type of guy who keeps things to himself. And he wants to take care of things himself, which is a good trait. But it could get him in trouble."

"Yes. I think the guy that's picking on him is huge, too."

"Right, but here's the thing. We've been watching James Skinner. That's the guy that's picking on him. And Billy's not the only one he's picking on. I've asked for help in the hallways from several of the teachers and coaches. I think we'll catch him in the act, and we'll handle it."

"That's great."

"And as for Billy's absence of yesterday. We can ignore it once. But any more unauthorized absences and he'll be looking at a suspension." She paused. "One more thing. Your Billy's tendencies to keep things to himself won't serve him well, later on. You need to encourage him to talk to you as much as possible. Start a journal, something. Don't assume things are okay just because he's quiet."

* * *

Emma was in her office reviewing her schedule and preparing for her next class when she heard a knock. She knew it was Angela. They'd made plans to meet at noon to review their projects and the interview schedule.

. "Come on in."

Angela entered the small office, a black leather backpack filled with papers hanging off of her shoulder. Her bangles clanked every time she moved her arm.

"Do you have time to grab lunch?"

Angela nodded. "Sure."

"Then don't put your stuff down. Let's walk over to Maple Street. We can go over things there."

The walk was brisk but lovely. Angela, who was tall and slim, loped along the sidewalks in her ballet flats, clearly enjoying the day. Her jet-black hair glistened in the sunlight. New Orleans was breathtaking in the spring. Azalea, wisteria, baby's breath, peonies, and jasmine were all in bloom, their fragrance infusing the air.

Lined with cobblestone, Maple Street was charming with its pastel cottages transformed into charming eateries and shops. They walked into one of Emma's favorite restaurants, housed in an old pink stucco structure with a beautiful patio. Emma ordered a salad niçoise which was served with an eggplant ragout. Angela ordered a Caesar salad with no toppers.

"So that's how you stay so thin? You don't eat?"

"I'm not that thin, and you ordered salad too." Angela grinned and took a sip of water.

"But my salad has potatoes, eggs, and a bunch of other stuff, including a ragout. I'm eating food. You're eating lettuce." She smiled. "And you are thin. But we didn't come here so I could pick on you." She took a sip of water. "I wanted to talk about Jeremy's case. I know you haven't had much time to arrange this, but have you made any headway about getting a psychiatrist and a psychologist on board to examine him? The judge asked us to expedite the process and sent an order setting the hearing date for Friday of week. The court-appointed psychiatrist must have already seen Jeremy, otherwise, he wouldn't have moved so fast to schedule this."

"Yeah. I heard from the psychologist, Dr. Ronald Parks, today. He's willing to give Jeremy the MFAST to see if malingering is an issue. And he said he'd do it free of charge."

"Wow! It's nearly impossible to find experts who will work *pro bono*, even in a case like Jeremy's. Did you also contact a psychiatrist?"

"Yeah. He's willing to examine Jeremy, but he doesn't have much time throughout the week. He said he'll try to get the examination done this weekend."

Emma knew she was lucky to have Angela on board in this case, but she hadn't anticipated Angela would get them access to experts, free experts at that!

"Amazing! How did you manage to get two experts on board and get them to waive their fees? I know I couldn't have managed that."

Angela smiled. "I took abnormal psych under Dr. Parks and did pretty well. Then he asked me to be his TA the next year. And we've kept up. He wasn't so excited about me going to law school. But I think I've finally convinced him that it was a good thing."

"Who did you get for the psychiatrist?"

"Thanks to Dr. Parks, Dr. Kenneth Tredway, who's his friend, and a psychiatrist, agreed to examine Jeremy. I told Dr. Parks what we needed. Then he called Dr. Tredway and asked him to do it as a favor. I'll verify everything later on today."

"That takes us to the LeFleurs. I contacted them right after my ten o'clock class this morning. They agreed to see me around four today. The sister and brother live together in the family home. It's over on Robert Street. That's a very nice area, and not too far from here. But I wanted to go over a few things with you before I head out."

Angela nodded. "Sure. I've got a little time before my next class."

"I don't know how old Holly and Brad are, but I think Bea told us that they're younger than Sally."

Angela nodded. "That's right. But it's weird they're living together."

Emma nodded. "Maybe there's a reasonable explanation for that. According to Dr. Rayford, Sally's father had been diagnosed with schizophrenia. Maybe she developed a fear of her dad, and Jeremy began to remind her of him." Emma shrugged. "The LeFleur siblings might give us some insight into Sally and why she left her family.

Emma sat back in her chair. "Is there anything else you think I need to ask about when I go?"

Angela thought for a moment. "Maybe you can get a sense of what their younger years were like, too. Sally's childhood would have been similar."

"I'm just going to talk to the LaFleurs and see what they can tell me about Jeremy and his mom."

Angela smiled. "I'm betting you're in for an interesting visit."

Chapter Eighteen

I t wasn't difficult to find the LeFleur home. Robert Street was one of the more prominent in the uptown area. Most of the houses there had been built in the 1920s or 1930s and were immense stucco structures. The trees which lined the street were massive, too. Oaks had been planted on both sides of the road more than a hundred years ago and had become so large their branches met, creating an elegant archway for cars and people alike. The LeFleurs's home was a Spanish colonial, painted a subtropical peach to compliment the red tile roof. Its main floor was raised one story in the event of a flood, creating a second-floor entrance. The ground level floor was enclosed, but treated as a basement. Green moss and a black discoloration were starting to encroach on the house's exterior walls. Some of the stucco had even started to crumble. Emma suspected the family wasn't able to keep up the yearly maintenance required in New Orleans's muggy climate.

When Emma knocked, her bare knuckles hardly made a sound on the solid, arched door. But she heard footsteps, and the door opened. A young woman's head appeared in the opening, her body hidden behind the door.

Emma introduced herself. "I have a four o'clock appointment today to speak with Holly and Brad LeFleur."

The young woman looked to be in her thirties. Her thick, almost black hair was cut short and jagged in the back, but longer in the front. She wore very little makeup on her pale face with the exception of coal-black eyeliner which encircled her eyes. Dressed entirely in black, offset by a demure pearl necklace, she would have been pretty if she hadn't looked so unhappy. She took the hand Emma offered and squeezed it. She was tall and thin and seemed fragile, but she had a strong grip.

"I'm Holly. Come on in."

Emma followed the young woman down a long hallway, bypassing the living and dining rooms, until they reached the kitchen. A man sat at a large round table at the back of the room, typing on a laptop. Pale and balding, what remained of his yellowish hair was plastered to his head. He had deep, purple hollows under his eyes, and seemed much older than Holly. His face was lined, especially at the corners of his mouth, which turned down. Emma doubted he'd smiled or laughed in years.

Emma glanced at the refrigerator to her left. Covered with calendars and agendas and a schedule for medicine, someone had been making check marks next to the separate days of the week indicating which medicines had been taken, and when. Emma and Holly sat down at the table, which was covered with stacks of paper, plates, and food crumbs. She glanced at one of the stacks and could tell it was a tax return. Crumpled paper littered the floor.

"Brad, this is Jeremy's lawyer, Ms. Emma Thornton. She wants to talk to us about Jeremy and Sally. Do you feel like it?"

"Sure." Brad didn't look up from his screen.

"Brad has his good and his bad days. That's why I'm here. He needs someone to make sure he takes his medicine and that he eats right. I never married, so it made sense that I help out."

Holly spoke about Brad as if he wasn't there.

Brad snorted. "Yeah, right, Holly."

Brad's tone was sarcastic. Emma hadn't known what to expect, but this wasn't it.

"I'd like to ask you both a few questions, but for starters, I have to ask one routine question. It's something the police will ask you, so I'd like to know your answer." She glanced at Brad. "What were you two doing on the night of Sally's murder?"

Brad was still typing as if she wasn't there.

Holly shrugged. "We were right here."

"Brad, what about you?"

He didn't move his eyes from the keyboard. "Yeah. That's right. Right here."

"Can you remember anything about the night? For instance, what time did you go to bed?"

"We always go to bed at ten o'clock."

"Does anything else about that night stand out to you? Do you remember the dinner you cooked, or maybe a TV show you watched?"

Holly sighed. "I think it was a Wednesday night, right?"

Emma nodded.

"We always have red beans and rice on Wednesdays. I know most people eat that on Mondays, or even Fridays, but we eat it on Wednesdays because that's the day I do the laundry."

"Did you watch TV that night?"

"On Wednesdays, we alternate between *Spin City* and *Third Rock from the Sun*. Brad likes *Third Rock*, I like *Spin City*. That's why we switch out."

Emma scribbled as fast as she could in her notepad to keep up with Holly. She was a little surprised that Holly and Brad had a scheduled routine and that they seemed to be involved in the same activities and ate the same food week after week. They were like an old married couple.

"Brad, do you agree? Do you have anything else to contribute about that night?"

Brad finally glanced up. "No. And she's right. That's what we always do." He turned toward the screen and started typing again.

"How did you learn of Sally's death?" Emma looked at Brad and then Holly.

"Todd called us. I guess the police came to see him. He called us after that," Holly said.

"When was the last time you saw or spoke to Sally?"

Holly cocked her head, but Brad, still consumed with typing, didn't respond.

"I haven't seen her for years. She came over here once. After Dad died. She brought a pie, but didn't stay long." She paused. "You know she left

Todd and the kids?" Holly said.

Emma nodded. "Do you know why?"

Holly shook her head. "No, I never understood that." She leaned back in her chair and sighed. "But I never had kids. Maybe it was justified." She looked down. "You know that Dad left us, too?"

Emma nodded. "I heard about that. I'm so sorry. Do you know why he left?"

Holly shrugged. "I'm not sure, really. I wasn't very old at the time. Maybe two or three? But I remember that about the time he left, he was doing odd things. Or maybe I just heard Brad talk about it. But I do remember that once I walked into his office and he started saying a bunch of words that didn't make sense. I can't remember what the words were now, but it was something like "run, cat, jump, dinner, pool, die." And he kept gesturing toward the floor like there was something there. I got scared. He wasn't always like that. But when I told him I didn't see anyone or anything there on the floor where he was pointing, he got angry."

Holly looped a strand of hair behind her ear. "I always thought he moved out because he didn't do well around other people. Other people, including me, seemed to agitate him."

"I'm sorry. That must have been frightening for you. How often did your dad have these episodes?"

"I'm not sure. A few times a year, maybe? I really don't know. I figured out later that he was okay when he was on his medication, but we discovered when we were older that he didn't always take it. He'd hold pills under his tongue. He even learned to drink water with those pills tucked away."

"Before I forget, when did your dad die?"

"I think it was 1990."

Emma placed a star beside her notes.

"Did you see Todd, or the kids after Sally left them?"

Holly nodded. "We did. Brad and I would go over to their house at Christmas sometimes."

"Did Becky and Jeremy seem okay when you made those visits?"

"Becky didn't live there, but she came by for dinner. I think the kids seemed okay. A little quiet, maybe, but okay." She looked down as she clasped her hands together at her knees. "And sometimes, after he'd gotten older, we'd see Jeremy walking around the uptown area. I heard that he liked to walk over to his mother's house. You have to like walking if you'd walk across the Huey P. Long bridge."

"Sally lived close to you, right?"

"She was a few blocks up, on Arabella. The few times I saw Jeremy, he was just strolling along, looking down at the sidewalk."

"You didn't stop and talk to him?"

"I called to him a couple of times, but he didn't even turn his head. Eventually, I just gave up."

"Do you know whether Sally had mental health issues?"

"I don't know." Holly paused. "We were never very close, so I know very little about her. There was too much of an age gap."

"She was older than you and Brad?"

Holly nodded. "That's right. She was ten years older than I am and about five years older than Brad."

"What was Sally's relationship with your dad like?"

"I think there was a time they were very close. She was twelve when he left, and I think that upset her a lot. And I know Dad would always get angry when anyone spoke about Sally's marriage to Todd. I don't think he ever forgave her for that. I always had the feeling there was love between Sally and Dad, but maybe even more hurt."

"You said you weren't very old when your dad left, right?"

"That's right. Two or Three."

"So, you didn't know your dad very well, either?"

"We had visits from him when we were younger. He'd come here, but Mom was always around. I think she insisted on that. Then, when we were older, we'd go over to his house. Check up on him. Make sure he had food and that he ate it." She paused. "Even though Dad moved out, my parents were never divorced. Did you know that?"

"Yes. Someone must have told me that."

"I think they loved each other, but my dad just couldn't cope with a full-time family situation. He just couldn't cope in general."

"How long have you lived here, in this house?"

"Well, I've always lived here except for a few years when I was in school. I left after I graduated from high school. Couldn't wait to get away. That was in 1981. But that didn't last very long."

"Why did you want to get away?"

"Doesn't every kid want to get away from home?" She smiled. "I wanted to go to college, so I enrolled at UNO. I attended classes for a few years, finished up my junior year, but didn't go back after that."

"Why not?"

"Dad had been paying for everything those first three years, then he started having some problems again and lost a lot of clients. He couldn't pay for college any longer, and I couldn't afford it. So, I came back home and got a job as a medical technician for a drug store, counting pills." She pursed her lips.

"Things were pretty tight because we had to have enough cash to keep mom in the skilled nursing place and had to pay for dad's apartment. Brad is a CPA, too. We decided that he should start working on getting Dad's lost clients back. That's when I stopped working and came home to help around the house. Brad had the potential to make a lot of money. I didn't."

"Has everything worked out the way you hoped it would?" Emma glanced at Brad. He was still typing on his laptop.

"Not exactly. Brad's had a few problems regaining the clients' trust. But it's not his fault. Dad accused his clients of lying to him and of cheating him out of his fee. And I'm sure a few were scared off when Dad started talking gibberish. And then, Brad's had some problems getting his own clients, too.

"Around that same time, Dad accused Brad and me of trying to poison him so we could get his retirement fund. So, we hired nurses to go out a couple times a week and check to see if he was taking his meds. Dad thought they were there to hurt him. He even said one of them sat on him and tried to break his arm." She shook her head.

"That must have been terribly upsetting for you. I'm so sorry." Emma glanced down at her questions. "I forgot to ask you about your mother. You mentioned she's in skilled nursing care?"

"That's right. She has dementia."

"What year did you put her in memory care?"

"A couple of years after Dad died. I think his death really shook her up. She went downhill quickly after that."

Emma paused. "Brad, do you have anything you'd like to add to what Holly has said today?" Emma tried to make eye contact with him, but he remained fixated on the computer screen.

Holly stood up. "Let's step outside for a minute. I'd like to show you our Carolina Jasmine. It just started blooming."

Emma and Holly walked out to the back deck which opened out to a lush garden. Emma could see the yellow petals of the Carolina jasmine in one corner of the yard.

"Brad's in a bad mood today." She sighed and sat down on one of the deck chairs. "He takes medicine for it."

Emma sat down next to Holly. "For his mood?"

She nodded. "It's okay. I know what to do for him."

Emma wasn't sure how Holly was coping.

"How do you help Brad?"

"I keep his environment calm. I make sure he gets the meals he likes at the time he needs them. And I keep a calendar of his meds, make sure he takes them."

Holly's eyes seemed glassy and little pinpoints of perspiration were gathering along her hairline, even though it was a cool day—by New Orleans' standards. Emma felt sorry for Holly. She must have found the discussion about her brother upsetting. Holly was trapped in an impossible situation.

Emma turned a page in her notebook. "I see. Do you know if Brad has a diagnosis?"

Holly nodded. "Sure. He's got what they call a mood disorder. I think he was around eighteen when he was diagnosed."

"He seems good today, busy, but okay."

"Yeah. But he doesn't like engaging with people he doesn't know."

Emma nodded. "Is there anything else you can tell me about Sally and

Jeremy?"

Holly shrugged. "Not really. I think Brad knows Sally better than I do. At least he's had some pretty strong feelings about her."

"And what are those?"

"He thinks she was Dad's favorite, and he thinks Dad stashed some money away for her and didn't leave us as much. He's always searching through Dad's accounts trying to find the hidden money under Sally's name."

"I'm guessing he didn't find anything?"

"No. I really don't think anything is there." She paused. "But he's obsessed about it."

"I'm sorry, Holly. I hope things get better for you."

"The house is paid for. So that's good. But we still have to pay taxes on the property every year, and they're pretty high. Dad inherited money from his family, which was set up in a trust. And we're living on the dividends and interest from our portion of Dad's accounts. If it weren't for that, we'd be in trouble."

"Do you know if Sally also received a portion of your dad's assets when he died?"

"I don't know. I think so, but I'm not sure. My dad's attorney took care of everything."

"What's his name?"

"Roger Lewis. He's got an office on Lafayette in the CBD."

That was the name of Sally's attorney, too. Emma wrote down his name in her notepad again. This time she circled it.

"Is there any reason you didn't make more of an effort to see Sally or her kids?"

"It always upset Brad. Just the mention of Sally's name sets him off. That's the real reason I thought we should step outside. Brad's face was getting flushed. That's the first sign he's about to blow."

As Emma walked to her car, she played the conversation she had with Holly back in her head. Holly was talking fast and seemed a little manic. Even her breathing was rapid. Brad's eyes didn't leave his computer, so it was hard to tell just what he was about. He seemed busy, but steady. And

Emma didn't see the flush on Brad's face Holly spoke of. She wasn't sure what to make of the siblings, or the afternoon's conversation.

When Emma opened her car door, she could still hear Brad's retort and his sarcastic tone when Holly spoke of taking care of him: 'Yeah, right, Holly.' What did he mean by that?

Chapter Nineteen

Emma pulled up to her apartment and sat for a moment, thinking about the day. Mental health issues had dominated the LeFleur family dynamics for years. She could see how children of parents with serious mental health problems might feel abandoned or insecure and could find adult relationships difficult because of it. Although he provided for his children when he could, Mr. LeFleur's problems had to have made his children feel anxious and unprotected.

Emma sighed as she gathered her belongings. She hoped Billy had a good day. She hadn't heard anything else from the guidance counselor and hoped that 'no news was good news.' She locked the car and walked up the stairs, checking her watch. It was a little after five.

The apartment seemed empty when she opened the door except for the families' perpetual greeters, Maddie and Lulu, their stubby tails wagging as fast as hummingbird wings.

"I'm home!" Emma shouted in the direction of the stairs.

Silence. Emma put her purse and briefcase down on the dining room table.

"Billy? Bobby?"

She started climbing the spiral staircase to the boys' bedroom on the third floor. As she neared the top, she could see the boys writing in notebooks, their heads bent over their work as they concentrated.

"This is quite a sight! My two boys, doing their homework without having to be reminded!"

"Hi, mom." They said in unison.

Emma squinted at them. Why hadn't they looked up? She walked closer and gently pulled Billy's face up toward her.

She caught her breath.

"What's this? A black eye, and a cut, too?"

She leaned over and raised Bobby's chin. "Oh, my God! You too? What happened? 'Fess up."

Bobby nodded toward Billy.

"Those guys were at it again, and this time I told them I wasn't going to fight them at school. I told them to meet me at that grassy patch in the back, behind the apartment, you know, next to the laundry machines." Billy kept his head down and picked at a hangnail on his thumb.

"So, you both got into a fight? Bobby, you too?"

The boys looked at each other and nodded.

Emma looked around the room and could see a couple of stained tee shirts thrown in the laundry basket. Neither Billy nor Bobby picked up after themselves without being forced to do so. This was an obvious attempt to hide the evidence.

She walked over to the hamper and pulled one of the tee shirts out. It was covered with grass and dirt stains, and little smatterings of blood. Someone had been hurt.

"You got in a fight with the kids who've been picking on you?"

Billy nodded.

"And Bobby, it was nice of you to help your brother, but why did you jump into this thing?"

"There were a couple of guys. That's why Bobby helped me. The guy who's been shoving me around is James Skinner. The other guy in the fight was James's friend, Terry Mitchell. You'll always find James and Terry together." Billy wiped his hands on his pants. His knuckles were scraped too.

Bobby nodded. "Yeah. They're big. It wouldn't have been a fair fight if it was just Billy against those two guys."

"Okay. I understand. How did it all end?"

"When they made a move toward us, we jumped in and started punching them. I think we got in as many hits as they did. One of them, Terry, I think, got a bloody nose, and after that, they pulled back and just walked away. Terry's eyes were watering."

"Do either of you have pain anywhere? Your noses, or anywhere else?"

Billy shook his head. "Not real bad. I just got a little banged up. But I'm okay."

"Me too," Bobby said.

"Do you think you'll have any more problems with them?"

They both shrugged.

"How do you feel about what you did, Billy?"

"I feel better. I mean, I hated it when they shoved me up against lockers and stuff."

"But now those guys know where you and the rest of your family live. Is that something to be concerned about?"

Billy sighed, and Bobby hung his head.

"I completely understand why you'd want to stand up for yourself against those boys. And sometimes, it's hard to think through all of the consequences. I can tell that you thought it through to a certain point. You didn't want to get suspended, so you decided to meet somewhere other than the school. But now those boys know where you live, which is in an apartment right on St. Charles. And the door that faces the street is shaky. If someone wanted to break in, they could easily find a way. That doesn't mean those boys will try to do that, but it's time to start thinking about the consequences of your actions. As beautiful as it is, we live in a dangerous city. Crimes are committed here every day."

Billy nodded. Bobby stared at his feet.

"But if I didn't ask James and Terry to meet me here, what else could I have done? I couldn't meet them in the park because people there might have called the police. And I couldn't fight them on the school's campus," Billy's face was beginning to turn red.

"Sometimes, the best thing to do is to not act. You could try to figure out a way around the fight, using your brain, not your fists. You're not little boys any longer, but you're not grown men, either. It's a tough time. And learning how to act in these circumstances is tough."

Billy nodded.

"So, what would have been the best thing for you to do?"

"Nothing, I guess." He paused. "But I couldn't just do nothing anymore." Billy's face became even redder. He blinked the tears from his eyes.

Emma ruffled his hair and kissed both boys on top of their heads. "Finish up your homework and come on downstairs for dinner around six. You can watch TV later on, too." She paused, glancing at both boys. "Thanks for telling me the truth."

Emma could feel the tension leaving the room as she walked down the stairs.

* * *

Emma and Ren had perfected their after-dinner routine. Ren always pitched in on the kitchen clean-up. Emma rinsed the dishes, and Ren placed them in the dishwasher, both smug about their ability to make things shine. And in good weather, they'd go sit on the balcony. Every night. Routines made them feel comforted, safe, secure.

Emma sat down in her favorite chair and looked over at Ren, pouring a glass of wine. He smiled as he handed it to her. She needed these quiet moments with him.

"How's your new case coming along?" Ren snapped the top off of his beer can.

"The ADA accused Jeremy of faking his mental illness, so the judge ordered psychological testing, which should take place soon. The judge has set the date of the next hearing for next week. Looks like the results of his testing are in already."

"What do you think they found?"

"I don't have a clue, except that I don't think Jeremy exaggerates his mental health symptoms, and I think the tests will prove that. The judge already signed an order transferring Jeremy to one of the psych floors at either the jail, or Charity for fifteen days. I'm hoping if the test results are favorable, Jeremy will be able to stay there through trial. And there's a good chance we could win the competency issue too."

"We reviewed Jeremy's case in our departmental briefings this morning. Someone said he has a drug problem, too." Ren glanced at Emma from the corner of his eye as he took a sip of beer.

Emma shrugged. "If I knew anything about that, I couldn't comment, but the truth is, I don't really know."

Ren raised his eyebrows.

"I'm looking into it. But let's just say he self-medicates sometimes. That doesn't mean he has a habit of drug abuse. One thing I do know is that there isn't any evidence that he fakes pain to get drugs if that's what you're thinking."

Ren shrugged. "I was just throwing that out for thought."

"Stephanie Manor pulled her malingering argument out of thin air. There's no evidence Jeremy's ever faked anything. But having to prove that he's *not* malingering prejudices his case. The jury will always keep the doubt she raised about him in the back of their mind. It's a dirty way to practice law."

Ren nodded. He knew when to be quiet.

"But I guess it's smart. Sneaky smart." Emma crossed her arms and looked out over the railing. There are so many hidden agendas in this case. She still wasn't sure why Sally left her kids. The husband she could understand. But not the kids. Even kids with troubles. Sally was a troubled woman, but a good mom – to Jeremy, anyway. Emma was afraid that Becky didn't receive the love and affection she needed from either parent. Had the kids become too much for Sally? She gnawed on her fingernail. There was a glaring information gap in every interview she'd conducted so far. She needed more information on Sally and her kids.

"The Shepherd family invited Jeremy's sister, Becky, to live with them after Sally left. But I suspect one of the reasons they took her in was to put her to work around the house. She's their indentured servant, and she seems resigned to that.

"Jeremy's dad, Todd, is a pretty quiet guy, a little removed, maybe. But he engages in roll-around-on-the-floor fights with his son, who's been diagnosed with a serious mental health condition. What's wrong with these people?"

"I don't think you should let yourself get worked up about this. None of the family's problems are in your control. I can see why you want to figure it all out, but you shouldn't allow yourself to get upset about it."

"And then there's Sally's younger siblings. They rarely visited each other over the last nine years." She paused. "Something's twisted here."

Chapter Twenty

April 7, 1997

E mma heard hurried footsteps approaching her office and a sharp rapping on the door. She was happy to see Angela's excited face when she walked in.

"Looks like you're in a good mood. What's going on?"

"Guess who called me this morning?"

"Dr. Parks, I hope?"

"That's right. And his friend Dr. Tredway. They both went out to the jail over the weekend and spoke to Jeremy. Neither one of them has prepared a report yet. They thought you'd probably like to speak to them first. But I took a few notes. Would you like to hear what they said?"

"Absolutely."

Angela scanned her notes. "Dr. Parks said the test," she glanced down, "The one for malingering, took a little longer than usual with Jeremy. He thinks Jeremy's solitary confinement intensified his mental health conditions. He seemed disoriented. The MFAST only has twenty-five items, and it usually takes five or ten minutes to administer. But it took him closer to twenty-five minutes. But they got through it." Angela flipped a page in her notebook. "There was no evidence that Jeremy had been faking psychiatric symptoms. He didn't report unusual hallucinations and had no extreme symptoms either. So, bottom line, according to the test results, Jeremy is not a malingerer."

Emma nodded. She never believed that Jeremy was feigning his symptoms, but was relieved to hear Dr. Park's report.

"I'm glad to hear that. And you spoke to Dr. Tredway too?"

"Yep. He administered a bunch of alphabet soup-sounding tests to assess his symptoms."

Angela flipped a page in her notebook. "He said he'd discuss everything with you during a lunch break sometime this week. But he was concerned the lack of privacy during the testing could have affected the accuracy of the results. They were in that same interview cell where we were when we spoke to him. The one with bars and no walls? Dr. Tredway was worried Jeremy might have been distracted by the noise and sounds made by the other inmates.

"But he agreed with Dr. Johnson. Jeremy's earlier diagnosis of schizophrenia was solid. He has positive symptoms, hallucinations, and delusions. A man speaks to him. Tells him that people want to hurt him, kill him. He's also convinced that people with blonde hair are evil. And, of course, Jeremy's personal hygiene has taken a nose dive recently. He doesn't take showers any longer. Doesn't comb his hair, or wash it. Dr. Tredway also said he had a flat affect. He remained expressionless during the assessment."

Emma was worried. The comment about blondes was exactly what the case didn't need. Did Freddy Kruger tell Jeremy to kill blondes?

"Sally was a blonde. I saw a photo of her at Todd's house tucked away on a shelf."

"Hmm. That's not good."

"I agree. It was a dishwater blonde, but definitely blonde." Emma paused. "Of course, I'm a blonde too." She grimaced. "Okay, I need to speak to both doctors before I make my final decision, but I'm pretty sure I'll use Dr. Parks' findings. So, once we have his report, we can prepare a supplemental brief. But I'm questioning whether we should use Dr. Tredway's findings. If the court experts agree with Jeremy's diagnosis, we won't use him. The evil blonde thing is a can of worms we just don't want to open."

Angela nodded and wrote down Dr. Park's and Dr. Tredway's phone numbers, and handed them to Emma.

"I'll call them and arrange a meeting this afternoon, after class."

Just then, Emma heard another rap at the door.

"Come in."

Sarah Kelly, the law clinic's secretary, walked into Emma's office and laid a handful of mail on her desk.

"I had to walk your way and thought I'd drop off your mail."

Emma thanked Sarah and shuffled through the envelopes. She pulled out two official-looking envelopes from the Orleans Parish Criminal Court. She knew what they were.

"What do you think these are? Three guesses."

"I don't need three guesses. That's got to be the reports."

"Let's see what they say." Emma tore into the envelopes, quickly reviewing the contents. "Yep. We have reports from a Dr. Abita on whether Jeremy is a malingerer and from a Dr. Lawrence on Jeremy's current mental state." She skimmed through the reports until she reached the final conclusion.

"Jeremy's test results show he isn't a malingerer, just like we thought. Also, Dr. Lawrence said Jeremy is currently experiencing positive symptoms of schizophrenia. Please put together something that briefly outlines the new reports and asks the court to dismiss the case for lack of competency."

"We don't have much time."

"Include only the essential details. The judge knows the case. Just make certain Stephanie Manor gets copies of it all. I don't want to give her a reason to have our pleadings struck. We'll need to get the sheriff's office involved for service."

Angela pursed her lips. "No pressure, Professor Thornton. No pressure at all."

Chapter Twenty-One

Ethyl Delacroix. That was the name of the neighbor who babysat Jeremy and Becky the day their mom left. Emma looked up the number Todd had given her. She had a little time between four o'clock and five thirty this afternoon for a visit. She picked up the phone and called Ms. Delacroix.

"Sure! Come on by! I'm not doing a thing." Ethyl sounded tipsy and more than just a little elderly. Emma feared the trip might be a waste of time.

She shaded her eyes from the sun as she peered at Ms. Delacroix's house. Sunlight struck the metal flashing along the roof line. It seemed brighter and more glaring on this side of the river than in the city. There weren't as many old trees lining the streets. A nice shady spot was a rare and welcome thing.

Ms. Delacroix's house had seen better days. The lawn was overgrown and full of weeds. Paint was peeling; Emma couldn't even tell what color the place had been originally. The front porch sagged and caused the house to list to the left, but the slant gave the place a jaunty, cheerful look.

Emma knocked. The door was opened by a spritely octogenarian. Her curly white hair, frazzled at the ends, framed her face like a fuzzy halo. Faded brown eyes sparkled out from hundreds of folds and wrinkles. Her round figure, dressed in a lime green jogging suit, reminded Emma of an elderly Kermit the Frog. Her toothless grin was infectious.

Emma couldn't help smiling as she introduced herself. "I'm so glad you were available to talk to me today."

"Oh, I love a little company! Come on in and sit down. Would you like

123

some lemonade? I have some plain and some with a little kick." Her eyes twinkled.

"Thanks, but I'm okay." Emma grinned. "I shouldn't be that long."

Emma sat down in an overly stuffed, green plaid chair. Emma had no doubt about Mrs. Delacroix's favorite color. She glanced around the room. It was sunny and bright, but messy, like a child's bedroom. Piles of crossword puzzles and other word games were stacked up on the coffee table. A pair of two-pound weights were sitting on the sofa next to Ethyl. Leftover Mardi Gras and St. Patrick's Day decorations were scattered over a sideboard.

"I just wanted to ask you a couple of questions about the day Sally Wilcox walked away from her family. That was about nine years ago. From what I understand, she asked you to stay with Jeremy and Becky that day. Do you remember?"

Ethyl raised her eyebrows. "Yes, I do. That was a sad day." She shook her head.

"Were you and Sally friends?"

"Not real close friends, but we were friendly. She asked me to watch the kids a couple of times, so she could make groceries. And sometimes, she'd come over for coffee."

"Do you know why she asked you to stay with her kids?"

"I think she said she had some shopping to do. Yeah," she nodded, "that's what it was."

"Did she tell you what time she was returning?"

"I don't remember her saying, but I don't think she ever stayed out more than a couple of hours. So, I thought we'd see her way before it was dinner time because that's when Todd got up. She always had his dinner ready around six o'clock.

"But that day, she didn't come back. I put something together for everyone to eat, but still no Sally. I ended up getting the kids to bed and staying the night. That was okay with me. A little inconvenient, but okay. I don't have no one to take care of anymore."

"Have you seen Sally since that day?"

"No, not once." She clasped her sun-spotted hands.

"Do you have any idea or suspicion about why Sally would leave her family?"

Ethyl hesitated. "I hate to guess about things like that. But sometimes, when she'd come over for coffee, she'd talk. I never said much then because I could tell she needed to work out some things, and talking helped. One time she told me that Jeremy reminded her of her dad and that her dad scared her. And she said she was afraid she wasn't a very good mother. That she wasn't good for Jeremy. I didn't know what she was talking about. She did everything for those kids. Well, maybe more for Jeremy. I couldn't help but feel a little sorry for Becky."

"Did you have an opportunity to see Jeremy and his mother together?"

Ms. Delacroix shook her head. "Not very often. But sometimes. I always thought Sally was trying hard, maybe too hard, to make him happy. Sometimes a kid has to learn how to deal with things that aren't going their way. Jeremy didn't have coping skills. But Sally seemed more worried about not rocking the boat than about teaching him how to live with other people. And Jeremy didn't live with others very well."

"What about Becky and Sally? How did they get along?"

Mrs. Delacroix shrugged. "Becky seemed to be one of those kids who takes care of herself. She did her own thing. She was always reading a book or taking a walk or something."

Emma nodded. She suspected as much.

"Did you ever see Becky and her mom together?"

Ms. Delacroix took several gulps of lemonade, the one with the kick, before answering. "I don't really think I did. She wasn't home-schooled like Jeremy. And she wasn't around the house as much as Jeremy. But I remember seeing her one time on the street with a bunch of other kids. I think they were playing kickball or dodgeball. They were right in the middle of the street and would run to get out of the way when a car came by. That day Becky tripped over something when she was trying to get away from a car, and fell, banging up her knee. All of the kids started laughing at her and calling her names. I think one of the things they called her was 'Klutzy Becky.' And they yelled that over and over.

"I was going to come out and tell them to leave her alone, but she turned to face them. She squinted her eyes and balled up her fists. When she took one step toward the girls, they ran off, except for one little girl who was so scared she tripped, right in front of Becky. Becky picked her up by her shirt, backed her up against one of the parked cars there on the street, and shoved her fist in her face." Ms. Delacroix made a fist and swung it in the air, mimicking an upper cut. "I couldn't tell what she said, but that little girl was crying when she ran away. I think Becky can take care of herself."

This was in keeping with Emma's impression of Becky, too. She was tough. There may be a vulnerable young girl underneath that tough exterior, but she didn't let it show.

"Have you seen anything like that since?"

"No. I didn't see her much after that, but when I did, she was alone."

Chapter Twenty-Two

There were no surprises at the second hearing on the motions in Jeremy's case. Emma and Angela won the motion to transfer, thanks mainly to the court-appointed psychiatrist's report. This meant Jeremy would be transferred to the tenth floor of the jail, or to Charity's third floor. And he would stay there at least until the end of trial. Emma was relieved. She wasn't surprised that they lost their competency argument, again thanks to the court's psychiatrist, but she was disappointed. The judge found that Jeremy was competent to stand trial, if medicated, stating that '...the nurses and staff at Charity would ensure Jeremy's compliance.' But Emma wasn't so sure. She still believed that keeping Jeremy properly medicated was going to be a bigger challenge than anyone realized.

Stephanie Manor sent an underling to the hearing, a lawyer so new to the practice that everything he wore, including his briefcase, was brand new. He'd even forgotten to remove the stitches which held the panels in the back of his jacket together. His hands shook every time he stood to speak. Emma felt sorry for him, but she realized that Stephanie's failure to show exposed a lack of faith in her own argument. Better to pass it off to someone else if it was a loser. And Stephanie's malingering argument, a major strategy for the prosecution, was a loser. A big loser.

Judge Quigley insisted that Emma walk the court's transfer orders over to the jail and hospital administrators, which she found confusing. It would have been perfectly acceptable to mail them, which is exactly what Emma had done with last week's temporary order. Why was it necessary to personally hand deliver the documents?

She had copies made at the clerk's office and prepared to leave. At least it was an easy walk. The jail was right across the street, and the hospital was only a few blocks away.

Emma took the elevator to the tenth floor of the jail, order in hand. She was hoping to see Jeremy, too, if the nurses allowed the visit.

The jail's head nurse stared at the order and shook her head.

"Jeremy's not here. He's still in solitary. But there's no room for him here anyway. Every bed's filled. We have inmates diagnosed with schizophrenia, just like Jeremy, and they've been here with the general prison population for years. There are about fifteen hundred of them. We can't accommodate your client or any of the others if there aren't any beds."

Emma was shocked Jeremy was still in solitary.

"Eight days ago, an order was signed transferring Jeremy to the tenth floor of the jail, and I mailed it here that same day. The order transferred Jeremy here for fifteen days. Now I have a new order which says that the jail or the hospital have been ordered to accept Jeremy as a patient for the duration of his trial."

The nurse looked down her nose at Emma. "I don't know what you're talking about. I never saw the fifteen-day order. If you mailed it like you said, it could take weeks to process." She stared at the new order. "But this one provides for an alternate placement at Charity." The nurse pointed to the language of the order. "I suggest you walk over there if you want him out of solitary."

Emma didn't argue with the nurse. And she had a new respect for Judge Quigley. He knew what he was doing when he had her walk the order over. She headed down Tulane Avenue toward Charity Hospital, still on foot.

Charity and the criminal court building were monolithic sisters, similar in so many ways. Both were built in the 1930s and were tall, gloomy art deco structures. And they both gave her the creeps.

Within five minutes, Emma handed the judge's order to Dr. Mary Goodwin, the hospital's Director of Admissions. Dr. Goodwin scanned the order.

"I know Jeremy, unfortunately. He has a strong propensity to run away. It exposes the hospital to liability. No one even knows how he's been able to do it." She hesitated and glanced up at Emma. "But I'm sure you know all of this."

"Placement at Charity is far better than putting him in a shared cell on a floor with the main prison population. And it's infinitely better than solitary confinement. I just spoke to the jail, and the tenth floor is completely full. I suspect you have more beds available than the jail. Charity is the only choice we have."

"We have about twenty-six hundred beds in total, but we only have about a hundred and thirty beds on the floor reserved for the mentally ill. I happen to know that many other inmates are in the same position as your client, and they're still in jail. No one is trying to transfer them. What makes him so special?"

"The court has ordered his transfer. There isn't any room for argument. If you have beds available here, and you don't open one up for Jeremy, the hospital will be in violation of a court order. Failure to comply with the order places the hospital in contempt of court."

Dr. Goodwin sighed. "I'll need to run this by the hospital attorneys to make certain everything is correct. When is this to take place?"

"Immediately." Emma pointed to the language of the order. "I'll prepare the paperwork required by the jail for the transfer."

* * *

Four days had passed since Jeremy's relocation to Charity, and Emma was beginning to relax. Things must be going smoothly, or she would have heard from Dr. Goodwin. That lady was looking for any excuse to return Jeremy to the jail, or anywhere else that would take him.

She was in her office preparing for her afternoon class when the phone rang. It was Dr. Goodwin.

"Looks like your client, Jeremy Wilcox, has escaped from the hospital again."

Emma was silent for a moment. *Damn!* She'd jinxed everything by thinking things were going well.

"Ms. Thornton?"

"I'm here." She sighed. "This complicates things."

"I'm upset, too. You knew Jeremy's history of escaping from Charity Hospital. Did you tell the court of his proclivities when you argued for his placement here? If something happens to him, it's on you, Professor. Our lawyers know about the role you played in getting him transferred. You can't run away from the fact that you knew of Jeremy's prior escapes. I think the District Attorney and the judge would be interested in that too."

It was easier to play offense, especially when you were vulnerable. But the hospital was liable for Jeremy's escape. They allowed him, a patient with a schizophrenia diagnosis who had escaped on numerous previous occasions, to run away from a floor that should have been secured. They were on notice it could and probably would happen again. Dr. Goodwin's bullying wasn't going to work.

"I think you have this backwards. The transfer was essential to Jeremy's safety. And the court's order must be honored. By both of us. Yesterday you admitted that Jeremy had run away from Charity so many times you lost count. It was on you to make certain he was properly secured. Did you lock the door? Did you restrain him, or get an officer to watch him?"

Dr. Goodwin sighed. "We locked the door, and I think an officer was outside of the door, too. I'll check on that. I know the door was locked, and he managed to escape anyway."

Emma hung up the phone. It was her guess that they didn't station a guard to watch Jeremy. And they should have. A missing Jeremy was bad news. She needed to act fast. She checked Angela's class schedule, and, seeing that her morning class was over, rang her cell phone. Angela was at Emma's office door within minutes. Emma filled her in on what had happened.

"As Jeremy's attorneys, we can't tell the police or anyone else about this unless we are certain that he has plans to commit a crime, or hurt someone. And we don't have any information which would indicate that. But this is a dangerous situation for him. If he's found by the police, I'm afraid he'd resist arrest. And that could be deadly.

"The hospital will report his escape to the police and the sheriff's department anyway, and the DA will find out about it pretty quickly after that. I'm sure someone will call the judge. We need to do everything we can to find him."

Emma frowned. "The hospital is already trying to make his escape my responsibility, but they're liable for this, and they know it." She sat back in her chair. "They're represented by Simmons and Robertson—a powerhouse of a firm. But we can't worry about that. We just have to find Jeremy."

Angela raised her eyebrows. "That won't be easy. "

"I know. We'll need to split up. Jeremy's dad is his official guardian, so we can talk to him. Could you give Todd a call and make an appointment to go see him? He's the guardian, so we can talk to him. And the quicker, the better. When you get there, see if he has any ideas about where we should look. He's dealt with Jeremy's escapes before.

Emma sighed. "There's a chance Jeremy could have gone to his mom's place on Arabella. I think the place is still empty. I'll call Bea and see if she has the telephone number of Sally's landlord. She's the one who found Sally. Her name, Nancy Bennett, is on the police report, but her phone number isn't. Hopefully, I can arrange a meeting with her.

Emma paused to check her notes. "Let's see if we can find any information about Jeremy. A sighting. Information about what he was wearing. Anything. And I'd like you to check whether any of the businesses in the surrounding areas have security cameras. Maybe they'd allow us to look at the footage. It wouldn't hurt to trace the steps Jeremy would take if he walked home." She sighed. "He's done this so many times before, he probably has an established route."

* * *

Sally's last residence, and the site of her murder, was a multi-colored Victorian home on Arabella, located in uptown, right off of Magazine Street. According to Bea, the landlord, Nancy, was another high school friend. The house had belonged to her parents.

Nancy was already at the house, parked in the driveway, when Emma drove up.

"What an amazing place!" Emma stopped to take in the three-story Victorian and its wrap-around porch. Located on one of the loveliest streets in the city, the home was breathtaking, spectacular with its many colors, but warm and welcoming at the same time.

She tried to quickly count the number of colors painted on the railings and banisters, and the ornate gingerbread decorations along the roof line, but gave up when she got to ten.

Nancy walked closer to Emma's car and smiled. "I could see you counting. There are forty-three colors. But that will change. Every time something shows a little wear and tear, we throw a 'paint the porch party.' Everyone pitches in to paint it another color." She grinned. "It's been fun. It was a wonderful house to grow up in."

"I'm sure." Emma paused. "But I'm here today for less than happy purposes. I represent Sally's son, Jeremy. He's been arrested for her murder."

Nancy shook her head. "I'm so sorry about all of this. It's such a tragedy."

"Do you know Jeremy?"

"No. I never met him. Sally talked about him and his sister sometimes, but I've never seen either of them over here."

"How long had Sally been renting this place from you?"

"I think it was about nine years. Sally moved in right after she left Todd and the kids. When she called me to see if she could rent this place, our last tenant had just moved out, so it worked perfectly for us. I was thrilled to have her since I knew she'd keep things clean and tidy."

Emma nodded. "The police report lists you as the person who found Sally the day of the murder. I'd like to talk to you about that. I also wanted to ask you about any businesses or homes with surveillance cameras in this area. I'd like to see if the cameras picked up anything, a person, a car, whatever, from the night Sally was killed or even during the nights following the murder. Do you know whether any homes on the street have security cameras?"

"I have several attached to the outside of this house. There's one, right on that corner." She pointed. "There have been some burglaries and even an armed robbery in the area recently. My husband's commercial real estate company puts surveillance cameras on all of their buildings, so I asked him to order some for this place, too. I thought it was a good idea to have some safety measures in place."

"Great. I'd like to get the tapes from March 19 and forword if they're available."

"The police asked for a tape too. I've already ordered it. I've been told that the security company keeps tapes for about six weeks. I'm not sure what I'll get, but you're welcome to whatever comes in. I thought it would have been here by now."

"Thanks. I'd like to see it before the police if that's possible."

"I don't see why not."

"Good." Emma smiled. "Is it possible to go inside the house and look around? Looks like they've taken down all of the yellow tape."

Nancy nodded. "The police have completed their investigation. You're welcome to step in. I can show you where I found Sally, if that would help." She motioned for Emma to follow and opened the door.

The home was as colorful on the inside as on the out. The walls were painted with intricate murals of bucolic scenes. An exquisite pianoforte, hand-painted with rosettes and golden scrolls, stood in one corner of the antique-filled living room. In the opposite corner, a huge brass bird cage, at least seven feet high, was home to a large, green parrot. The bird nodded his head up and down as soon as they walked into the room and squawked, 'you-whooo, you-whooo!'

Nancy laughed. "That's the sound Charlie makes when he recognizes someone. He's such a sweet bird."

Massive faux-marble, hand-painted columns held up the second story. It was a visual feast - an exquisitely decorated, delightful home. Not a likely venue for murder.

Emma's eyes widened. "This place is amazing."

Nancy smiled. "I left all of my parents' furniture here. It looks just like it did when I was a girl. I know it's museum-like, but I found it impossible to disassemble their things. And then there's Charlie, an Amazon green parrot. My parents' love. He's twenty years old. I'd love to have him, but my kids and my husband are allergic to feathers, and I don't know where that cage would fit into my home. So, I come over to take care of his cage and to visit with him several days a week. The tenants always feed him and give him water. But the cage chore seems like a little much to ask of a tenant, even though, so far, I've only rented to friends. Plus, I love seeing Charlie."

"I was surprised to see him in the corner in that massive cage! He's gorgeous!"

"He's a good watchdog. Want to go into the kitchen? That's where I found Sally."

The kitchen floors and counters were marble, elegant, and white, with the exception of one section of the floor, which was stained with a light, reddish-brown color.

Emma pointed to the stain. "Is that what I think it is?"

"Unfortunately. I didn't realize it, but the police leave the crime scene clean-up to the property owner. I thought they'd clean everything. By the time I got around to it, the blood had stained a portion of the floor. It's been professionally cleaned, but marble must be porous. It's so disturbing to have that stain there. I'm tempted to replace it." She sighed.

"I was looking for a stain. I don't think most people would notice." Emma stepped back to scan the area. "So, Sally was at the kitchen counter when she was killed."

"Yes, and I'm pretty sure she grabbed one of those knives to defend herself. The knife was still grasped in her hand. And another knife is missing, too. Both knives had been in that knife block on the counter for years."

"A second knife is missing?"

Nancy shrugged. "Looks that way. I drove over that morning. Sally should have been at work. Must have been about ten o'clock. When I walked into the kitchen to refill Charlie's water tray, there she was." She paused, putting her fist over her mouth. "I'm sorry. It's overwhelming. I'd never seen anything like that before." She sniffed. "That's when I noticed that there wasn't any electricity." She closed her eyes for a second. "It was terrible. I don't think I'll ever get that image out of my mind."

Emma shook her head. "I'm so sorry. Would you like me to stop? We can step out of the kitchen."

"No, I'm okay. I'd like to tell you everything I know."

Emma looked around the room. "You said the lights were out. Where's the fuse box?"

"It's on that wall, behind that calendar." Nancy pointed.

Emma stepped over to the calendar and lifted it up from the wall. "I'm so glad to finally be able to see this. The fuse box is hidden, so you'd have to know where it was if you wanted to turn off the power."

"That's exactly right."

"Have you ever seen Jeremy at his mother's house, or walking nearby?"

"No. Not that I recall. But I'm not sure I'd recognize him."

"Does everything seem to be in place here since the house was professionally cleaned?"

Nancy wrinkled her forehead. "Are you asking whether someone has broken into the house?"

"I'd just like to make certain nothing has changed since it was cleaned."

Nancy glanced around the room and nodded. "Everything seems to be in place." She stepped back and squinted at Emma. "What does Jeremy look like?"

"He's a tall, thin, dark-haired young man."

"I'll keep an eye out for him. And that reminds me, when I was driving over the day Sally was killed, I saw Brad LeFleur peddling a bike down Magazine Street, right by the entrance to Arabella. I thought it was strange at first, but the LeFleurs were known for that."

"Known for what?"

"They're a little eccentric."

* * *

Emma was unlocking her car so she could leave when her cell phone began to ring. She fumbled around in her deep bag, cursing her stupidity for having such a huge purse, and finally felt her phone.

"Hello?"

"It's Angela. You need to get over to the Wilcox place right away. Jeremy's dad, Todd, is dead. Looks like he was murdered."

Chapter Twenty-Three

Emma waved to Angela who was standing in the crowd of neighbors gathered in the Wilcox's front yard. Angela ran over to Emma's car and got in, slamming the door. She looked at Emma, her face ashen.

"I can't believe he's dead!"

Emma could feel her heart rate increase. She was worried. Jeremy had just escaped, and now his father was dead. This didn't look good.

"I can't either! It doesn't seem real. Do you know what happened?"

Angela shook her head. "When I got here, cop cars were in the driveway, and the ambulance was pulling up. They took Mr. Wilcox out of the house in a body bag a few minutes ago." Deep pink blotches were beginning to appear along Angela's neck.

"Are you sure he was murdered?"

"See that guy in the orange hat over there?" Angela nodded toward a man in an orange baseball cap, dressed in jeans and a faded flannel shirt. "His name is Andrew Cummings. I asked him what had happened. He said that he and Todd carpool to work at the refinery every day. Today was his turn to drive, so Alex came by around seven o'clock and honked, as usual. When Todd didn't come out, he got out of his truck and knocked on the front door. The car was in the carport, so he thought Todd might have overslept. But after a few minutes of knocking and ringing the doorbell, he got worried that something was wrong. He walked around to the back of the house. The door to the kitchen was ajar, so he went in. That's when he found Todd, bleeding on the kitchen floor. He'd been stabbed. He wasn't breathing. Mr.

Cummings thought he was dead."

"So 'murder' is a pretty good assumption."

"Right. People don't stab themselves."

Emma nodded. "I'm not sure that's correct, but I'm sure most suicides aren't stabbings. Did you speak to any of the other people?"

"I didn't speak to anyone else."

"It doesn't seem like a great time to ask anyone about Jeremy sightings. It could raise unnecessary suspicions about him, especially since he just escaped."

Angela nodded. "I agree."

"What about this morning? Didn't you call Todd before you left? Did you get him on the phone?"

Angela shook her head. "He didn't answer. And I called several times."

"He could have been dead already. There's no way to know for certain. If Jeremy hadn't escaped, we could share that information with the police. It might help them pinpoint the time of Todd's death. But right now, talking to the police could put Jeremy in jeopardy."

Emma hesitated. "I see police officers pulling a few folks over to talk to them." She nodded toward the carport, where police officers were speaking to about five neighbors and taking notes.

"We don't need to be on the list of people who talked to the police after Todd Wilcox was found stabbed to death. The DA would certainly want to know why we were here."

Angela nodded. "I'm sure Stephanie will find out about Jeremy's escape, but we don't need to be the ones who tell her about it." She turned around and peered through the back window at the line of cars gathering behind Emma's."Before I got here this morning, I was able to talk to a few stores and even one neighbor down the street who was outside, working in her garden. No one who worked in any of the local stores knew Jeremy. But the neighbor, Mrs. McDonnell, did. But she also said she hadn't seen him this morning."

"Do you know how long Ms. McDonnell had been out in her garden today?"

"Since about eight o'clock. She was trying to avoid the mid-day heat. But she also admitted that she'd kept her head down most of the time, digging up weeds. So, she could have missed him. I gave her my telephone number and told her to call me if she saw him."

Emma stared at the crowd surrounding the police. "Did the police ask you to stay so you could be questioned?"

"I didn't hear them say that."

"Then we should leave. I've got a late afternoon class, and I need to finish preparing for it. Let's get together tomorrow morning to discuss our next steps. How's nine o'clock?"

* * *

Sarah McLachlan's *Building a Mystery* was blasting on the car radio as Emma drove home. She turned up the volume. Music, played as loudly as she could stand it, helped her calm down. She felt her heart rate drop as she sang along for several stanzas, breathing deeply as the wind tossed her hair around the car. But she knew she couldn't escape this latest problem. It was a time bomb waiting to explode.

The police would soon discover that Jeremy was missing from the hospital, which gave him the opportunity to kill his father. At least it opened the door for the police to consider him a suspect and investigate. And when they did that, they'd discover that the same type of weapon was used to kill both of his parents. That was complicated by the fact that the police could also discover that Jeremy had more than one motive to murder his father. The house had to be covered in Jeremy's fingerprints since he'd lived there for years. She just hoped there wasn't any other evidentiary link to Jeremy at Todd's murder scene.

She turned into her parking spot, grabbed her mail, and ran up the stairs. She'd promised the boys spaghetti tonight. She sprinted through the door, surprised to see Ren sitting on the couch. He usually ran a couple of miles when he got home if the weather was good, but he was still in his work clothes. She could hear music from Billy and Bobby's bedroom on the third floor. She shouted a 'hello boys' and hoped homework was in progress.

She ran over to the couch, planted a kiss on Ren, and threw her purse on the coffee table, giving Maddie and Lulu the required scratches and kisses.

"I've got to hurry if I'm going to get this spaghetti sauce done in time for dinner. We can talk while I cook if you'd like."

Ren stood up and took Emma's hand. "Why don't you sit down? I have something to tell you."

Emma could feel her heart in her throat. She sat down next to Ren.

"Not again. What happened?" Her voice sounded as if it was a hundred miles away.

"Billy didn't come home from school again. Bobby's here, but he didn't see Billy after school let out. Billy didn't get on the bus. Bobby talked to a few of their friends, and none of them had seen him either."

"Bobby, please come down!" Emma called from the couch. Her hands were shaking.

Bobby walked down the stairs, much more slowly than his usual pace. He edged toward his mother, then sat down next to her.

"I don't know where he is."

"Who were those boys who were picking on Billy?"

"James Skinner, and Terry Mitchell."

"Do you know where they live?"

"I think Mitchell lives on Napoleon somewhere."

"And that's on a different bus line, right?"

"Yes."

"What about Skinner?"

Bobby shook his head. "Nah."

"Have you ever been to the Mitchell's house?'

He hesitated and then nodded. "I think we told you about that, didn't we?"

"We can re-visit that a little later. But right now, I'd like to know whether you would recognize the house if you saw it?"

"Yeah. I think so."

"Why is Billy with that guy? I didn't think you were friends. You just got in a fight with him."

"We got in a fight with James, but not with Terry, really. We're friends with Terry, now. James not so much."

Emma looked at Ren. "Let's go. Maybe he's there."

"I'll drive, Emma." Ren held out his hand for the key.

"No. I've got to do this. I might go crazy otherwise."

Emma, Ren, and Bobby piled in her car.

"Is Terry popular at school?"

Bobby shrugged. "Maybe a little more than James. No one likes James."

Emma frowned. "I didn't think you and Billy liked either one of them. I thought they were bullies. I don't understand why you're friends now."

"James is the bully. Terry just kind of went along with him. And Terry doesn't want to hang out with James anymore."

"He wants to hang out with you two instead?"

Emma glanced in her rear-view mirror as Bobby shrugged.

Emma turned onto Napoleon, a very busy, but beautiful tree-lined street. It was dusk. The sky, no longer illuminated by an overhead sun, had started to turn various shades of purple and pink. Emma loved this time of day, but it was difficult to see details from a distance in the subdued light. She definitely wanted Billy home before the sun dipped below the horizon. New Orleans was a dangerous city after dark.

"Keep an eye out for the house and your brother."

"There it is! That pink one over there. I remember that the house was pink."

Tall, century-old palm trees swayed in several of the yards on the street, including the home of Terry Mitchell. Emma pulled up in front of the pink house. She expected to see Billy and the other boys sitting outside on the steps. But no one was there.

"Think we should knock on the door?" Emma looked at Ren.

"Could they be at the mall instead? Or maybe out by the levee somewhere?" Ren looked worried, too.

"They could be *anywhere*. I can't drive all over the city." Emma turned around and looked at Bobby in the back seat. "Do you have any ideas? Did you hear Billy talk about going anywhere?"

Bobby cleared his throat and looked down.

"Bobby! Would you please answer me?"

"Mom. I don't want to be a snitch. I think he'll get home soon. He probably just lost track of time."

Emma clenched the steering wheel and shut her eyes for a moment. Losing her temper right now wouldn't help.

"If you know anything about where your brother might be, you have to tell me. He could be in danger."

"I doubt it."

"Bobby Thornton, if you don't tell me what you know, you'll be restricted for three months."

Bobby sighed and ran his fingers through his hair. "I don't know anything for sure. But that day, Billy and I went over to Terry's house after school. Terry said he knew how he could get some beer for us."

"*What?*"

"Yeah. He said he knew a guy who worked at an uptown bar and that the guy could get us some beer, maybe even a keg."

"What in the world would a bunch of fourteen-year-olds do with a keg?"

He shrugged. "I don't know. I think he was going to store it under his parent's house, somewhere. He said they never go down there. And then we would drink a little at a time."

"Oh my God, Bobby. I can't believe this. Where's the bar?"

"It's right off Maple Street."

"Is the name of the place 'Jake and Baked'? The place that has a decorated Christmas tree out front?" Ren turned around and frowned at Bobby.

"I think so."

"You need to stay away from that place. Any keg this person would sell you would have to have been stolen from the bar. You don't want any part of this, Bobby. If you want to drink beer, and if your mom approves, you can have a few sips with me at home. But no underage drinking in public. And participating in the purchase of a stolen keg makes you as guilty of stealing the keg as the employee."

Bobby looked down, picking at his fingernails.

"This is a discussion for another time. Right now, we have to find Billy." Emma put the car in gear and pressed the accelerator just as a group of boys rounded the corner, walking toward James's house. Emma pulled over, searching for Billy.

Ren pointed. "There he is!"

Emma squinted. Her heart fell. Her baby boy, her sweet child with rounded cheeks and gentle ways, was smoking a cigarette. Where had she gone wrong? She turned the car off and stepped out of the car. Her hands were shaking, and she couldn't speak. She pointed toward the back door of her car.

The ride back home was quiet. Emma fought back tears. She wasn't ready for this. A missing client, a missing child, and the discovery that her fourteen-year-old twins were attracted to the wrong side of things. She remembered her grandmother always said she was so happy when her sons finally got over 'fools hill'—the time in a boy's life when he ventures into the wild side. And she knew that girls could be just as attracted to all of the fun and partying. But she had two sweet boys who, for some reason, needed to prove to themselves and to others that they were cool. That they could smoke and drink beer. She sighed. According to her grandmother, this dangerous, giddy time was up around age twenty-five. She didn't know if she could make it that long.

Chapter Twenty-Four

Emma felt numb. She'd been confronted with so many new problems throughout the day and evening she'd stopped reacting to anything. She shut down. She knew she needed to get a grip. If she didn't, she was going to lose her boys.

When Billy and Bobby climbed the stairs to their bedroom that night, she followed them up and talked to them for a while. They promised her they'd go straight home from school tomorrow and every day. That they wouldn't hang out with Terry. But her trust in them had been breached. She now knew they'd lie about important things and that they'd lie to protect each other from her anger or her discipline. And that was heartbreaking.

Emma threw away the pizza boxes on the counter. It had been too late to start her spaghetti sauce when they'd gotten home, so Ren had ordered pizzas. She appreciated his silence. She knew they'd discuss everything later. She just needed some time to gather herself and her thoughts.

She heard her cell phone ringing from inside her purse. Instinctively, she knew the call was about Jeremy. She checked the number. The call was from Angela.

"I just got a call from Mrs. McDonnell. You know, Todd's neighbor on the West Bank? She'd gone outside to grab her trash cans when she saw Jeremy. She said he was walking down the street with a knife in his hand. She saw him stabbing at a couple of tires on cars parked in the street. And then he started walking towards her. She thought she heard him say, 'Kill me.' She ran into her house, and he kept walking down the street."

"Oh, my God. I'll drive down to see if I can find him, but I'd bet he's not going to be there."

Ren would be furious if he knew that she was going to look for Jeremy in the middle of the night. Especially if he knew about the knife. But she had to. Jeremy could be a danger to others and certainly was putting himself in jeopardy. She'd call 911 if she got in trouble. She gathered her purse and keys.

"Ren, I need to go out for a little while. Something's come up in the Wilcox case."

"What in the world would require you to leave your home at this time of night?"

"I can't really say, but trust me. I need to go." Emma cringed. Nothing she was saying made sense, even to her.

"This doesn't sound safe. Stay here and handle whatever it is tomorrow morning."

"I don't expect you to understand, but I have to go. I feel like I have no choice. And I need you to stay here and make sure the boys are okay, please." She ran down the stairs before Ren could say anything else.

Ren shouted down the stairwell. "You always have choices, Emma."

But Emma was already in her car.

* * *

Emma had no real hope of finding Jeremy, but she had to try. If she found him, she didn't have a plan for what she was going to do. Calling the police would be the safest thing to do for herself, but the most dangerous thing for Jeremy. If he still had a weapon in his hand, and she called the police, she couldn't rely on him to cooperate. He might be shot. The mentally ill didn't fare well in confrontations with the police.

She drove toward the Huey P. Long Bridge, following the route she usually took down Claiborne Avenue. It was well after dark, and she crept down the roadway. She was afraid she wouldn't be able to see Jeremy. She kept her eyes peeled for anyone walking along the side of the street.

Emma turned left at the bridge's ramp, then right, onto the bridge itself, slowing her car to a crawl. The bridge was not illuminated at night except for the lights from passing cars. But tonight, there were no cars. It was eerily quiet. Emma stared into the inky darkness, creeping up the cantilevered structure, cautiously searching for Jeremy. The Huey P. Long was scary, even when she was able to keep her eyes on the road.

An approaching train made the bridge quake. Emma felt her heartbeat in her throat. Train tracks on the bridge were sandwiched between two separate vehicular traffic lanes, all spanning the Mississippi River. She heard the train's haunting horn growing louder as it crossed—its narrow beacon of light shining along the tracks. The bridge towered one hundred and fifty feet above the river, where the wind gusts climbed as high as seventy miles per hour and even higher during hurricanes and storms. Years ago, four train cars were thrown off of the bridge by heavy gusts of wind.

The bridge began to sway from the power and weight of the approaching engines. Emma fought an urge to close her eyes as she slowly climbed. At the bridge's apex, she saw a thin figure standing by the bridge railing, his hair and white tee shirt blowing wildly in the wind. It was Jeremy, grasping the railings and looking out over the water. Emma edged her car closer to the bridge railing. She pulled her parking brake and hit the emergency blinkers. Her car lights shone on Jeremy's back.

She rolled down her car window. "Jeremy, get in the car!" She had to yell to be heard over the wind.

Emma squinted to see more clearly. When Jeremy turned around, he shielded his eyes from her car lights. He was holding something metal in his hand. A rod, or a pipe? Something from a construction site? It wasn't a knife.

How could she convince him to move toward her car? Especially if he was in the middle of an episode. If he became agitated, he could lose his footing, slip, or even jump.

Wind gusts pounded Jeremy. He was in danger of losing his grip on the railing. Although he was tall, he was thin and could easily be blown over the bridge. Emma put her car in drive and edged closer toward him. She could see that he was shaking. He was cold or quaking from the fear of being so high off of the ground.

She reached across the passenger seat, cracking open her car door. The wind slammed it open.

"Jeremy, get in the car! I'm here to help you."

Jeremy shook his head. "I have to kill myself. The voices," he put his hands over his ears. "They won't stop until I die. I'm going to jump!"

But he was afraid. He grabbed the railing, showing no signs of letting go. His instinct to survive the adverse circumstances of wind and the roiling waters below seemed to be stronger than the voices in his head. Jeremy didn't want to jump.

"Get in, Jeremy! Grab the car door!"

He shook his head.

She reached out to Jeremy. "Please get in!" She hesitated, waiting for Jeremy's response. "Aren't you cold? I have a blanket in my car. Would you like the blanket?"

Emma reached over the back of the car seat and grabbed her 'emergency' blanket from the back. It was a throw she used to protect her back seat from dogs, plants, and whatever else she was hauling. She held it up for Jeremy to see.

"I have something to warm you up!"

Jeremy turned his back on her and put his foot on the bottom rail.

Emma didn't want to step outside of the car, but Jeremy was clearly positioning himself to jump. She moved across the front seat of her car and stepped out of the passenger's door. She gripped the door, partially protected from the wind.

Emma reached her hand out again. "Get in the car, Jeremy. You'll be safe and warm there."

Jeremy turned around, staring at Emma for several seconds, then took a step toward the open door.

Emma stepped aside, giving Jeremy a clear path to the car. He was still gripping a metal pipe. As he moved closer, she took his arm and led him in, shocked that he followed.

Once he was inside the car, she handed him the blanket. He pulled it up to his chin, shivering. She walked around to the driver's side and climbed in. Now her hands were shaking.

"Is that better?" Emma acted much calmer than she felt. But she remembered what Katherine Green had told her. When Jeremy is in the middle of an episode, he needs grounding, a reminder of who and where he is.

Jeremy nodded. Shivering, he began to curl up in the front seat, his head resting on the car door, the metal pipe still gripped in his hand.

"I'm your attorney, and you are Jeremy Wilcox. We are on top of the Huey P. Long Bridge, and we're going to drive to the bottom of the bridge and turn around. Does that sound okay to you?"

Jeremy nodded.

Emma touched the metal pipe. "You might be more comfortable if I move this to the floorboard, here, right by your feet."

Jeremy sat up and looked at Emma. Then nodded and put the pipe on the floor of the car.

She wiped the sweat from her palms on her pants. She didn't realize until now how nervous she'd been. She inhaled deeply trying to calm down, then put her car in gear. She climbed the remaining span of the bridge, then made a U-turn at the bottom. She was taking him back to Charity, but she didn't want him to know.

She looked at Jeremy. He was still shaking.

"Are you still hearing voices?"

Jeremy shook his head.

"Let me know if you'd like me to stop and get you something to eat or drink."

He shook his head again.

Emma hesitated. She wasn't certain how he'd react to her next question, but she decided to plunge ahead.

"Jeremy, how were you able to escape from Charity? Are you a magician or something?"

Jeremy, still shaking, smiled. "It's a secret."

"The door to your room is locked, right?"

Jeremy shook his head. "Not the door to my room. The door at the end of the hallway is locked."

"Do you know how to unlock that door?"

"I know the code. The officer sitting down at the end of the hall, Officer Nelson, falls asleep when he's on duty, and if he isn't asleep, he's down in the lunch room." He nodded again, smiling to himself and pulling Emma's blanket tighter around his shoulders.

"When I want to leave, I make sure Officer Nelson has nodded off. And that's easy because he snores really loud. I usually head out when it's late. Like two o'clock in the morning. Since I know the code to the door, all I do is enter it and leave."

"How do you know the door code?"

"I saw Officer Nelson entering it. The electricity went off one day, and he had to reset the code. I watched him do it."

"And that's all there is to it?"

He nodded.

"They never changed the code?"

"One time. But I watched him make the change. I guess they don't realize that we pay attention to what's going on."

"What about security cameras?"

He fished around in his pocket and pulled out a roll of masking tape, and showed it to Emma. "That's where the tape comes in." He smiled.

"You tape over the lens?"

He nodded. "Nobody ever notices. I could walk out right in front of those nurses, and they wouldn't look up. They pay more attention to what they're writing in their charts than to us. That and making sure we take our medicine."

Emma shook her head. "Well, you're full of surprises." She smiled. "I see you're wearing your regular clothes, not the prison uniform. Where did you get your tee shirt and jeans, Jeremy?"

"I got them at my dad's house. I have stuff there."

"Why were you at your dad's house?"

"I needed some money. My dad keeps money in the house." Jeremy was still shivering. "I don't feel very good." He paused. "I need some Oxy."

"I don't think more Oxy is the answer. Did you find any money at your dad's house?"

"You're wrong. Oxy helps." He started breathing heavily.

Emma did not want him to become agitated, especially when she was driving.

"But you got some money from your dad?"

"Not from him. I found it. He always has some in a jar in the kitchen. Sometimes, when he's asleep, I'll sneak in and get the money in his wallet."

"Was he sleeping when you were there?"

"No. I didn't see him."

"Was it daytime or nighttime when you went to your dad's house?"

"It was dark outside."

Emma sighed. Jeremy must have been there at a time when his dad wasn't home. But it would be impossible to prove.

"You told me before that you buy Oxy from a friend. What's the friend's name?"

He giggled. "I was kidding you. It's not a friend. It's Becky."

Chapter Twenty-Five

"Do you mean Rebecca, your sister?"

Jeremy nodded. "Becky."

Emma leaned her head against the neck rest, squinting at approaching car lights. It was late. She was beginning to feel the effects of her day, which was filled with more emotional angst than she normally experienced in an entire year. Her head hurt, her eyes hurt, and her heart was broken. She didn't want to face the problems with her sons. She just wanted to crawl into bed with Ren and have him hold her until she fell asleep.

Instead, she was driving to Charity Hospital, in the middle of the night, with Jeremy Wilcox shaking beside her. She wanted to get home, but that wasn't going to happen anytime soon.

Jeremy stirred under his blanket. "Where are we going?"

"We're going somewhere where you can get a nice hot shower, some food, and some medicine to help you feel better."

"I don't want any medicine."

"You said that voices were telling you things. You even wanted to jump off that bridge because they were telling you that was the only way to get rid of the voices. Do you remember that, Jeremy?"

He nodded.

"But if you'd take the medicine the doctors give you, the voices will go away."

"Yeah, but that stuff makes me twitch and feel weird. I don't like it."

"Would you consider letting the doctors change your medication until they find something that doesn't make you twitch?"

He shrugged.

"The oxycodone could make you feel bad too. How often do you take it?"

Jeremy shook his head. "The oxy makes me feel a lot better. I feel good when I take it, and bad if I don't." He paused. "My hands don't shake when I take it. I feel relaxed." He looked down at his trembling hands.

"How long has Becky been supplying these pills to you?"

He shrugged again. "I don't know. Maybe a couple of years?"

"How does she get them to you?"

"She usually comes by the house."

"How many times a week does Becky come by?"

"Maybe once a month. Maybe not that much."

"How many pills would she usually bring you?"

He shrugged. "Maybe five or six. But she only lets me have them one at a time. Dad would leave for work around eight o'clock in the morning, and would come home after six. So, she'd usually come by after school, but before Dad got home." He took a deep breath. "She got the stuff from other people. Like that lady where she's living." He laid his head back on the neck rest. His breathing was labored. And he was still shivering.

"Are you cold?"

He nodded, and Emma switched on the seat warmer.

He swallowed loudly. His mouth was dry. "I need something to drink."

"We'll get something for you soon. We're almost there." Emma was on Claiborne Avenue. The hospital wasn't that far away.

"Sometimes, me and Becky would look for stuff in Dad's bathroom. Sometimes we'd walk to Mom's."

"Why did you walk to your mother's?"

"We'd leave her messages. And she had pills too."

"Messages?" Emma glanced at Jeremy. He was asleep.

She pulled into the Charity Emergency entrance. She couldn't take the chance of leaving him in the car while she spoke to the ER attendant.

She touched his shoulder. "Jeremy, we're here."

Jeremy opened his eyes, blinking. "What? Where are we?"

"This is where you can get some food and a shower. You'll feel better soon."

"No! This is the hospital! I'm not going in, and you can't make me!" He bolted from the car and started running down the driveway.

Emma dashed after him, guessing he was at least five strides ahead. A hospital security officer who had been standing at the ER entrance made two quick leaps and caught him, quickly placing him in a bear hug, both of his arms encircling Jeremy's shoulders.

"What's going on here?" He frowned at Emma. "I know Jeremy. He's run away so many times from this place most of us know him by now."

"He was admitted yesterday and ran away sometime after he checked in. I found him tonight on the Huey Long bridge."

"Good for you." He hesitated. "I need to call the third floor. I don't know if he has to go through the readmission process or not." He walked Jeremy into the ER, one arm still around his shoulders, Emma's blanket dragging on the hospital floor. Emma trailed behind them.

The officer turned and looked at Emma. "Who are you, by the way?"

"I'm Jeremy's attorney, Emma Thornton."

"What you did tonight was foolish. Why didn't you call the police?"

"I was afraid something would happen to Jeremy.

"You need to trust your community's law enforcement a little more than that." He asked the ER intake nurse to put him in touch with the third-floor nursing station. He was connected immediately.

"They said to bring him on up."

"Plus, they have a court order requiring Jeremy's admission."

The officer gestured to an orderly standing in the hall who pushed over something that looked like a wheelchair with extra straps. Emma held her breath as Jeremy sat down. As soon as the orderly attempted to fasten the straps around his ankles, Jeremy jerked his leg away and tried to stand up, forcing the officer to hold him down while the remaining straps were secured. Jeremy pulled against the straps, straining, screaming, kicking, trying to stand up.

Emma felt as if she couldn't breathe.

The officer nodded to the orderly. "Go ahead and bring him up. Third Floor. They'll take it from there." He looked at Emma. "I'd tell you to go up too, but it's after visiting hours, and you're not family." He smiled. "And by the looks of things, you need some rest. It's late. Go on home. We'll take it from here."

"Jeremy tried to commit suicide tonight on the bridge. The nurses will need to know this."

"I'll go up and let them know. The NOPD may want to talk to you about it. Let me get your telephone number."

Emma gave him her card. "Will he be restrained once he gets up there?"

"I don't know. After what he did the last two nights, probably."

"He told me that he knows the door code on his hallway. That's how he's been escaping. So, if they'd change the code, they wouldn't need to restrain him. And they'll need to make sure he's not around when they do it. He watches."

"I'll let them know."

"Does anyone know what time he ran away last night?"

"I don't, but I can find out for you." He handed Emma his card. "You can call me tomorrow morning. I should know by then."

Emma tucked the card in her wallet. "Jeremy told me that he's hearing voices, and they're telling him to do harmful things to himself. Please tell the person in charge tonight that I said someone should watch him twenty-four hours a day. If he escapes again, it could be fatal."

* * *

Emma's mind was swirling. She was overwhelmed, physically and mentally. And she was worried. She knew that all violent acts leave behind some trace evidence, either fibers, gunshot residue, hairs, fingerprints, or blood. What, if any, trace evidence did Todd's killer leave behind? And did any of that evidence belong to Jeremy?

Chapter Twenty-Six

I t was late when she got home. Ren was awake, sitting up in bed. Even though he was down the hallway, one look at his face made her turn around and grab a glass and a bottle of wine from the kitchen before she entered the room.

"Want anything? A beer or something?" Emma poured an extra-large glass of wine for herself.

"No, you know I don't drink anything, but especially not beer, right before I go to sleep." He hesitated. "But I am anxious to hear what you've been up to tonight."

Emma sighed. She didn't like the edge to Ren's voice. Plus, she really didn't want to get into what had happened. "Like I said, I thought it was an emergency. And I was right. I needed to be there, but everything's okay now. How were the boys after I left?"

"The boys were quiet. They went to sleep right after you left. I think they're dreading their punishment."

"No hanging out on the rooftop smoking?"

"Not that I noticed. That is something we should look out for, though. But you changed the subject. I wanted to know what *you've* been up to. Leaving your home in the middle of the night for a client 'emergency' is not situation normal. And I've asked you before to let me at least know where you're going. You ran out of here without saying much of anything. I didn't know where you were, or what you were doing, and," he glanced at the clock on the bedside table, "now it's after midnight. This is crazy."

Emma drained her glass.

"Were you with the client with mental health issues last night?"

Emma raised her eyebrows.

"Come on. You've always told me a little something about your cases, so I wouldn't worry. What's it about this case that's making you so secretive?"

"I don't mean to be secretive. There are certain things I can't say, though."

"There have always been certain things you shouldn't say, and it didn't bother you so much before. You're more guarded than usual about this one."

"I don't know if that's true. But I've probably had better intuition about my other murder cases. I knew Stacey Roberts, for one thing. I didn't believe she had it in her to kill anyone. And, early on, I had the sense that both Adam Gannon, and Louis Bishop were set up.

"But this case makes me feel lost. I don't have a clear sense of anything. I've done my research. I know that people with schizophrenia are more likely to hurt themselves than other people. But that doesn't mean I know what Jeremy is capable of doing." She paused. "I left tonight because I felt as if Jeremy might be in danger. People with mental health issues who get themselves into confrontational situations with the police lose almost every time. I didn't want that to happen."

Ren shook his head. "You left because you didn't want to face your problems here. The boys needed you more than your client."

Emma drew in a breath. That stung. "I'm sorry I worried you. I won't do it again." Emma turned and walked out of the room. She grabbed the bottle of wine from the kitchen and brought it out to the balcony. Three glasses of wine later, she fell into bed.

* * *

A part of Emma knew that Ren had been right last night, but she wanted to ignore what he said. She wasn't a perfect mom, but she tried. She tried hard. And she hadn't anticipated the evening she'd had with her boys. How could Bobby lie so blatantly? How could Billy take off with those kids to buy beer at a bar and walk back smoking cigarettes? Why couldn't they stand up to peer pressure? It all made her feel like a failure. Her boys were perfect, and she was singlehandedly messing them up.

She flipped open her calendar. She couldn't afford to wallow in misery all day. She'd scheduled a meeting with Dr. Washington, the psychologist who had taken over Dr. Rayford's practice, at noon. She needed help.

* * *

Dr. Washington stepped out into the waiting room and motioned for her to follow him. He looked very much as he had when she first met him. He was wearing a different version of the casual buttoned-down shirt he'd had at their first meeting. Sleeves rolled up as before, glasses on top of his head, a notebook in his hand, he was ready to listen. She was happy something in her life was consistent.

They sat down in his office.

"What's up, Emma? You sounded a little stressed when you called."

Emma told him what had happened to Jeremy over the last twenty-four hours.

"The thing is, I knew that Jeremy had escaped from Charity before. But it wasn't my place to tell the judge. Jeremy will always try to escape from that place. He hates it."

"It's common in people with schizophrenia. It's called absconding. This isn't your fault."

Emma nodded. "But if I'd known Jeremy was going to attempt suicide, I would have told the court, or anyone else who would listen."

"I don't think you need to fret about that. And I'm not making light of the situation. Psychologists have to make the same decisions all the time. The doctor-patient privilege is just as strong, maybe even stronger than the attorney-client privilege. And sometimes, those rules conflict with what you might think is the best thing for your client or your patient. So, just accept what you did. It was the best thing you could do in the moment. Unfortunately, suicide is a known risk for people diagnosed with schizophrenia. Had they cared to look into it, the court and the DA could have figured that out for themselves. And the DA could have easily discovered Jeremy's history of escaping from Charity."

He looked down at his notepad, where he had scribbled some notes. "But, in running out in the middle of the night to find him, you put yourself in danger. That might be something you should look at. Do you have 'rescuer syndrome'?"

"I don't think so. I hope not. I never think of myself that way. Last night I was told that Jeremy was seen in his father's neighborhood with a knife in his hand. I was afraid if the police saw him with a weapon and stopped him, it might not end well."

"That sounds like a dangerous situation. And you *were* being a rescuer – to your detriment."

"I was being protective. That's true. And there's probably more to it, but I'd like to move on." Emma wasn't in the mood for questions about her motivations.

"Okay. But someday, you need to look at that. Honestly."

Emma nodded. She appreciated Dr. Washington and his position. But she didn't feel like taking an honest look at herself at the moment. "When I left Jeremy last night at Charity, I was told they'd probably restrain him. I guess that means in bed. And to bring him up to the third floor, they strapped him into a wheelchair. It was awful. Medieval-like. He was strapped up like cargo, from his head to his feet. He hadn't been that agitated before, but after they buckled him up in that contraption, he went wild. And I don't blame him. He started kicking and screaming. I told him they'd give him something to eat. He hadn't eaten in forever. But I didn't see anyone offering him food. It seems like I put him in worse circumstances by bringing him to Charity."

"I don't agree. And what else could you have done? He was ordered by the court to be admitted to Charity, and they had to accept him. And just so you know, they can't restrain him in a chair longer than two hours."

"But even that's a long time."

"I know. But look. The hospital will stabilize his meds. Once he's stabilized and doesn't hear the voices in his head, he'll be much better off. This is the best course."

"Will Jeremy be competent to stand trial after he's medicated?"

"Of course. From what you've told me, when he's not in the middle of an episode, he's a smart, pleasant guy, talented guy, fully capable of understanding what's going on. The important thing for you to remember is that at some point, Jeremy will have to come to terms with the importance of the medication. And he will never do that unless it's explained to him. And he may not be able to hear or understand that explanation unless he's medicated. How can you listen or understand anything if you're hearing a chorus of voices in your head?"

Emma nodded. "I get it. But the medicine makes him feel badly. I'm not sure anyone will be able to talk him into taking it regularly."

Dr. Washington nodded. "Finding the correct treatment is a challenge."

"I'm not sure he's going to find it at Charity after what I saw last night."

"There has been a lot of improvement there and everywhere else since the 1970s. I think he'll receive proper treatment. And now they know to watch him vigilantly. By the way, I saw Dr. Rayford last night at the grocery store."

Emma was surprised to hear that. What was that man up to?

"Really? He told me he was taking a trip through Europe, on the Orient Express. But at Jeremy's hearing, the prosecution submitted an affidavit signed by Dr. Rayford on April 2, the day after he and his wife were supposed to leave. I thought he wasn't scheduled to return until sometime in early May. Also, this sounds crazy, but I've been seeing a silver car that looks a lot like his all over the city. If I didn't know better, I'd say he was following me."

"That is strange. We talked for a few minutes at the grocery store. He told me that he and his wife had no plans for the summer, and that they'd been doing some spring cleaning and had been working around the house all month."

No way. Dr. Rayford was not the 'spring cleaning' type. Emma suppressed a laugh at the thought of Dr. Rayford in cleaning clothes, waving his black cigarettes all over the house.

"That's so weird. Why would he tell me he'd be out of the country?"

"Maybe they had to change their plans for some reason."

She shrugged. "I don't know. Stephanie Mason, the ADA, invited me to call him, ask about his travel plans, so maybe I will."

* * *

Emma grabbed her purse and prepared to leave Dr. Washington's office, inhaling deeply as she slung her bag on her shoulder and walked into the lobby. She noticed that Clare, Dr. Rayford's former assistant, was at the front desk. Emma walked closer to the glass partition.

"Thanks again for your help the other day with the Wilcox's medical records." Emma smiled.

Clare glanced up at Emma, squinting. Her glasses made her eyes seem at least twice their size. "Wasn't that about a month ago?"

"You're right. It was. I spoke to Dr. Rayford afterwards. He told me he was going out of the country, to Paris, to catch the Orient Express all the way to Istanbul. That must be so exciting. I think he said he's coming back sometime in May?"

Clare shook her head. "I don't know where you got that from. He's here, in New Orleans. He called me yesterday. He wanted a copy of some old records. I think they were the same records you got that day you were here."

"Records from the Wilcox case? Did he say why he wanted them?"

"No, Mrs. Thornton. But if he did, I couldn't tell you."

* * *

Emma started her engine, still perplexed about Dr. Rayford's lie. Why would he feel the need to tell her he was going out of the country when he wasn't? And if that was his silver car she found in her rear-view mirror nearly every day, why was he tailing her? Was he trying to intimidate her?

From what she'd seen of the man so far, Dr. Rayford did more harm than good. Especially with his patients and his insistence on applying antiquated theories to their problems. In contrast, Dr. Washington had opened her mind to an entirely different way of looking at mental illness. Before today, she'd found Jeremy's outbursts, even the prospect of an outburst, alarming.

Now she could see them for what they were, a reaction to the thousands of voices in his head. She needed to remember that sometimes Jeremy was struggling through the chaos in his head to think and to be heard.

Chapter Twenty-Seven

Emma grabbed the mail from her clinic cubbyhole and flipped through her correspondence as she walked down the hallway. One item stood out. A letter from the Orleans Parish Police Department. When she reached her office, she found Angela waiting outside her door.

"Good morning. What brings you here?"

"I got another call from a neighbor on Sally's street. Someone I'd spoken to earlier. She said she saw Jeremy early this morning, walking down the street from his mom's house on Arabella."

"That's impossible, unless Jeremy's managed to take off from Charity again. I checked him into the hospital last night. They seem to be on high alert now. I doubt if they'd let him slip away again, especially so soon after his last escape. But, when we finish, please call the hospital and confirm that he's there. I'd hate to be mistaken about that." She held the door open for Angela.

She ripped into the envelope from the police department.

"It's the complete homicide report we requested weeks ago." She scanned the first page. "Most of the report is prepared by a patrol officer."

Emma finished reading the report.

"Looks like we already know most of what was reported. He said she was ready for bed when she was attacked. So, she wasn't expecting visitors."

"There's also a report from a criminalist, Dr. Steven Jacobs, who examined the blood spatter in the kitchen. Dr. Jacobs' report states that that every blow struck placed its 'signature on the room' with corresponding spatter, with one exception. There was an approximate three-foot-wide span directly in front of Sally." She looked up from the page. "He said that was where the killer stood." Emma raised her eyebrows. "That seems to rule out suicide. And I'd bet the killer has a blood-spattered shirt hidden away somewhere, unless he's already gotten rid of it."

"He probably has the missing kitchen knife, too," Angela said.

"Dr. Jacobs also examined the knife Sally was holding and found traces of blood and DNA on that blade. She must have tried to defend herself. The DNA on the knife blade isn't a match for Sally, but Dr. Jacobs said that it's the DNA of a close relative."

"Oh, crap."

"Right." Emma shook her head and flipped another page. "The Medical Examiner prepared a preliminary autopsy report, too." She ruffled through the pages. "The ME described all of the wounds. They were all abdominal wounds, and each wound was fatal." Emma frowned. "Says here that the ME ruled the death a homicide."

Angela pursed her lips. "I think we're going to have to accept the fact that it's not looking good for Jeremy."

"Yes." Emma sighed. "The revised report also repeats some of what we already knew. The tennis ball and shoe prints are listed as evidence from the scene, but there are a couple of new findings. They also found a box of hand-written notes from unknown persons in Sally's vanity in the bedroom and a prescription for oxycodone in the bathroom. There were Gitanes cigarette butts on the porch, in front of the living room window, and at the back of the house, by the back door. The one that leads to the kitchen." She looked up from the report. "We don't know whether Sally smoked. We need to confirm that one way or the other. But I do know that that's Dr. Rayford's brand."

"Gitanes are French?"

"I think so. Dr. Rayford bought his from one of the smoke shops in the Quarter. Do you have time to go to one of those shops and see whether they know who sells them?"

Angela nodded. "Sure."

"Also, as soon as you can, please call Nancy Bennett about those security

163

tapes. If she has them in, please schedule a time for us to view them. I'll get in touch with Dr. Rayford, Brad LeFleur, and Becky. I need to find out more about Becky's and Jeremy's drug use."

She paused. "I almost forgot. Today I was flipping through Dr. Rayford's notes again. I couldn't understand some of his handwriting when I scanned his notes the other day, but today I think I figured most of it out."

Emma pointed to the note. "It looks like he wrote, 'She said she wanted to kill herself.' The report was dated August 2, 1988. That's about a month before Sally left her family."

"She must have been very depressed."

Emma nodded and turned the page, and pointed to another hand-written note. "I guess I skipped this page earlier. This note says, 'Sally's been having dreams that she killed both of her children, which echoes her father's attack on her brother years ago. She's afraid she might wake up one day to discover that she seriously injured Jeremy and Becky. She thinks she should leave before any harm is done.'" Emma showed Angela the note.

They stared at each other, both stunned.

"Oh, my God! That's why she left. Sally was afraid she'd hurt her children, like her dad. Walking away from them was an expression of love, not indifference. How sad."

They were silent for a moment. "Sally needed help, but all she got from Dr. Rayford was judgment, and harassment, and an oxycodone prescription."

"Also, Bea said that Sally had been receiving harassing phone calls from a man. Clare got me some of Dr. Rayford's phone records. Dr. Rayford made repeated calls to Sally and must be the person who harassed her, but I'd like to subpoena all of her phone records, and Dr. Rayford's, too. That should prove it. Also, please make an appointment for us to review all of the physical evidence the police have."

Angela nodded and added the items to her 'to-do' list. "What do you think is going on with Dr. Rayford?"

"I'm not sure. I hope to find out soon."

Chapter Twenty-Eight

Emma walked back into her office after her afternoon class. She was exhausted and still a little queasy from the night before. She should be leaving for home soon, but she was dreading it. She and Ren still weren't on the best of terms this morning. She looked up Dr. Rayford's telephone number. She had time for one call.

"This is Emma Thornton again, Dr. Rayford. Stephanie Manor, the ADA in Jeremy Wilcox's case, suggested that I call you to clarify a few issues. You and I spoke several weeks ago at your house. I was there a couple of days before you were scheduled to leave for Europe. You're back home earlier than I thought you'd be."

"Actually, Ms. Thornton, we never left."

"Did you change your plans? Your trip sounded so lovely."

"We decided to put it off until later. Our house needs some work. You know how it is."

Emma didn't believe him. For one thing, he was a little old to make his own house repairs. Plus, if they were actually in the process of a renovation, scheduling it around a European trip would have been ideal for a retired couple. Something wasn't right. And he'd obviously lied. Why did he want Emma to think he was out of town? Was he trying to avoid her or her questions?

"I see. Also, you told me you hadn't been asked to testify in the Jeremy Wilcox case, but you submitted an affidavit in support of the ADA's position. You'll be subpoenaed for trial."

"The only thing in my affidavit is my diagnosis of Jeremy when he was

165

my patient."

"No. That's not true. In fact, the ADA is using your affidavit to support her position that Jeremy is a malingerer." Emma could hear the pace of Dr. Rayford's breathing quicken.

"I can't comment on it. I am a witness for the prosecution now, and I can't talk to you. And I couldn't give you an opinion about his later diagnosis anyway because I didn't see him during those years."

That was a load of crap. But Emma didn't think she'd get any more information from him today. He was antagonistic, slippery, and more than a little strange. Emma didn't believe anything he said.

"What type of car do you drive? I saw a glimpse of it when we met at your house, but I'm not good at recognizing car brands."

"Why do you want to know that? It's none of your business."

"I was asking because I've noticed a silver car almost everywhere I go these days, and it's usually following a few cars behind. Are you tailing me?"

"Of course not. Your questions are exhausting. I'm not entertaining them any longer. If you need something to do, why don't you get that ten-year-old Volvo of yours repaired? It's got a right-sided dent you can see from a mile away. And just leave me alone."

Emma caught her breath. He couldn't have seen the right side of her car the day she was at his house. He entered his car from the garage, opening the door on the driver's side only. Her car was parked in front of his. The right side of her car wouldn't have been visible. There it was. He was stalking her.

"You have been following me."

"Don't be ridiculous. It's not my fault if I'm going about my business and you happen to find your way in front of my car." Emma could feel him smiling.

"Stalking is a crime."

"Clare told me you were difficult. Even demanding. That's the way it always is with beautiful women."

"That's enough, Dr. Rayford. Misogyny is considered a bad thing these days."

"I'm no misogynist. I love women."

Emma had had enough of Dr. Rayford.

Emma closed her notebook. But she wanted to ask one more question. She was interested in his reaction.

"Did you have an affair with Sally Wilcox?"

Dr. Rayford paused. His breathing became quicker. She'd surprised him. "That's another thing that's none of your concern. I'm not in the practice of having affairs with clients. But even if I did, so what? It's not any of your business."

"Is that a 'yes', or a 'no', Dr. Rayford?"

"Good day, Ms. Thornton."

Emma smiled as she hung up. She was glad she'd made him uncomfortable. He deserved it. She would file a report against him for stalking the next time she was downtown.

She gathered her belongings and locked her office door. This was the first time she could remember not looking forward to going home. She didn't feel like facing the tension in the house or any of her responsibility for it. Ren was justified in being upset with her. She should just acknowledge that. She should have called him last night and told him she was going to be late. And she could have told him where she was going, even if she didn't want to give him all of the details.

She sighed. This was not going to be a fun evening.

* * *

"I'm home." She directed her voice toward the boys' upstairs bedroom.

"Hi, Mom!" Bobby and Billy shouted in unison.

She walked into the kitchen, surprised to see the oven light on. She opened the door and peeked in to see salmon lined up on the left side of a cookie sheet, a row of broccoli in the center, and little discs of sweet potatoes lined up along the right side. Ren had copied one of her dinner ideas. She smiled.

He wasn't in the apartment, which meant he was out on a run. She threw her purse and briefcase on the bed and quickly changed clothes. Things were looking up.

Emma heard someone running up the stairwell in the hallway. She opened the front door, smiling at Ren as he sprinted up the steps, two at a time. When he hugged her, she burst into tears.

"What's the matter? Is everything okay?" Ren looked down at her, his face worried. "Tell me what's going on."

"I'm sorry I messed up last night." She sniffed. "I understand why you were upset with me. I feel like such a failure." She put her hands over her face. "The boys are getting into trouble. And the case I'm working on is a mess. We've been working on it for almost a month and have almost nothing to show for it. Everything is up in the air. And it's all my fault."

"I doubt that, but I'm sorry I didn't realize things were so bad."

"I'm so afraid the boys are going to be like their dad. I've told you about his drinking problem. He's struggled with alcoholism for years, but I've never really talked to the boys about it. Obviously, that discussion is past due." She sniffed. "So, I don't think I can condone the drinking at home thing with the boys like you suggested. I just can't do it."

"Whatever needs to be done with the boys, we can do together. I shouldn't have thrown out any new idea without talking to you first."

Emma nodded and put her arms around Ren's chest.

"And I promise I'll do a better job of letting you know what's going on. I'm sorry I didn't let you know what I was doing last night."

Ren squeezed her shoulders. "Yeah. You need to do a better job at that."

Chapter Twenty-Nine

Since it was a Friday, and Emma had no classes, she decided to check on Jeremy and take a look at his living conditions at Charity. She wanted to make sure that a hospital staff member, or a security guard had been assigned to him to prevent another escape.

Emma took an elevator to the third floor. She'd always found walking down the hospital's long dark hallways a little frightening. Twenty floors high, Charity was a massive structure, smelling strongly of antiseptic. The thousands of fluorescent lights lining the corridors did nothing to brighten its colorless, dingy walls. Best known for its trauma unit and for serving those without insurance, the reputation of the psych ward had always been questionable. No one bragged about Charity's third floor.

Emma didn't know the policy for visitors on the psych ward, realizing suddenly that she should have called first. She approached a nurse sitting at a desk close to the third-floor elevators.

"I'm the attorney for one of the patients on this floor, Jeremy Wilcox. Is it possible for me to see him?"

She shook her head. "He's just been given his meds, and it was a rough go. It's not a good time to see him. The best thing for him right now is sleep."

"What are you doing to make sure he gets his medicine on time?"

"We talk to him." She looked at Emma. "None of the patients on this floor want to be here. And they don't want to take their medicine because it makes them feel bad. Some of the patients also have side effects from it. Tardive dyskinesia isn't an easy thing to cope with. So, we tell them they'll get out earlier if they take their meds. It's a big motivator. We do everything we can to avoid forcing them to take their medicine. But Jeremy is especially difficult. He fights it every time."

"I see. Have his meds started to work yet?"

"It takes a few days to see a significant improvement, but he'll get there eventually. He always does."

"So, you know him?"

"Oh, yes. He's been here, on and off, for years. Nice guy when he takes his meds."

"Unfortunately, both of Jeremy's parents are now deceased. I'll need to do something about having a temporary guardian appointed for him."

"If you don't get someone soon, the state could step in. Once they figure out what's going on, they could do that pretty quickly."

"Thanks for the heads up. Also, can you tell me whether guards or staff members are watching him? I'm sure you know about his escape the other night."

"Yes. There's a NOPD unit, Unit 1826, assigned to the ward. They pick up people having mental health crises, either from their home, or on the street, and bring them to us. We call them the 'Disoriented Express.'" She laughed. "They also guard patients who are known escapees and inmate patients. Especially the patients who are under court order, like Jeremy. They're on to him now. I don't think he'll escape again."

Emma left the ward, worried about finding a temporary guardian for Jeremy through trial. She didn't want the state to make decisions for him, or control his money. The only person she could think of to ask was Holly LeFleur, Jeremy's aunt and Sally Wilcox's baby sister. Holly had never taken an active interest in her sister's children, and Emma was afraid she wouldn't now. But she had to ask. Plus, she wanted to speak to Brad.

* * *

Emma pulled up to the LeFleur's driveway on Robert Street and knocked on the massive oak door. There was no response. Emma knocked again, and waited several minutes, then turned to leave. As she was walking down the steps, the door creaked open.

"Can I help you?"

Emma turned and stared at the open door. She couldn't see the person speaking, but recognized Holly's voice. She explained what had happened to Todd Wilcox.

Holly peeked around the door. "Come on in."

Emma stepped into the foyer. "I should have called first, but Jeremy is at risk of becoming a ward of the state. I'd like to do what I can to avoid that, and need to move fast."

Holly led Emma into a dark, dingy-looking front parlor. A layer of dust coated everything, including the baby grand, which occupied one corner of the room, and the Oriental carpet thrown over the top. The drapes were drawn. She and Holly sat down in over-stuffed brocade chairs which belonged to another century.

"Right now, Jeremy is fine, or at least as good as he can be. He's at Charity through his trial. But he will need another guardian appointed since both of his parents are dead. I was hoping you might consider it."

Holly raised her eyebrows. "Sure! That's something I know I can do. The guardian controls the person's property, right? That might be something I can help with." She swallowed loudly. "I'm really busy here, but I might be able to squeeze in a little time to help balance Jeremy's budget. I do that here, for Brad and me. I'm really good at it." She smiled. "But Jeremy's a problem. He'd be hard to work with. Sometimes he's rude; sometimes he talks to people who aren't in the room, sometimes he loses his temper. He'd be better off staying at Charity on a full-time basis."

Emma had a feeling she was going to regret this.

"Like I said, I'll try to keep Jeremy at Charity throughout the trial. But I'm concerned about what might happen to him afterwards. Financial issues could come up. The family home will have to be dealt with. I think Todd told me that Sally paid off the house he was living in so Jeremy would always have a place. But it would be great if a family member could keep up with all of that. We're going to need some help getting in recent medical records. A guardian could be instrumental in getting all of that done."

Holly nodded. "Sure. That's understandable. I'd be happy to help."

"Good. I'll start the process." Emma paused. "Is Brad here today?"

"Yes. He's in the kitchen."

Emma noticed a purplish scar on Holly's arm, barely emerging from her sleeve. The scar was in the later stages of healing. She hadn't noticed it earlier.

"Is that new?" She nodded in the direction of Holly's arm.

Holly pulled her sleeve over the healing wound. "Yeah. I got it a few weeks ago. I burned myself taking something out of the oven."

"Kitchen burns can really hurt." Emma paused. "I'd like to speak to Brad today, if he has a few minutes. I don't have many questions."

"I'll see. He's working on somebody's late-filed return." Holly walked down the hall to the kitchen where Brad was working.

Seconds later, Holly returned to the living room. "He can't take the time today. His client wants his return finished immediately."

Emma sighed. She had anticipated this. "Nancy Bennett was your sister's friend and landlord. She was the one who found Sally the morning after her murder. She also said she saw Brad that morning, riding his bicycle on Magazine Street, right where it intersects with Arabella. Do you have any idea why Brad would have been riding his bike so close to his sister's house?"

"No. I don't. How could I?"

"Does Brad ride his bicycle every day?"

"Not that I know of."

"How often does he ride?"

"I don't know. I really don't pay that much attention."

Emma didn't believe her. She paid attention to everything Brad did.

"I'd like to ask Brad about this. It shouldn't take long."

"Suit yourself. But just so you know, irritating Brad will not work in your favor."

"I'll make it short." Emma stood up. "I remember the way."

The sound of Brad's typing led Emma down the hallway to the kitchen. It didn't seem as if Brad had moved since the last time she saw him. His back was facing her. He was looking at spreadsheets.

"Mr. LeFleur, I'd like to speak with you for just a minute or two."

There was no response.

Emma cleared her throat. Brad wasn't wearing earphones. He should be able to hear her.

"I only have one question, Mr. LeFleur."

Brad spun around in his chair. "What? Can't you see I'm busy?"

"You were seen on Magazine Street and Arabella on the morning after Sally's murder. Can you tell me why you were there?"

"I don't remember, but I like to ride my bike. And I get out as often as I can. It's good exercise." He ran his fingers through his hair, which only made it seem greasier.

"What shoes were you wearing that morning?"

"How am I supposed to remember that?"

"Do you own a pair of Converse All Stars?"

Brad sighed. "I'm not answering your stupid shoe questions."

* * *

On the way to her car, Emma noticed a utility room or shed at the top of the LeFleur's driveway, next to the house and garbage cans. She scrambled through her purse and fished out a few used Kleenex, then tossed them in the trash cans. The utility room was adjacent to the cans—its door cracked open. She took a couple of steps toward the door and peered through the opening. There she saw a bike and a pair of Converse All Stars draped over the handlebars. She pulled her camera out of her bag and took a photograph.

Chapter Thirty

Emma decided she needed what her mother called a 'come to Jesus' meeting with Becky. It was time for her to tell the truth.

"Hi, Catherine. I'd like to arrange a time when I could come by and see Becky. I'd like to ask her a few questions."

"If you're going to come by today, you'll need to get here in the next fifteen to thirty minutes. I asked her to do some grocery shopping for us, and that's got to be done pretty soon."

Emma wasn't surprised Catherine was keeping a tight grip on Becky and her activities. Becky was controlled, used. From what Emma could tell, Catherine didn't even allow Becky to answer the phone. The Shepherds lived in an elegant home, but Emma didn't know how Becky tolerated her living arrangements.

"I'll be there in thirty minutes."

The drive over the Huey P. Long bridge was always difficult, but, after Jeremy's suicide attempt, it held new horrors for Emma. She shook her head, trying to forget the memory of Jeremy stepping onto the bridge railing, and was relieved when she finally made her way to the other side.

Jeremy said Becky sold drugs to him, but that didn't seem to square with everything else Emma knew about her. Becky didn't seem to desire many creature comforts. She was a minimalist. A person who dressed in jeans and tee shirts. She kept her hair short, her words succinct. Dealers were willing to risk their freedom, and sometimes their lives, for money. Emma had seen no sign of that from Becky.

She parked her car in front of the Shepherd's home and rang the doorbell.

174

Catherine, dressed in another pastel frilly pants outfit, answered.

"I'd like to speak to Becky if she's still here."

Catherine's mouth twitched into a smile. "Becky! Ms. Thornton is here to see you!" Catherine pointed to the sunroom. "Make yourself comfortable, Professor."

Emma heard Becky's shoes beat a quick rhythm down the stairs. She scurried into the sunroom where Emma was waiting and flung herself into the couch.

"Nice to see you again, Becky. Do you have any more news about the St. Stanislaus admission?"

Becky shrugged. "I haven't heard a thing. But I still have a few months. And if I can't get in this semester, there's always the next. But I'd like to get out of here sooner rather than later, if you know what I mean."

"I thought your plans were to stay here during school so you wouldn't have to pay rent."

"Those are Catherine's plans. Not mine."

"I see. What are your plans?"

"I'd like to get a job. A real job. St. Stanislaus offers night classes, so I could work and go to school. A lot of people do that. I'd rather be on my own even though I wouldn't have to worry about money if I stayed here."

"I understand." Emma checked the list in her notepad. "I'd like to ask you a few questions today that could be difficult to answer. I'd appreciate it if you would try your best."

Becky nodded.

"Do you know when Jeremy started taking oxycodone?"

"Like I've told you before, I haven't lived at home for nine years. I was ten when I left. I don't know anything about Jeremy's drug use, or if he even has a drug problem."

Emma's pressed her lips into a straight line. "Not according to Jeremy. He asked for oxycodone a few days ago when I was with him. I asked him where he usually got the pills, and he told me he got them from you."

Becky stared at Emma without changing her facial expression.

"What do you have to say about that, Becky? Have you supplied painkillers

175

to your brother?"

"I'm not going to answer a question like that." Becky lowered her head and peered at Emma from under her heavy bangs.

"I'm trying to pin this down for a few reasons. The first thing I need to figure out, obviously, is whether Jeremy was at your mother's house on the night she was killed. It would be great if you have any information that could help me with that."

"And the answer to that would be 'no.'"

"Okay. Then, just between us, assume for a minute that he was there and that he did stab your mother. I'll need to figure out whether his behavior was related to his mental illness, or opioid use, or both in order to mount a defense. Insanity can be a complete defense to a crime, but..."

Becky interrupted. "Would it be enough if Jeremy was high on painkillers when it happened?"

Emma shook her head. "No. I know it sounds backwards. But intoxication isn't a defense to a second-degree murder charge. That's what the state has charged Jeremy with—second-degree murder. Killing someone in a drunken rage *is* second-degree murder. So, I'd like to know if you can tell me whether Jeremy has a problem with painkillers?"

Emma met Becky's gaze.

"I don't know whether he has an addiction or a problem with them. I do know that he uses painkillers sometimes."

"How did you learn that?"

Becky sighed. "He told me."

"When did Jeremy talk to you about this? I thought you only saw each other once or twice a year."

She shrugged. "I lied about that. A few years ago, Jeremy called me. He said he needed help. So, I went over to his house, and we started getting together about every week after that. But I don't want to tell you anything that's going to get me or Jeremy in trouble."

"Jeremy's already in trouble, and there's no question about whether he needs help. What do you know about Jeremy taking painkillers?"

Becky stared at Emma, crossing her arms across her chest.

"This is important. Is he still taking them? And don't worry; I'm not going to use anything you say against you," she paused, "unless you're the murderer." Emma pressed her lips together.

Becky frowned. "I didn't kill my mom, and as far as I know, Jeremy didn't either. I loved her, and so did Jeremy, but everything was so messed up. And she was so messed up." She pulled her legs up on the couch and hugged her knees. "Jeremy got into my dad's medicine cabinet like four years ago and tried one. My Dad hurt his back at the plant, and a doctor prescribed the pills for his back pain. This was right before the time Jeremy was diagnosed. He doesn't feel good when he's having an episode, and was looking for something that calmed him down, or calmed down the voices in his head. When Jeremy took Dad's pills, he got sleepy, but the voices went away for a little while."

"I can understand that, but what I don't get is how and why you got involved in this."

"Jeremy skipped school a lot. Not while mom was homeschooling him, obviously, but later. Dad would go to work, and Jeremy wouldn't get on the bus. I did the same thing. I'd act like I was going to school, then sneak back in the house. Catherine never knew.

"The day he called me, we were both cutting school. I walked over to his house that day, and when I got there, he was about to take a handful of Dad's pills. I took them from him. I was really surprised he let me do that. But I convinced him that he could only take one pill at a time. I was afraid he'd OD. Jeremy's really a good guy. If voices aren't screaming at him, he'll listen."

"Did Jeremy keep the pills, or did you?"

"I did. I didn't think I could trust him to take only one consistently, especially if he was having an episode. But he was okay taking only one pill at a time if I was handing them out to him."

"Interesting. So, did you run out of your dad's pills?"

"Yep. But I knew that Mom used to have plenty. At least, I knew that her pills looked just like Dad's. So, Jeremy and I walked all the way to her house when she was at work one day."

"You walked? How long did that take?"

"It takes a little over two hours to walk it from the West Bank." She paused. "Not bad."

"How did you get inside your mom's house?"

"Mom always kept a key to the house hidden somewhere by the back door. We guessed she'd do the same thing at her new place, and we were right. We found a key under the mat and opened the door to her house. We wouldn't ever stay very long. We'd just get some pills, but never all the pills. Sometimes we'd leave a note. And then we'd leave."

"You'd leave notes?"

"Yeah. Little messages to Mom. We left them around the house to surprise her."

"What sort of messages?"

"Just silly stuff, like 'guess who?' or 'we came by to say 'hi!' Stuff like that. One time Jeremy drew her a picture and left it on her nightstand."

Poor kids. Emma couldn't imagine the pain they'd gone through throughout their life. They were orphans even before their parents died.

"You missed her?"

She nodded. "Yeah. Especially Jeremy."

"Did your mom ever write back? Did she ever leave anything for you?"

Becky nodded. Emma could see her eyes watering. "She did. She'd just tell us she missed us and that she loved us." She shook her head. "I don't know what it was, but something terrible made her stay away. Something she was afraid of. Jeremy never understood, and I'm only guessing. But I think she loved us."

"I'm sure she did. Do you think she knew that you were taking her medicine?"

"She had to have. But we didn't take that much. Jeremy never had more than one pill a day, and he usually took them when he was having an episode. He doesn't hear voices all the time."

"Did you get the pills from any other source?"

Becky nodded. "I got in the habit of checking other people's bathroom cabinets for them, too. You'd be surprised how many people take painkillers."

"By other people, do you mean the Shepherds?"

Becky smiled, then nodded.

"Do you think your mom had a pain pill addiction?"

"I wouldn't know. All I know is that she always had them, and she had a lot."

"Did you ever see anything at your mom's house that stood out to you as unusual or even dangerous?"

"I noticed a guy in a silver-colored fancy car parked there a few times. There was a little black horse on a yellow shield on the back of the car. I think it's a Ferrari."

"How often would you see that car?"

"I don't know. Five times for sure. Maybe even more. I wasn't counting." She shrugged. "And we'd see black cigarette stubs at the back door and sometimes on the front porch. It was like someone had been standing there, staring into the window and smoking.

"And once, when we were leaving, we saw an older guy get out of that car. He left something in a plastic bag in Mom's mailbox. It looked like pills, white ones."

"Did anything else happen when you and Jeremy were over at your mom's place? Did a neighbor see you, or did you ever break anything of your mom's? Does anything stand out in your memory?"

"I don't know." She hesitated. "I'm guessing that neighbors saw us, because people are always out, working in their yards over there. And every time we walked in the house, the parrot would say, 'yoo-hoo.' He's a cute bird.

"Then one time, it might have been the day Mom was killed, we were over there to get a few pills. I'd started cutting Jeremy back—giving him fewer pills because he seemed to want to take more and more. I didn't think it was good for him. Anyway, we heard something outside. It sounded like a car door slamming in the driveway. We got scared and left through the back door."

"Was anyone in the driveway?"

"Nothing was in the driveway. But that silver car was parked in front of the house. I didn't see anyone in it."

"Did you leave on bikes, or were you walking?"

"We were walking. And when we were about halfway over the bridge, Jeremy reached in his pocket and screamed, 'my ball!' He wanted to go back to get it, but I wouldn't let him. He was pretty upset."

Emma paused, taking in everything Becky had just told her. Now she knew why Sally had put up with Dr. Rayford over the years. She had a pain pill addiction that he not only encouraged, but fed.

She was certain that the police had found Jeremy's fingerprints at his mother's house, but now, if Becky would agree to testify, she could explain why. And she had an answer for why Jeremy's ball was at the scene of the murder. But the biggest reveal was Becky's compassion. She wasn't selling drugs to Jeremy. She was trying to help her brother, even though she may not have used good judgment. She was a kid, and didn't seem to grasp the consequences of what they were doing. But it was clear she cared about her brother.

"I'd like you to consider testifying at trial about breaking into your mom's house to leave messages. But there could be problems with that testimony. The prosecution might wonder why you didn't just put your notes in the mailbox. But your testimony would also explain why Jeremy's DNA and fingerprints were in your mom's house."

"My testimony could also get me arrested. But I'll think about it."

Emma nodded. "It could come out that you were trying to steal painkillers for your brother. And that's illegal."

Becky nodded. "I'll let you know what I decide to do."

Emma didn't blame her for being worried. This would be a tough decision for anyone. Testify and risk jail, or remain silent, and watch her brother serve time for murder.

"Thanks. And one more question. You said you and Jeremy were at your mom's house the day she was killed. What time of day was it when you left?"

"We left at three o'clock. We had to get back before Dad got home. I didn't have to worry about Catherine. I never see her unless she sends me on an errand or gives me another chore."

Chapter Thirty-One

Angela rushed into Emma's office without knocking.

"Boy, do I have some stuff to tell you!"

Emma smiled. "I hope it's good news. I could use some."

"It's definitely news." She raised her eyebrows. "I'll leave the interpretation of it to you." Angela took a deep breath. "Nancy Bennett has received the video tapes from the night of the murder. The security company keeps the tapes for six weeks, so she received tapes from a couple of weeks before Sally's death, and the tapes from about a month afterwards."

"Did you review them?"

"I did. But I think you should go by to see them too. Nancy hasn't called the police yet, but she will. It's evidence, so as soon as they hear about it, they'll run over and pick it up."

"And? What did you see?"

Angela pressed her lips together. "Jeremy was at his mom's house the night of the murder. He was wearing his usual jeans and tee shirt. But he had a hoodie on over his shirt. His tennis shoes looked like Converse All Stars. He was also wearing a baseball cap. He walked around to the back of the house and picked up the mat, obviously for the key, and then unlocked the back door. That's not all I saw, but that was plenty."

"What time was this?"

"Around midnight."

Emma's heart sank.

"Are you sure it was him? Jeans, tee-shirt, and a hoodie don't exactly make him stand out in a crowd. Was there anything you saw that made him unique? Glasses, a watch or bracelet, a necklace? Anything?"

"No. I didn't notice anything. Except, the streetlight illuminated him when he walked by the front of the house. I was certain it was him. There was that shock of thick, black hair hanging in his face. His hat had pushed his hair down into his eyes. I guess the face wasn't really that clear. And I could have been fooled by the hair. But it looks like him." She shrugged. "I'll look at it again when we go back."

Sometimes the imagination could play tricks, filling in the blanks to make an image seem something it wasn't, something expected or familiar. Like the face of someone known to the observer. Emma hoped these videos weren't as clear as Angela imagined.

"Okay. Let's go together. Did you ask about a time?"

"She said tomorrow's good. What time works for you?"

"Tomorrow's a Saturday. How about 1:00? That gives me some time to spend with the boys."

"Okay." She paused. "But that's not all. There are a few other segments of video that might pique your interest."

"What's that?"

"Footage, all on different nights, showing a car that pulled up in front of Sally's place and parked. A man was inside the car. It was definitely not a female. He stayed parked in front of Sally's place, for hours. But sometimes, he'd get out and walk up to her porch and leave a bag of something in her mailbox. Then he'd light up a cigarette and peer into the window. Once he even walked around to the back of the house."

"That's creepy. What did he look like?"

"I couldn't see facial features, but I think he might have been an older guy. He wore little round glasses and had a mustache. He didn't exactly limp, but he walked like he might have arthritis in his knees. He was wearing a hoodie, which is weird for an older guy."

"Not necessarily."

"Still, the whole thing was strange, especially when he sat on her porch in the middle of the night. Smoking. And when he was done with his cigarette, he'd throw it right on the wooden floor of the porch. That house is ancient.

The whole place could have gone up in flames."

Emma's eyes narrowed.

"That's got to be Dr. Rayford on the tape—the smoker. I'm pretty sure he was leaving opiates in Sally's mailbox. It's clear that he was obsessed with her. But I don't know what he was trying to accomplish by giving her drugs. Did he want her to depend on him, need him? She'd been taking oxycodone for years."

"That's all pretty weird."

"Yes. Sally didn't want to have anything to do with him. But she didn't refuse his offer of painkillers. Would that give him a motive to kill her, or am I making more of this than there really is?"

Angela flipped through Sally's records, pausing to read several reports. "Of course, it could. I've heard you call Dr. Rayford an egomaniac. A narcissist. He called her all the time. He stalked her. He supplied her with opiates. And her murder doesn't feel like a crime committed by a stranger. It was passionate. Nothing was stolen. There aren't any other obvious motives. He was spurned, and her murderer was out for vengeance."

"My thoughts exactly." Emma paused. "If we can convince the jury that there is a reasonable doubt and another explanation for Sally's murder, we might be able to avoid a conviction.

"But then all the prosecution has to do is to show Jeremy on the video, walking into his mother's back door right before her murder." Emma sat back in her seat. "And if the jury believes Jeremy was in the house, they'll be convinced he's the killer. If this case goes to trial, we have to put on everything we have against Dr. Rayford."

"I agree."

"Also, I spoke to both Brad and Holly LeFleur today. And as I was leaving their house, I peeked in their utility room at the end of the driveway. Guess what I saw?"

"I have no idea. Is it trespassing to peek inside a shed?"

"No. I didn't walk in. And they had the door open." Emma paused. "Anyway, when I walked by, I saw a pair of tennis shoes, the same brand as Jeremy's, draped over the handlebars of Brad's bike. All it means is that Brad had some tennis shoes just like Jeremy's. But I'd like a little more information about Brad and what he was doing the night Sally was killed. The only thing he and his sister said about that night is that they were together watching TV."

Angela nodded. "There are a bunch of people connected to this case who wear Converse All Stars—Jeremy, Becky, and now Brad. I'm not sure what to make of that."

Emma shrugged. "It's a popular tennis shoe. My sons both have a pair. But Holly also said that there was no love lost between Brad and Sally. He's jealous of her and believes their father had squirreled away money for her to the exclusion of the rest of the family. I'm not sure I can trust Holly, but she said Brad was obsessed with finding that money. I never seriously considered him a suspect before I saw the tennis shoes, but I do now. Something's not right. I'm just not sure what."

Angela shook her head. "But the prosecution and the police don't have anyone but Jeremy in their sights."

Emma sighed. "Right. The fact that the murderer found the back entrance, and the key that was kept under the mat isn't so exceptional. Many people hide a key at their back door somewhere. But, when I visited Sally's house, I had to search for the fuse box. It was hidden behind a calendar. The murderer had to know where the fuse box was located."

"That means that the murderer had to have been in Sally's kitchen before. Maybe they saw her flip a fuse or something."

"If that's true, the killer knew Sally. But, all of our suspects knew Sally. That doesn't narrow down anything." Emma leaned back in her chair. "I haven't told you about my visit with Becky yet."

"No, what happened?"

"She's been carefully meting out painkillers to Jeremy for years. Their parents' painkillers." She shook her head. "So, their DNA and fingerprints have to be all over both parents' homes."

Chapter Thirty-Two

Emma was waiting for Angela to pick her up in front of the coffee shop. She'd walked over a few minutes before and picked up her usual latte. She got one for Angela too and was still mulling over the morning she'd had with the boys and Ren.

It was a Saturday, and she'd made oatmeal thinking Ren and the boys needed something healthy in their stomachs. Billy had scooped off the top of the oatmeal, eating only the brown sugar, and Bobby chased the contents of the bowl around without ever putting any of it in his mouth. Her healthy efforts were totally wasted.

The twins didn't seem excited about soccer practice, which was right after breakfast, or anything else that morning, but she was glad they'd be outside and running around all day. That was so much better than hanging around a mall with friends who'd hand them cigarettes. Plus, she had the remainder of the day for Jeremy's case.

Even though there were a few positive turns in her investigation, the case wasn't looking good for Jeremy. The police were still processing and analyzing forensic evidence from Sally's house, where they were sure to find Jeremy's fingerprints. Becky's explanation about Jeremy's tennis ball and how it ended up at Sally's house was helpful, but also proved that Jeremy was at his mother's house the day she was killed. To make matters even more difficult, the revised homicide report probably wouldn't be released until much closer to the trial date. She was shocked she'd received even the partially amended police report.

Angela pulled up in front of 'What's Perkin' and Emma hopped in the car.

"Do you know where Nancy lives?"

Angela nodded. "I called and got her address. Jefferson Avenue."

Emma raised her eyebrows. "Fancy!"

Even though Emma was expecting to see a beautiful house, she wasn't prepared for the extravagance of the Bennett home. It was huge—a magnificent Greek revival, painted in the lightest shade of gray she'd ever seen and trimmed in a creamy white. Emma nearly lost her breath when they walked through the front door, stunned by the quiet beauty of the curved mahogany staircase and dripping chandelier that greeted them in the foyer.

"I'm glad you came by. I called the police to come pick up the tapes. They'll be here at any moment." She gestured toward the hallway. "But come on through the house. We'll look at the tapes in the family room. I think you've got enough time for that."

Nancy led the way through a sea of white marble that had to have been a kitchen. Emma was trying not to gawk. The 'family room' would never have done for her family. Matching couches covered with white linen flanked the fireplace, and a delicate antique Italian day bed stood by itself in one corner.

"Do you have children?" Emma couldn't help herself.

"Yes. But they're in school. I miss them." She picked up a VHS tape, inserted it into her VCR player, and clicked a button.

The room got quiet as the tape flickered on. Glare from the sun's rays bounced off the pool and splashed across the television screen. Nancy closed the drapes.

"There. That should be better. I'm going to step out, so you two can view this in private."

The tape was dated March 19, 1997, 11:45 p.m., the date and approximate time of the murder. It was dark, grainy, and difficult to see.

"They didn't use the best quality tape, did they?" Angela said, squinting her eyes. "Nancy said the security company installed cameras that had audio and video recording capabilities. There are several cameras at the house, and they're set up all around the place. There's one on the front porch that captures people walking in front of the house and people walking up to the door. She said they get a lot of homeless people who walk right up to the door and ring the bell. Then they have cameras on each of the four corners of the house."

"Hmm. I don't remember seeing so many."

"I think they're right under the gutters, attached to the eaves. They're up pretty high. She said about twelve feet. One of those cameras is directed at the back door. There's a street light at the corner, but it doesn't illuminate much—just the activity at the front of the house."

At first, Emma saw movement on the tape and then the clear figure of a person walking in front of the house on Arabella.

"Can you freeze this so we can see who that is?"

"Sure." Angela clicked a button, and the video stopped.

It was difficult to discern facial features. The video was way too dark and grainy for that. But the closer the person in the film walked toward the street light, the clearer he was. Angela froze the film just as the light hit him.

"You're right. This person does have a unique head of hair." Emma squinted to see.

Angela clicked the video button, and the image began moving again. A gust of wind blew in, probably from the river, causing the street lights to flicker. The baseball cap blew off of the young man's head momentarily, but he bent over and pulled it back on.

Angela popped in a video from a second camera that captured movement down the side of the house. The young man walked down the driveway and turned toward the back of the house. A third video which captured the area along the back door, showed the young man retrieving something from under the doormat. He then pulled the hood from his sweatshirt over his baseball hat and opened the door to the house.

"Can we go back to the place where the wind blew the hat off?"

Angela inserted tape one, rewound it, and then started it again.

"Okay, now freeze!" Emma pointed at the screen.

Angela stopped the tape right after the wind blew off the intruder's hat.

Emma stepped closer to the TV screen, so close she was mere inches away.

"I don't think this is a young man, like I thought earlier." She pointed to the screen. "I see breasts. They're small, but they're unmistakably breasts." Emma pointed to the intruder's chest area.

"I don't think that's any more than a wrinkle in the hoodie fabric. If that is a girl, you'd never be able to tell from that video." Angela squinted at the screen.

"Maybe. But I see two distinct lumps." Emma pointed to the image.

Angela frowned. "Maybe."

They allowed the tape to run a few more minutes. Then they heard it. "Youuu Whooo!"

Emma turned toward Angela. "Did you hear that?"

"Yeah. I did. Sounds like Charlie the bird had seen the intruder before. So, we've got a couple of reasons to believe that the killer knew Sally and had been in her house."

"All we have to do now is to figure out who among our short list of suspects had previously visited Sally." Emma closed her notebook.

Angela sighed.

"Okay. Nancy's already notified the police that she's got the tapes. They could drive up any minute, and I don't want to be here when they arrive." She stood and began gathering her belongings. "We'll request a copy from the DA's office."

* * *

Angela started her car as Emma climbed into the passenger seat, and slammed the door.

Angela glanced at Emma.

"So, what did you think of all that?"

"I'm still not convinced the person on the video was Jeremy. There are other members of his family who could have been at Sally's house that night. The fact that Jeremy's already been charged with her murder will influence how that tape is interpreted."

"I think you're right. Plus, the video just isn't that clear."

Emma nodded. "Yes, that too." She paused and glanced at Angela. "We've got a little time. I think we should pay Brad a visit. I've got a few questions about his relationship with Sally."

"Today?"

"Yes. If you have time."

"I do, but shouldn't we call first?"

"No. I'd like to take him by surprise. We're pretty close to his house, anyway."

Chapter Thirty-Three

"I wonder if they're home. I don't see any lights." Angela peered at the front window of the house.

"I'd bet they are. I don't think those two ever go anywhere."

"They have to grocery shop, and we know Brad likes to bicycle."

"Let's see." Emma and Angela walked up the driveway to the front door of the LeFleur home and rang the doorbell. No one answered at first, but, based on her last experience, Emma waited. Sure enough, a few seconds later, the door creaked open.

"Who is it?"

"It's Emma Thornton and Angela Burris. Angela's working on Jeremy's case with me."

The door widened, and Emma and Angela stepped in. Holly was standing behind the door; only her head and shoulders were visible.

"We'd like to speak to your brother, Brad." Emma took a few steps further into the hallway.

"He's busy, but I'll ask. Do you want to wait in the parlor or in the hallway?"

Emma didn't want to sit in the spooky parlor again. "We'll just wait here." She watched Holly walk down the corridor and into the kitchen.

The tap, tap sound of typing stopped. She heard hushed voices. Then, a higher-pitched voice said, 'No! That's not a good idea,' followed by a lower 'go get her.' Then, Emma could hear footsteps on the kitchen floors. Seconds later, Holly appeared in the hallway.

"Brad would like it if you'd step into the kitchen. He's working there."

Emma and Angela followed Holly down the hall to the kitchen. Emma

190

was surprised by the tidiness of the room. There were no stacks of paper on the table, or crumpled-up papers on the floor. The counters were clear of coffee cups and dishes, and there were no food crumbs on the table. Brad turned around when Emma and Angela walked into the room.

"I'm sorry I wasn't able to talk with you the last time you were here. I had to get some late returns filed. Sometimes I find myself at the mercy of others." He smiled.

"Oh, that's fine. Holly explained everything to me. I'd like to speak to you about a few things Holly, and I talked about the last time I was here."

Holly quietly walked into the room and stood next to Brad.

Brad nodded toward the kitchen table. "Please sit down. I'll join you there."

Emma and Angela sat down at the table as Brad and Holly sat down across from them. Emma cleared her throat.

"When we were here earlier, Holly explained that you were trying to find proof that your father left more money in his will to Sally than to you and Holly. Did you ever discover any proof that your dad had hidden away money for Sally?"

Brad frowned. "None of that's true. Holly was mistaken. I can't imagine why she said that." He looked at Holly and raised his eyebrows.

Emma leaned back in her chair.

"Is someone not telling the truth here?"

"None of this is your concern. But even if it was, I have no reason to lie to you. And, of course, the simple explanation is that Holly just got the facts wrong. She does that sometimes."

Emma studied the siblings sitting across from her. Brad was tall and blonde and appeared older than his years. He was also considerably heavier than Jeremy. But Holly bore a striking resemblance to both Jeremy and Becky.

"I've noticed that several members of your family resemble each other. One might even be mistaken for another."

Brad crossed his arms. "Again, I'm not sure why you're telling me this."

"For instance, you and Jeremy have very similar builds. You're both over six feet, you're both thin, although you have a heavier frame. If it weren't for the differences in hair color and texture, you could easily be mistaken for one another."

"What are you talking about, Ms. Thornton? I'm sorry, but you're not making any sense."

"I'm proposing that you were the one who entered your sister Sally's house around midnight on March 19, and you were the person who killed her."

Brad snorted. "Sorry, but that's ridiculous."

Emma was surprised that Brad had maintained his composure. She was doing her best to provoke him.

"What's so ridiculous? You hated your sister. Jeremy loved his mother. What reason would he have to kill Sally?"

"I didn't hate my sister. You're way off base."

"The last time I was here, I saw a pair of Converse All Stars draped across your bike's handlebars. The police found Converse shoe prints at the murder scene."

"I don't own Converse All Star tennis shoes. I never have." He hesitated, then looked at Holly, his eyes widening.

Holly turned and walked to the kitchen. Emma could hear her pulling glasses down from the shelf and placing ice cubes in each glass.

"I'm sure millions of people have Converse All Stars. That doesn't make them guilty of my sister's murder." Brad frowned as he watched his sister pour water in the glasses.

"You told me earlier that you and your sister Holly get to bed every night around ten o'clock. That's good information, but it isn't as strong as a specific memory, or an interaction you had with someone else that night. Can anyone verify that you were at home on the night of the murder? Could Holly? Would your phone or billing records indicate whether you spoke to a client or anyone else that night?"

"I'm not sure why you're asking me these questions, Ms. Thornton. I'm not a suspect. And you certainly are not the police. I doubt if I spoke to anyone that late. I'd never call a client after six o'clock in the evening. I don't know why you're here, and I am not compelled in any way to answer your questions. So, we're going to shut this down."

"Are you saying you have nothing which would prove where you were on the night of the murder?"

"I just said that we're shutting this down. I'm not going to help you with your process of elimination. You'll have to find your answers some other way." He squinted his eyes.

Suddenly Emma could detect movement and felt a quick brush of wind at her left side, followed by a loud thud. She jumped and turned, shocked to see that Angela had crumpled to the ground and that Holly was holding a wooden rolling pin. She was poised to strike again.

"Stop!" Emma shouted. She lunged toward Holly, reaching for the rolling pin in her grip. Brad rushed toward Emma, grabbed her around the waist, and pulled her away from Holly. Angela wasn't moving. Blood was pouring from the wound on her head.

"Holly, what are you doing?" Brad shouted. He held Emma by both of her wrists.

"You need to call an ambulance for Angela. She's bleeding, and I don't even know if she's breathing!" Emma struggled against Brad's clasp.

"Didn't you hear her? She's going to try to pin Sally's death on us." Holly was breathing heavily. The rolling pin was grasped in both of her hands and raised to her shoulders, as if she were about to hit a baseball.

"You were there that night, weren't you? You took my bike. I could tell it had been used. There was mud all over the tires." Brad's mouth gaped open.

"Shut up, Brad."

"I can't think. I don't know what to do." He was breathing heavily. "We have to put them somewhere until I can decide what to do." Brad dragged Emma toward a door in the hallway. She guessed that the door would lead to the ground-floor storage area.

"Keep an eye on the other one. I'll come back and get her."

Brad opened the door and shoved Emma down the stairs. She tripped but regained her footing, pushing against Brad as she tried to make her way back up the steps. He grabbed her, placing her in a choke hold with his arm around her throat, and dragged her down the steps.

Once he was at ground level, he searched the darkened room, grabbed some twine from a shelf, and wrapped it around Emma's wrists and ankles. He ripped off a strip of cloth from the bottom of his shirt and tied it around her mouth.

Brad charged back up the stairs and returned minutes later with Angela slung over his shoulder. He flung her onto the floor and tied her just as he had Emma, wrist to wrist and ankle to ankle. Her body was curled into a fetal position on the concrete floor. Her head wound had already made a small puddle of blood.

Emma tried to swallow. "Why are you doing this?" Emma's words sounded muffled. "You're getting deeper and deeper into this. If you're innocent, you need to call the police. Anything you do now will be considered aiding and abetting. My husband is also expecting me to return home at any minute. He's a New Orleans police officer. A detective. He'll search for me, and he'll find me."

"If you don't want to end up like your friend here, you'd better shut up. And don't even begin to think of screaming. It could be the last sound you make." Brad stomped up the stairs.

Emma looked over at Angela, who still hadn't stirred or made a sound. Angela could have a concussion, or her skull could have been fractured. She could have bleeding in her brain. Emma's thoughts were racing. Angela could die, and it was Emma's fault.

"Angela, can you hear me?"

Angela didn't move. Emma listened to Angela's breath sounds. They seemed normal, but she wasn't trained to hear irregularities.

Emma could hear shouting upstairs. She held her breath and listened.

"What in hell came over you? You've done some stupid things, but this is by far the dumbest thing you've ever done!"

"I was just trying to help you." Holly was crying. "With Sally dead, you would get everything. All of Dad's money. Whatever Sally got that you were supposed to have. I did it for you. So, you wouldn't worry anymore." Holly sniffed.

Emma froze. What did that mean?

"God, Holly! You could have killed that girl. She still might die. You've made such a mess of things. I don't know what to do." Brad's voice was shrill, his breath rapid.

Holly began sobbing. "I didn't mean to make things worse."

"Sit down."

Emma could hear walking. Just a few steps. They were probably at the kitchen table. Brad spoke in lower, almost hushed tones. It was difficult to hear.

"How could you have done this?"

There were several seconds of silence. Emma strained to hear.

"I thought it was what you wanted." Holly's voice was shaky.

"No, Holly. I never said anything that would give you that idea. You're very confused."

"Yes, you did! You said that! And don't tell me I'm confused. You said Dad left everything to Sally!"

"No. We got money from Dad's estate. And Sally did too. Remember? We met over at Sally's house to talk about everything before we met with Dad's attorney, Mr. Lewis."

"But you hate Sally."

"No, I don't hate her."

"Well, I do. I've always hated her. She always got everything she wanted." Holly screamed.

Then, low murmuring sounds and a scream. "No! They will tell the police about this! We have to kill them, Brad!"

She heard a drawer being pulled open and sounds of someone clamoring through metal utensils.

Emma looked around the dark room. It was filled with old furniture and cardboard boxes. Rusty bicycles stood in the corner. It was illuminated by one bare light bulb, which Brad had flicked on when he climbed back up the staircase. But the light bulb did very little to brighten the space.

It was common to see ground-floor storage spaces in New Orleans, but Emma had never been inside one. There was a large double door which faced the street. It appeared to be chain bolted on the outside. Looking upwards she could see that a small window was on one wall, close to the ceiling, but it was partially covered by stacks of boxes. The boxes were piled on top of a workbench.

Emma began biting the strings that bound her wrists together, but they didn't loosen. Then she began pulling her wrists in opposite directions from each other, and the string began to stretch. She continued pulling and working the string until her wrists began to bleed. She was able to work one hand out of the binding, and when she did that, the strings fell off the other wrist. She untied her feet, pulled the rag from her mouth, and listened. She could still hear Brad and Holly arguing upstairs. That was good.

Hiding Angela was her priority. After that, she'd work on an escape. She needed to go get help. But she didn't know if she had the time for any of it. Her heart was beating fast. Trying not to panic, she breathed deeply to steady her hands.

Angela was still unconscious and was badly injured. Emma didn't want to move her for fear of injuring her further. She began gathering boxes and small items of furniture and placed what she could around Angela. She ripped open a couple of empty boxes and laid them on top of her, making sure there were openings so she could breathe. Stepping back, she examined her work.

She was glad the room was dark, but that was the only thing working in their favor. The dim light bulb cast more shadows than light, so that helped too. But she was certain Brad would find Angela if he started looking for her.

Emma hoisted her legs up on to the workbench and stood, cursing the ten-foot-tall walls. She'd never be able to reach the window without help. She'd have to build a structure or pile up some boxes to get access.

She moved all of the boxes to one side of the bench, then selected a few of the heavier, sturdier ones and pushed them toward the back wall. Lighter, smaller boxes were stacked on top until she had constructed a facsimile of steps to the window.

Holding her breath, Emma began scrambling up the boxes to the window. She still didn't know if escape was possible. The window was an old casement style, hinged on one side, and designed to crank open in an outward direction. They could be difficult. She grabbed the crank and pushed hard, but the window was frozen shut.

She scanned the room, looking for tools to force the window open, then, realizing she was sitting on top of a workbench, scrambled down the boxes and began searching for anything that could be used to pry open the window. She grabbed a couple of screwdrivers and a hammer and jumped back on the bench, trying not to think about how injured Angela could be. She just wanted to get out of the window and get help.

Emma could still hear Brad and Holly arguing as she climbed up the boxes to the window. When she got to the last box, she was high enough to see the corrosion and rust lining the bottom of the casement and circling the handle. She wedged a screwdriver into the joint of the crank and began tapping the plastic end of the tool ever so lightly with the hammer. She jiggled the crank every few minutes until it finally loosened. Then she began moving the crank back and forth, as far as it would go, until finally, it gave a little. She pushed against the crank with all of her strength and was thrilled when she felt it give way.

The window, which was about thirty inches wide and twenty-four inches deep, was smaller than Emma realized. She could squeeze through, but it would be difficult. And it was awkwardly placed, about a foot from the ceiling.

Easing her legs out of the window first, she teetered for a moment on the casing. Then hanging onto the window frame, she began scooting down the outside wall of the house, feet first. When she'd edged down the wall as far as she could, she let go, falling several feet to the driveway below.

She was shaken and slightly banged up, but all of her senses were on alert. She looked down the street. No one was out. No children were playing. It was approaching the dinner hour. Not knowing what she'd face if she knocked on a neighbor's door, she began running, as fast as she could. One of her favorite restaurants was on the corner, a couple of blocks away. She knew she could get help there.

Chapter Thirty-Four

Emma was breathing heavily by the time she approached the waiters and waitresses of Le Chateau de Crepe. They were in front of the restaurant, on the sidewalk, unfurling white tablecloths, and setting out menus for the restaurant's tiny outdoor dining space.

"I've got to call the police. It's an emergency." She coughed, winded from her run. Even though she was used to running, her knees were wobbly, and she was nauseated from the terror of the last thirty minutes.

A waiter quickly ushered Emma into the restaurant and handed her the telephone. Her hands shook as she dialed 911.

"I am calling to report a kidnapping and an attempted murder." Emma told the dispatcher what had happened to Angela and gave her the address for the LeFleur's home. "Please ask them to hurry. I'll get back there as quickly as I can."

Emma hesitated. Then she called Ren.

* * *

Emma checked her watch as she approached the LeFleur's home. It had taken her nearly fifteen minutes to walk back, which meant it had been around twenty-five minutes since she'd escaped the storage space. That was plenty of time for Brad and Holly to discover that she was gone. And they could easily find Angela under those broken-down boxes.

Sirens wailed from a distance. Emma's heart pounded. She turned toward the entrance of the street as the sirens grew louder. She waved police cars over to the LeFleur's home. Ren would be here any minute.

"I'm the person who called. I haven't gone back in the house since I left." She was trying not to panic, but she'd started to shake. She needed to sit down.

"What's going on?" Several other NOPD officers gathered around.

Ren pulled up and parked in front of the police cars. He sprinted toward Emma.

"Are you okay? What happened?"

"I'm fine, but I'm worried about Angela."

Ren put an arm around Emma. She felt her body relax.

Emma told Ren and the officers what had happened to Angela and to her, then pointed to the storage area. "When I escaped, Angela was in there, and Brad and Holly were in the kitchen. I don't know what happened after I left to get help."

"We'll find out," Ren said. "Is Angela injured very badly?"

Emma nodded. "She could be. And, before I left, I think they were going to take us somewhere. But I don't know where."

"Okay." Ren motioned to an officer. "Do you carry bolt cutters?"

The officer nodded. "Yeah. We got one." The officer popped his trunk open and pulled out something that looked like a giant pair of pruning shears.

"Before you do that, I'm going to ring the doorbell. Let's see if they'll answer."

Ren motioned for an officer to follow him as he stomped up the driveway. Several minutes later, he yelled down to Emma.

"No one's answering. We'll try that storage door."

Emma met Ren and all of the officers in front of the double doors. An officer snipped off the chain as if it were made of cream cheese. Both doors slowly swung open.

Emma followed the officers into the room, running to the spot where she'd left Angela. She started moving boxes and throwing them aside. "She was right here, under these boxes." She swiveled around, her eyes flashing with terror. "I used the boxes to hide her from Brad and Holly, but they found her, and they've taken her somewhere." Emma's eyes watered.

"Wait, wait, wait!" Ren pointed. "There's blood right there on the floor. And everything you just touched is evidence. You have to go back outside. You're going to contaminate the site."

"But my fingerprints are already all over the place. I was thrown down here too."

"I'm sorry, sweetheart, but you still have to leave. You know the protocol."

Emma backed out of the room. "I have an idea where Angela might be. But first, I'd like to run up to get our keys and purses. They're upstairs. Is that okay?" Emma knew the answer.

"No. I'm sorry. You have to leave everything for now. Everything here, both upstairs and in this storage place, is evidence." Ren put his arm around her shoulders again. "I'm so glad you're okay." He squeezed her. "Where do you think she is?"

"If I had to guess, I'd say Arabella. Their sister's house on Arabella."

"Do you know the house when you see it?"

Emma nodded.

Ren motioned to another officer. "J.T., get some yellow tape around this place. Emma and I will drive down to Arabella. You guys follow. Emma, while we're driving there, I need you to tell me everything."

* * *

It was dusk and quickly getting darker, except for the street light, which had just begun to glow. Sally's house was dark.

"Sally kept a key under the doormat at the back. I doubt if it's still there, but it wouldn't hurt to check."

Ren led the way, his flashlight making a bobbing trail of light, stopping at the back door. Emma searched under the mat, but didn't find a key. Then she tried the door knob. The door swung open.

"You want to go first?"

"I have to, Emma. There could be someone in here. In fact, you need to stay outside." Ren motioned for the officers to follow him.

Ren entered the back door, sweeping the light from his flashlight across the room as he walked. Emma peered into the kitchen, praying that Angela was there and that she was okay.

The beam from the flashlight danced across the walls.

"She's here, and she's alive!"

Emma rushed through the back door to the kitchen, where she saw Ren huddled over a figure lying on the floor.

"Angela!" Emma dropped onto the floor next to her. Angela had bled profusely. Blood was caked in her hair and had soaked into the front and back of her shirt.

One of the officers clicked on his hand-held radio. "I need an ambulance. And put a rush on the bus."

Angela turned her head and opened her eyes. "My head hurts." Her voice sounded scratchy. She struggled to swallow.

Emma ran to the sink and filled a glass with water. She dipped a clean towel in the water and moistened Angela's mouth with it.

Ren shined his flashlight in Angela's eyes. "The ambulance will be here soon. Please try not to move."

He motioned for Emma to join him a few feet away from Angela.

"I never would have expected that she'd be here."

Emma shrugged. "This was just a guess."

"It was a good one. Do you have any ideas about where that brother-sister team – the LeFleurs? – may have gone?"

Emma leaned against one of the kitchen cabinets. Her hands were still trembling. "It's just a guess, but I'd say that they might have gone to Todd Wilcox's house on the West Bank to hide out. That house is empty too. Todd was the husband of Sally Wilcox. He was killed four days ago. If they're not there, I don't have any other ideas. They could be anywhere."

"Didn't you say the Wilcox place is in Jefferson Parish somewhere?"

Emma nodded.

"That's not our jurisdiction, but I'll give the Bridge City police a call and send some officers down there to check it out."

"I think Brad's calling the shots, but he seemed genuinely shocked by

Holly's attack. And she was out of control. I don't think any of this was planned. And I think Brad panicked. He's trying to protect his sister, not Angela."

"Yeah. Looks like he just wanted to get rid of her."

An ambulance pulled into the driveway. The EMTs checked Angela's vitals, then lifted her onto the gurney and placed it in the back of the vehicle.

"Shouldn't I go with Angela?"

Ren nodded. "You need to get checked out too. I'll let them know what happened to both of you." He handed Emma his business card. "Write down the exact address for the Wilcox place if you know it." He squeezed Emma's arm. "I'll be right behind you."

Within minutes Emma was buckled up in the front seat of the ambulance and on the way to the hospital. She turned around and looked toward the back of the vehicle. The medics were securing an oxygen cannula into Angela's nose. Her eyes were closed. But Emma could see her chest rise and fall.

Chapter Thirty-Five

Angela was rushed to a room at the back of the ER. The hospital refused to allow Emma to follow and told her to sit in the waiting room until her name was called.

Within minutes Emma heard her name. She was triaged and taken back for a CT scan of the head and neck. As she was being wheeled back to her room, Ren pushed the ER doors open. He helped the orderly tuck Emma into her bed. She braced herself for a lecture.

"How are you feeling?" He leaned over and kissed her forehead. "Do you have the results of the CT scan yet?"

"No results yet, but I'm fine. I don't think I even needed to come here. I just wanted to make sure Angela was okay." She reached out and grabbed Ren's hand.

"Okay. So." Ren sighed. "What happened? Why did Holly attack Angela?"

"I'm pretty sure she thought we were threatening her brother. But I was the one asking all the questions, not Angela. I think Angela was just in the line of fire. I think she got hit because she was closer to Holly than I was."

"Holly was blindly swinging?"

Emma nodded. "It all happened pretty fast, but I think so." She paused. "After I get my results, we'll need to wait here to see whether Angela will be discharged. If she is, we'll have to take her because her car is still in front of the LeFleur's house."

"Sure."

An ER nurse stepped inside Emma's room. "Your friend is asking for you. We're going to let her go. She didn't have a fracture, and the CT scan didn't detect bleeding in the brain. But she will need to take it easy for a few days. If there's any sign of a concussion or if her headache worsens, she'll need to return. We can do an MRI then. Oh, and you're free to go too."

By the time Angela was up and seated in a wheelchair, Ren had pulled his truck into the patient pick-up area. She and Angela piled in. The drive to Angela's apartment was unusually quiet. Even though Angela was capable of walking, they helped her up the stairs. Her roommate promised to watch her for the next several days.

"Don't hesitate to call me if you need anything. Ren and I will get your car and bring it to you as soon as we can. You need to take it easy for a couple of days, anyway."

Emma wasn't looking forward to the ride home.

* * *

Ren was silent for the first mile. Then, when they were almost to the apartment, he spoke, keeping his eyes riveted on the car in front of him. That was not a good sign.

"How did this happen? I thought you were going somewhere to review a tape. How did that turn into a potential kidnapping or attempted murder, with you right there in the middle of it all?"

"We did review the tape, and then I thought it would be a good idea to go see the LeFleurs. I wanted to ask them a few questions. We'd interviewed them before and hadn't had any problems. I couldn't have anticipated this."

"You have to have had your suspicions about them, or you wouldn't have wanted to go over there, right?"

Emma didn't want to answer that question, because Ren was right. She did have her suspicions. And she should never have taken Angela into such a dangerous situation. She couldn't have anticipated the LeFleurs' reaction to her questions, but she took a risk. She couldn't avoid responsibility for what happened.

"You're right, although I hate to admit it."

"You're missing the point. You suspected the LeFleurs might be dangerous, yet you walked right into the situation and brought a student with you. You seem incapable of foresight, but I know that's not true. So, what you were doing was ignoring all of the alarms and whistles that had to have been going off in your head and just plowed forward with your plan. And why did you do that? Because you were curious? Really?" He paused for a moment, breathing heavily. "And what about all of the 'truth and honesty lessons' you've been giving the boys? I've asked you to tell me where you're going and what you are about to do, but you didn't today. You didn't because you knew it was dangerous. So, on top of being rash and foolish, you were also dishonest."

The veins on Ren's head had popped out, and his face and neck were beet red. She'd never seen him so angry. She exhaled loudly. She didn't have a good answer to Ren's questions. And he knew it.

"I was trying to do a little research on a couple of defenses in Jeremy's case."

"That doesn't validate your rash behavior. It was a stupid move, Emma, and you're not stupid. You'll be lucky to keep your job. What happened to you to make you so eager to put yourself in danger? Don't you think your life is important to the people who love you?" He looked at Emma. "You matter to me and to your sons, and I'm sure you matter to many others, too. You need to start using those instincts of yours to protect yourself. Billy and Bobby want you safe. We all want you to be safe."

* * *

That night Emma, Ren, and the boys ordered their favorite pizza and rented *The Untouchables.* Emma thought they all needed a break. After watching the movie, the boys went up to their room. They'd stay awake playing computer games for hours, but she was okay with that, too. A little fun didn't hurt them, even when they were grounded.

Ren stood up and grabbed his empty beer can. "You coming to bed?"

"Not right now. I have a couple of things to do."

"You'd do anything to avoid another talk, wouldn't you?"

Emma grinned. "No. That's not it. I need to make a few notes about the day. I won't be long."

Ren kissed Emma. "I know when I'm being asked to leave. Don't stay up too late."

Emma watched Ren walk out of the room. She loved spending time with him most of the time, but tonight they both needed a little space. Plus, she had to get her thoughts together. She grabbed a notebook and a pen.

Chapter Thirty-Six

Emma leaned back against the couch and closed her eyes. She hadn't had a moment to digest all that had occurred at the LeFleur's. It had been a brutal day.

Everything had happened so quickly it was difficult to process, and she was still uncertain what some of it meant. She was shocked by the conversation she'd overheard between Holly and Brad. She closed her eyes even tighter, trying to remember each word. Emma picked up a pen and began to write down what she could remember.

With Sally dead you would get everything. All of Dad's money. Whatever Sally got that you were supposed to have. I did it for you. So, you wouldn't worry anymore."

It was bone-chilling. What did '*I did it for you*' mean? What did she do? Was Holly talking about her attack on Angela, or was she talking about Sally?

And nothing that Holly had told her about Sally or Brad had been true. Holly hated Sally. Not Brad. It was becoming clear to Emma that Holly was the unstable one of the pair. Brad had called her 'confused.' But she was much more than confused. She was violent, out of control.

The video from the night of the murder hadn't been clear enough to distinguish between Jeremy, Becky, and Holly, but one thing seemed certain to Emma. She didn't believe the person captured in the video walking in front of Sally's house was Brad. Although his physique was similar to his nephew's, his craggy facial features should be easy to distinguish, even on blurry footage.

Holly, who had emerged in Emma's mind as a new primary suspect, was in a different category. She didn't look much older than Becky and Jeremy, and together, they could be confused for triplets. And didn't Brad say something about Holly using his bicycle on the night of the murder? After what happened today, it was obvious that something was amiss with the LeFleur siblings.

Whoever it was, Charlie the parrot had made clear that the killer had visited Sally's house before. And Holly said she hadn't visited Sally in the past nine years.

Emma's head was spinning. She put her notes away and turned on the bath water.

* * *

Monday morning, Emma saw the boys off on the school bus and ran upstairs to finish getting ready. She'd already called the law offices of Roger Lewis, the LeFleur's estate attorney, and had been told to come by. She had a hunch he might be able to answer some of her questions.

Emma parked on the street in front of Roger Lewis's office. The impressive space almost made her wish she was in private practice. Located on Lafayette Avenue, the office was in a narrow, old-brick industrial building, renovated with lush fixtures and furniture, velvet drapes, and elegant wallpaper. She was surprised when Roger Lewis walked out of his office in a pair of jeans; his shirt sleeves rolled up to his elbows. He waved her back. Unshaven, the bright copper stubble of his beard was a few shades lighter than his disheveled auburn hair. He didn't match his resplendent offices.

"Your office space is stunning."

"Yeah, well. My wife does all that. I just hand her the checkbook." Roger spoke with the sort of southern drawl one didn't hear much in New Orleans. He rubbed his beard. "You'll have to forgive my casual attire. I wasn't planning on coming in today. Then something came up." He laughed and looked down at his jeans. "If I could get away with this every day, I would. But New Orleans is a little fancier than Madison, Mississippi, where I'm from."

Emma glanced at the diploma on the wall. It was from the University of Mississippi School of Law, Ole Miss. Emma had been there once for a moot court competition. She loved the idyllic town of Oxford and the campus.

"I represent Jeremy Wilcox for the murder of his mother, Sally. I understand you were Sally's attorney, as well as the attorney for the LeFleur family."

"I did all of the estate work for Sally's father, Henry LeFleur. His kids, Brad and Holly, and Sally, too, for that matter, have seen me on a few occasions. We even met over at Sally's place a couple of times. And you're right. I also represented Sally." He shook his head. "This is sad business."

"Yes, it's a tragedy. Did you ever meet Jeremy?"

"No, but Sally and I spoke about him on many occasions. She worried about him a lot."

"Have you started the probate process on Sally's estate yet?"

"No. There was no need to probate the estate. All of her accounts were TOD. They transferred immediately to her beneficiaries, Jeremy and Becky, when she died. She didn't owe anything, so there wasn't much to do."

Emma wasn't surprised Jeremy and Becky benefitted from Sally's death. Parents almost always leave assets to their children at their death. But most parents' cause of death wasn't murder.

"What would happen if one of the beneficiaries was also the murderer?"

"If that happened, the trust would be overridden. There's a legal presumption that the victim, in this situation, Sally, would change her mind about leaving anything to her murderer. So, a murderer can't inherit from his victim."

He cleared his throat. "I know this might sound strange, but I don't think that presumption works in Sally's case. Even if Sally had a minute to think before she died, and she knew that Jeremy killed her, she'd want him to inherit, so he could be taken care of. But that's not how the law works."

"I'm a mom. I understand that." Emma paused to scribble down what Roger had said. "Can you tell me why you met with Sally, Brad, and Holly before the execution of her trust?"

"We met to discuss Sally's estate and how she wanted it handled following her death."

"Can you give me any details?"

"Typically, I couldn't because it would be privileged. But Sally insisted on having her brother and sister over to discuss everything, even though I told her that she'd violate her own privilege if she did. She just didn't care. I suggested that she put everything she wanted down on paper, to be read after she died, but no. She wanted eye to eye contact with her siblings. So, as I think you may have suspected, Sally broke the attorney-client privilege. I made certain to put a letter documenting my warnings and recommendations in the file."

"You don't seem too happy about that."

"I'm not. But there it is. Sally didn't like the way things were going between Jeremy and his father. So, in the event of her death, she wanted her siblings to be appointed powers of attorney. She wanted Brad to handle the finances and Holly to be Jeremy's medical power of attorney. This gave them both a lot of control. In those positions, they would manage Jeremy's and Becky's money. And Holly would manage Jeremy's residential placement."

"Residential placement? Like whether he lives in a group home or was institutionalized?"

He nodded. "Yes. Jeremy and Becky didn't get much, maybe $100,000 each. And they got the house."

"Is Brad still the financial power of attorney?"

"Yes. He doesn't have a role now as trustee. But, he's still financial power of attorney for both of the kids. He has complete control of their money. So, let's hope he's trustworthy."

Neither Brad nor Holly were trustworthy. This was looking bad for the kids.

"Did you know that Todd was also killed?"

"I read about that when it happened. Hard to believe two people, especially a husband and wife, could be killed in two separate, unconnected incidents."

Emma nodded. "Now that Todd isn't living in the West Bank house, could Brad, as financial power of attorney, sell it?"

Roger raised one eyebrow. "Yes, he could."

"If he did that, would he be legally bound to reinvest that on behalf of Sally's kids?"

"He has a fiduciary duty to the kids. But who is watching over him to make sure he does the right thing? I haven't been retained to represent the kids or anyone else in their family. You've discovered a weakness in the system. Financial and medical powers of attorney have complete control. If they're dishonest or negligent, the incapacitated person they're supposed to be protecting and helping can be stripped of everything they own. You can bring them to court for their misdeeds, but it's hard to recover the money they lose or misappropriate."

"But the power of attorney can be revoked if you find wrongdoing, or negligence, right?"

"That's right. Jeremy and Becky would need an attorney for that. If you find that Brad or Holly have acted inappropriately, let me know. Sally brought me a lot of business. I'd be happy to help out her kids, free of charge, but I can't do anything unless I'm retained."

"Thanks. I have one more question. I was told that someone had been calling Sally, harassing her, really. But she never went to the police about it. I was also told that she was going to speak to you about it. Did she ever do that?"

Roger nodded. "Seems like she might have."

"And?"

"We're into privileged territory again. But let me see if I can answer your question hypothetically. Stalking and harassment are misdemeanors in Louisiana, so both acts are crimes, and they're punishable by a small fine or about a year in jail. But if the victim and her stalker-harasser were involved in other criminal activities together, it might discourage this victim from going to the police. I hope that makes sense."

"Are we speaking about the illegal distribution of painkillers?"

"We could be, hypothetically, of course."

"In that scenario, the stalker would have distributed the drugs to this hypothetical client?"

"That's right."

"And this client wanted it to continue, so she never filed a report against the stalker?"

Roger nodded.

"You can't tell me the name of the drug dealer?"

"No. But I can say that she knew him. She knew him well."

Chapter Thirty-Seven

Emma wasn't sure who to call about Brad and Holly. She didn't write down any of the names of the NOPD officers who searched for them. But Ren always answered her calls. She dialed his number.

"Can you talk?"

"Sure."

"Do you know if the NOPD officers were able to go by Todd Wilcox's house over the weekend?"

"They drove down there late Saturday afternoon, right after you left in the ambulance. But they didn't see any sign that anyone was at the house. No lights were on. The only vehicle in the driveway was an old truck. They looked up the tag, and it belonged to Todd Wilcox."

"Did they go inside?"

"No. They didn't have a warrant and couldn't have gotten one based only on your hunch that the LeFleurs could be there. If they were ever there, they're gone now."

"Did they look in the windows?"

"Of course. There were no signs of life. I really don't believe they're there."

Emma sighed. "Okay. Can you call me if you hear anything?"

"Sure. Do you know anything about the car the LaFleur's drive? Color, make, anything?"

"I remember a white car being parked in their driveway, but I can't tell you the make, or the year."

"Okay. I'll try to find car registration information. I'll call you if I find anything." He paused. "How are you?"

"I'm okay. I'd be better if someone could find Brad and Holly."

Emma sighed and hung up the phone. She had been putting off her talk with the Dean about what had happened to Angela last Friday. She had wanted to report that Brad and Holly were found. But that wasn't possible. She leaned back in her chair. She'd never seen Dean Munoz lose his temper, but she had a feeling she was about to test his self-control. She grabbed her keys and locked up her office. She'd rather tell him in person.

* * *

Emma knocked on Dean Georges Munoz's door, halfway hoping he wasn't in. Dean Munoz and she had been close throughout her career, especially since he'd offered her the only job she'd had since graduating from law school. A recognized legal scholar, the dean was an expert in legal procedure and ethics. He'd taught her Federal Jurisdiction and how to think like a lawyer. But more than that, he was her mentor and friend. She hated disappointing him. Her heart sank when she heard his booming voice.

"Come in."

Emma walked in and closed the door.

"It's good to see you. I haven't seen you much lately. Guess you've been busy?"

Emma nodded and glanced down at the floor for a few seconds, trying to find her courage.

"I need to tell you about something that happened this past Friday. It was late when I got home, so I didn't call you." She took a deep breath, trying to ignore the dean's frown. "Do you know Angela Burris?"

"Yes. I had her in my Federal Jurisdiction class. Excellent student. She'll make a great lawyer."

"I think so too." Emma attempted a smile, then told the dean about Angela and her visit with Brad and Holly LeFleur last Friday afternoon.

"So, you went there to ask the aunt and uncle a few more questions about the night of the murder?"

"Yes."

"And you were invited to their house?"

"Not exactly. We were close by and thought we should drop by to ask a couple of questions."

Emma didn't like the look on the dean's face.

"Didn't it occur to you that you should have invited them to your office instead?"

"Not at the time."

"You wanted to take them by surprise?"

Emma nodded. "I thought the element of surprise might shake them up. I thought they'd have less time to prepare answers to my questions."

"It doesn't sound like a safe situation and not one you'd want to drag a student to. Are you here because something you hadn't planned occurred last Friday?"

Emma swallowed. "That's right. Holly LeFleur, Jeremy's aunt, didn't like our questions and attacked us. And Brad, Jeremy's uncle, did his best to get rid of us. I wasn't hurt, not very much, anyway, but Angela was banged up pretty badly."

"My God, Emma. When you mess up, you really mess up."

Emma nodded and told the dean the rest of the story. "We still haven't found the LeFleurs."

"There should be no 'we' in that sentence, Emma. You're not a police officer. You have no business looking for anyone. Your zeal is admirable, but it gets you in trouble. Angela should not have been in that situation, and neither should you."

"I understand."

"Where is Angela now?"

"She's back at her apartment. She needs to rest up for a few days, but she's okay, thank God."

"She's okay by the grace of God, and no thanks to you."

"I understand."

"I hope so. This type of thing can't happen again. If it does, President Ackerman will close the clinic down. He's not crazy about students working on actual cases anyway. Thinks it will expose the school to liability, and this situation is a perfect example of just how that could happen. It will be surprising if Angela doesn't sue the school after all of this. And if she does, that's it. President Ackerman will jump at any excuse to shut it all down."

"I'm so sorry, Dean Munoz. I never would have expected something like this to happen."

"I realize that, but that's why you don't do things that leave you in a vulnerable position. You exposed yourself and Angela to people you are beginning to suspect of a crime. I'm not sure why you did that. And just so you know, if the President catches wind of this, the clinic is not the only thing at stake. You could lose your job."

Emma met the dean's eyes. "I know."

Emma walked out of Dean Munoz's office shaken. She'd expected the dean to fire her right then and there. She realized she was lucky. The dean had always appreciated her work and her work ethic. He wasn't going to tell President Ackerman about the situation with the LeFleurs and Angela unless he had to. But she had to be careful. The dean's message was clear. She couldn't screw up again.

Chapter Thirty-Eight

Emma's hands were still shaking when she got back to her office. The Dean was holding back his anger because he liked her. That made her feel even worse.

She would have loved to have gone home for a quick run and try to get her head straight. But she couldn't. She had a class at one. Plus, the judge's clerk had just called. He wanted to schedule a telephone conference on April 25, only four days from now.

The way things stood, Emma needed a delay, any delay. The farther out the judge set the trial date, the better. She wasn't ready, but she guessed the DA was. The evidence against Jeremy was overwhelming, and even though Emma had a few theories about who may have killed Sally, she had very little proof that would support a defense, or elevate Jeremy's 'reasonable doubt' argument. In fact, if she were on the jury, she'd seriously question Jeremy's innocence.

But she did have several other ideas that were worth exploring. She'd start with a chat with Becky.

* * *

Becky was available for the next hour, but Emma wasn't going to get her hopes up. Her goal was to persuade Becky to testify at Jeremy's trial and she was prepared to do all she could to convince Becky that it was the right thing. Unlike prosecutors, who could offer witnesses immunity, Emma couldn't offer Becky anything in exchange for her testimony. And serving Becky with a subpoena for trial could make her hostile. It was a dilemma.

Emma reached the other side of the bridge, realizing she was only a few blocks from the Wilcox house. She couldn't resist a drive-by. Maybe the NOPD officers missed something.

Several minutes later, Emma turned on to the Wilcox's street, taking extra care to park a couple of houses away. She squinted in the direction of the bungalow, looking for the LeFleur's white car. Seeing nothing in the driveway, Emma approached the house.

Ren was right. There were no signs of life. Emma walked up to the porch, and peered into the large picture window. The drapes were partially open. Emma leaned forward to get a better view, then felt an excruciating pain at the back of her skull.

* * *

Emma woke up to a high-pitched whirring sound. Surrounded by darkness, she attempted to stretch out her arm to feel the sides of the compartment she was in, but couldn't. Her wrists were taped together. And she'd been gagged.

Within seconds Emma realized she was in the trunk of a car. The vehicle jostled back and forth, and occasionally one of the tires picked up a pebble, and spat it back out at passing cars. Her neck was at an awkward angle, and the trunk smelled like gasoline. She was starting to feel dizzy, but she had to think quickly.

Whoever had knocked her out had made at least one mistake. They taped her wrists together at the front of her body instead of bringing her wrists back where she couldn't get to them. And, they'd used duct tape. She brought her wrists up to her mouth and began tearing at the tape with her teeth. It might take a while, but she knew she could rip it open.

She could hear a muffled conversation from inside the car. A man and a woman. She scooted toward the back of the trunk, straining to hear.

"What's your plan? That lady's on to us. What are you planning to do with the stuff in that bag?"

Emma recognized Holly's high-pitched voice.

"Clean it, and then bury it. Shouldn't be so hard to do."

That was Brad. Emma strained to hear.

"Bury it? We should just throw it all in the river. It would never be found."

"It's too busy there. We might be seen, even at night. But there are a lot of abandoned buildings—old factories, even old motels—along River Road. I'm thinking of that old refinery. The place's deserted. I haven't seen a car or a person there since it closed. I'm going to bury it all. No one will find it, and if they do, they won't know what it is."

Emma was still working on the duct tape on her wrists. She had ripped through at least an inch of it.

"That's way too uncertain for me. And I still can't believe you killed Todd. This is such a mess. Every time I turn around, your nasty temper is getting us in trouble."

"I'm not the only one who's killed someone, and I'm certainly not the only one with a temper. So, give me a break. Todd was a problem. We'd never have been able to have controlled the money with him around. He'd have lawyered up and fought us on everything."

The car was slowing down, then came to a stop.

"This is it."

Emma could feel the car turning toward the right. They were on a gravel road. It was much bumpier, and little pieces of gravel hit the bottom of the car, sounding like machine gun fire.

They pulled to a stop again. Emma heard two doors slam.

She bit down on the tape around her wrists and pulled, relieved when it finally tore. One more tug, and she was free. She pulled the tape from her wrists and stretched out her arms, searching the trunk, in vain, for a latch. Her heart raced. She was beginning to panic. She needed to move fast. They could be back at any moment.

Emma braced herself against the back of the trunk, burrowing her back between the two tail lights, and kicked the back seat. She kicked over and over, with both feet, praying the traffic sounds would drown out the noise she was making. Finally, she felt the back seat give. She kicked again, and the seat back cracked. She gave one final kick, and the back seat flopped over. Keeping her head as low as possible, she peered out of the back window. She didn't see Brad or Holly.

Emma crawled out of the trunk to the back seat, then propped the seat back up. She stepped out of the car, quietly closed the door, and started running toward River Road faster than she'd ever run in her life.

Emma saw the lights from a convenience store up ahead. She ran toward the light, ignoring everything but the thought of making it there safely. Minutes later, she tried to catch her breath as she spoke to the store clerk.

"Could I use your phone?" Emma was gasping for air.

"We don't allow customers or anyone else to use our telephone."

"I was just kidnapped. I need to call the police, please." Emma took a deep breath, trying to calm down so she could communicate. It was difficult. Her breath was jagged. She tried breathing in and out slowly.

"Oh. Okay." The clerk reached under the counter and handed her the phone.

Emma dialed nine-one-one and explained her situation to the dispatch operator.

"We'll send out an ambulance for you and police officers to the site."

"Could you also alert Detective Ren Taylor to the situation?"

"I'll see if he's working today and will let him know."

Thirty minutes later, an ambulance rolled up. A NOPD patrol car pulled into the convenience store shortly afterwards.

Emma's vitals and the back of her head were quickly checked by the EMTs.

"Could you drop me off to my car? It's just a mile or so up the road."

"Sorry, ma'am. You were hit pretty hard. We'll need to bring you in. Do you have a preferred hospital?"

Emma sighed. "Just bring me to Charity. I've got to check on a few things there, anyway."

Just then Ren drove up and parked in the convenience store's driveway. He did not look happy.

Chapter Thirty-Nine

"I didn't think I'd have to put you in another ambulance again, or at least not so soon. Are you okay?" He pulled her aside. "This is my wife, officers."

"Okay." The EMTs stepped back.

"I'm fine." Emma told Ren what had happened. He took notes as she spoke.

"So, both of the LeFleurs killed someone?"

"Brad seemed to admit that he killed Todd. I'm not as clear about Holly. I don't know what Brad meant when he said, 'I'm not the only one.' That could mean anything. He didn't speak about Sally's murder. But they both spoke about burying 'stuff' somewhere on the grounds of the plant."

"Go ahead and let the EMTs put you in the ambulance so they can take you to Charity. You could have a concussion, and you need to get it checked out. I'll be there shortly. I've got to talk to these officers."

Emma was released from the ER at Charity two hours later. She was shaken, but not injured, except for a huge hematoma at the back of her head.

Ren arrived at Charity's ER shortly after Emma. He sat grim-faced in the ER, waiting for her discharge. They hardly spoke when he drove her back to Todd's house to pick up her car.

Emma had considered not calling him from the convenience store and not telling him about her kidnapping. But she didn't want to lie to him again. Plus, she knew he was right—she needed to be more protective of herself. But she obviously had a hard time living within those boundaries.

"Thank you for coming out today and for taking me back to pick up my car. I have one more thing I need to check out. I'll be home shortly."

"Can we talk about what just happened?"

"What do you mean? I told you everything about what just happened."

"Yeah. Too late." He turned toward Emma, his face contorted with anger or sadness. She couldn't tell which. "I asked you to stay in touch with me about your plans, but you didn't. I asked you to be safe, and you deliberately put yourself in harm. You could have died several times over the past few weeks. I think you need to look at that, and you need help with it, too. I've told you this before, but it's as if you think your life isn't important. But so many people depend on you. Especially your boys, and me too.

Ren brushed something from his face. "I've bet my life on you, on living with you, and being with you until we're both old. I don't want to get short-changed. I don't want my time with you cut short because you stubbornly refused to be just a little sensible."

"I understand."

Ren shook his head. "I don't think so. You always say you're going to do better, but you don't. I think you need to see a psychologist and get a deeper understanding of what's going on in your head. I love you, but I can't sit by and watch this anymore. For our marriage to work, you have to make that much of an effort."

"Okay."

"Can't you say anything but 'okay?'"

Ren spun out, scattering loose pebbles as he drove away. Ren, the man who never got angry, was furious.

She would make an appointment with a psychologist like Ren wanted her to, but she was so close to unraveling the case. The answer was right in front of her; she could almost touch it. She couldn't afford to give up now. She'd call Dr. Washington as soon as she had some free time.

* * *

Emma was convinced that Brad had killed Todd, and from what she'd overheard, there was a possibility that Holly murdered Sally. She couldn't be sure. No charges had been brought against Jeremy or anyone else for

Todd's death, which meant the police were still investigating the case. She hoped that they'd search the grounds of the refinery thoroughly and would let her know what they found. She scoffed. That was a pipe dream. She was Jeremy's attorney. They weren't going to tell her anything. But, Ren might. If he wasn't too angry with her.

She decided to drop by Nancy's house on the way home.

* * *

Nancy answered the doorbell wearing an apron.

"Am I interrupting dinner?" Emma offered her hand to Nancy. "I can come back another day."

"Oh no. Dinner's in about an hour. Come on in." Nancy smiled and pushed a lock of hair from her eyes.

"I'm sorry I didn't call first." Emma walked into the hallway, then turned around to speak to Nancy. "Have you given the security tapes to the police yet?"

"Yes, but only one. I gave them the tape that captured the person walking down to the back door."

"You didn't give them everything?"

"No. That's not what they asked for. They only wanted the tape that showed the person breaking in with the key."

"I didn't look at all of the tapes, and I'd like to."

"Sure. The VCR and tapes are still set up in the TV room. Just find what you want to review and turn it on. The tapes are all dated."

Emma thanked Nancy and walked into the family room. She found two tapes which were dated March 19, 1997, the day of Sally's murder. She had never seen either. She popped one in the VCR and turned it on.

The quality of the film was poor, but Emma could tell that the camera was positioned above the front porch, and captured activity at the side of the house that was only partially illuminated by the porch lights. This was a different angle from the tape Nancy had given the police. Minutes ticked by as Emma watched the hazy video. Then she saw a blur as a figure wearing a baseball cap walked in front of the camera at 11:48 p.m. Emma rewound and stopped the tape, studying the features of the person who had strolled by.

Jeremy, Becky, and Holly were all tall, and thin, and had the same skin tones and hair color. The only distinction she could think of was Holly's haircut. Styled in a sharply angled bob, her hair was longer in front than Becky's and Jeremy's. It framed her face and dipped nearly as low as her collar bones and then sharply angled in the back up to the base of her skull.

Emma stared at the still frame. The baseball cap hid most of the intruder's hair. Then Emma saw what she thought was a shadow behind the right ear. She zoomed in on the photo. It wasn't a shadow. The camera had captured a lock of hair that had escaped the baseball cap and trailed down her neck, almost to her collarbone.

Several minutes later, a medium-built man entered the camera's view. His glasses caught the light from the front porch for a few seconds, and Emma could see that he was smoking a cigarette, the bright light of the lit end glowing as he walked. The man took a left turn and walked down the side of the house opposite to the driveway. Emma hesitated. She hadn't considered that two people could have been in the house at the time of the murder.

She popped in the second tape, which was even more difficult to see than the first. The camera in this video was directed along the back of the house which was poorly lit. Even though the moon shone brightly, Emma struggled to see. She eventually detected movement at the back door and saw a tall, thin person wearing a hoodie over a baseball cap. He searched under the mat, then entered the house.

Emma paused the tape. Nancy should have passed this video along to the police as well. It showed someone retrieving something from under the mat, and that's what they'd asked for. Why didn't Nancy give them this tape?

Emma reversed the video a few frames, then stopped it, capturing a dark figure reaching for the mat. Then she noticed something she hadn't seen before. Something dangling out from under the tee shirt. It was a necklace, a glowing, white necklace. Could that be the pearls she'd seen Holly wear?

Was it possible that this tape might be used to help prove Jeremy's innocence instead of his guilt? One thing was sure, if she wanted to use it, she had to get it to the police, as well as the DA.

She restarted the video and saw, in the foreground, a flicker of movement, then a man's shoe crushing something. A cigarette?

The man with the mustache and glasses came into focus as he crept to the backdoor and peered into the window. He stayed at the back door, looking through the window into the house for several minutes, then turned the knob and walked in.

Chapter Forty

When Emma got in last night, Ren had already gone to bed. And he left for work before she woke up. She'd never seen him like this before. He was unapproachable, furious, and hurt. She didn't know what to do. Except, of course, call Dr. Washington.

But she was also in a time crunch. The telephone conference with the judge was in three days. After that, she could call Dr. Washington, then sit down and talk with Ren, tell him she was sorry. Maybe three days would give him the time he needed to cool off.

She had awakened early to take Nancy's security camera tapes to the school's audio-video department so they could make copies. She planned to ask them to make two copies – one copy for her and one for the DA. The originals would go to the police. And she wanted one of the copies enhanced. Even though she couldn't use it in court, she'd like to see a clarified image. That would give her the confidence she needed to proceed.

She made sure the boys got off with a little breakfast in their stomachs and dropped off the tapes. She was back at the law school campus before nine o'clock.

But she was starting to panic. The security tapes had convinced Emma that Jeremy was innocent, but she didn't know if anyone else would agree. She wasn't at all certain the details on the tapes were clear enough to convince a jury of Jeremy's innocence. Even something as bright and white as a pearl necklace was difficult to see.

She and Angela were planning to file a motion to dismiss so she could get the tapes and her argument in front of the judge. But dismissals were rare in criminal court without the consent of the DA. And even though a reasonable DA might dismiss the charges based on the tapes alone, ADA Stephanie Manor wouldn't. She wasn't reasonable. She wanted a conviction. Nothing else mattered. Plus, she had plenty of evidence against Jeremy to convince a jury that he was guilty.

The tapes showed two people entering Sally's house on the night of the murder, but didn't show what happened once they walked inside. If Holly was one of the killers, as she suspected, the motive was obvious. She wanted to gain control over Sally's estate and over Jeremy. But Dr. Rayford's motive for murdering Sally was less clear.

Dr. Rayford was a stalker. Emma suspected Sally hadn't been the only patient he'd harassed, and that, at some time in the past, complaints had been lodged against him. That could be important, especially if Sally was one of those patients.

Emma flipped on her office computer and typed "Louisiana State Board of Examiners of Psychologists" in the search bar. When the website popped up, she clicked 'disciplinary actions', and there it was. Dr. Rayford's license had been revoked in 1996. He was prohibited from practicing because he had violated state statutes and rules prohibiting sexual harassment. Emma stared at the screen. Why hadn't she thought of that earlier? That's why he stopped practicing. He was a peeping Tom and a predator, and maybe even worse. The names of the patients who had filed complaints against Dr. Rayford weren't listed, but she had a strong hunch that Sally Wilcox was one of them.

Emma was also certain Dr. Rayford left cigarette butts along the back of Sally's house the night of the murder, but that had been a little over a month ago. None of the police reports mentioned them. And the cigarettes could have disintegrated by now, especially since it had been raining on and off for the past several weeks. But she needed evidence, anything which would show that Dr. Rayford was there that night. She'd run by Sally's house to check the back yard after her two o'clock class. She was only looking for Gitanes.

* * *

Emma turned onto Arabella, surprised to see a familiar-looking silver car parked directly in front of Sally's house. She pulled up to the curb and grabbed her notepad and a pen to write down the license plate number. She had no doubt that this was Dr. Rayford's car, the car that had been following her for weeks. But no one was in it.

Emma had a choice. She could continue her investigation, even though Dr. Rayford was probably in the back yard. Or she could drive home. She glanced down at her watch. It was the middle of the afternoon and a bright, sunny day. And it was scheduled to rain tomorrow, which would ruin any remaining evidence in the yard. She took a deep breath. She wasn't afraid of Dr. Rayford. She could outrun him.

She walked down the side of the house, tracing Dr. Rayford's steps from the night of the murder, scanning the windows as she passed, searching for signs of life. The house appeared to be unoccupied; she saw no movement and no lights.

She stopped at the corner of the house to examine the ground, stooping over to pick up a twig she mistook for a black cigarette.

"Looking for something?"

Emma started, but she wasn't surprised to see Dr. Rayford standing in front of the back door. He was clearly the man from the video.

"Nice to see you again, Dr. Rayford."

He took a step toward Emma. "I'd forgotten how beautiful you are." He took another step.

Emma stood and took a step backwards. She wasn't afraid of Dr. Rayford, but he was a creep. She was prepared to run.

"So, what brings you here? Playing detective?" He laughed and shoved his hand in his pocket, and pulled out a clear plastic bag. "Looking for these?" Dr. Rayford held up the bag. It held black cigarette stubs of various lengths.

"What makes you think I'd be looking for those?"

"Because I've been watching you. You think you're on to something. And you're curious, maybe a little too curious. That gets you in trouble, doesn't it, Ms. Thornton?"

Emma ignored him. "I know you were here the night Sally was killed. And I've got proof."

"You don't have proof, or at least not the sort of proof that ADA Manor would need to drop the charges. Jeremy's been violent for years. I knew he was from the first time I saw him. Ms. Manor needs my testimony. She's not going to buy any of your silly ploys to incriminate me. And she's not going to allow someone like you to step in and redirect the trial."

"I think you're wrong, Dr. Rayford. There were two people in Sally's house the night she was killed. Jeremy wasn't one of them, but you were. Was Holly there too? Did you and Holly act together, or did you kill Sally all by yourself because she filed a complaint with the psychology board? A complaint which detailed how you stalked her and harassed her." She hesitated, watching Dr. Rayford's reactions. "Or did you watch while Holly stabbed Sally to death? Did you enjoy that, Dr. Rayford?"

"You're delusional, and you just made it clear that you don't have a clue about what happened." He sneered. "Delusional disorders are serious. I'd be happy to recommend someone to help you."

"Goodbye, Dr. Rayford." Emma began to walk toward the street.

"You can go, but I'll always be able to find you, Ms. Thornton."

"Is that a threat?"

When he didn't answer, Emma turned around to see his reaction, shuddering when she saw the smile on his face.

Chapter Forty-One

Emma picked up the copies of the tapes, which had been delivered to the law clinic's receptionist. She was surprised to see Angela Burris standing next to her door when she got back to her office. She hugged Angela's neck.

"Oh, my God! I'm so surprised to see you! It's only been a few days, but it seems like forever. How are you feeling?"

"I'm okay. Just a little sore from the staples in my head." Angela smiled. "That was quite an adventure."

"Yes. One we can't afford to repeat. I feel so responsible for what happened to you. Are you sure there isn't anything you need?"

"No. You ask me that every time you call." She smiled. "It looks worse than it is. And please don't feel bad about what happened. No one could have anticipated that."

"Well, come on in. I've got to call Dr. Washington. Dr. Rayford is scarier than I realized."

Emma was relieved to see Angela looking so well. Except for a vicious-looking set of staples in her head, she seemed to be doing great.

Emma filled Angela in on her encounter with Dr. Rayford, then dialed Dr. Washington's number.

"Dr. Washington? This is Emma Thornton and Angela Burris. Do you have time for a couple of questions?"

"Sure. I have about ten or fifteen minutes."

"I have a few hypothetical questions about stalking and sexual harassment. Do you feel comfortable discussing those topics?"

"I've had patients who were stalkers and patients who were victims of harassment and stalking. So, I've studied those two behaviors. I feel pretty confident talking about them."

"Okay. My hypothetical question is about a stalker in the medical profession who followed a former patient for years, and he sexually harassed her as well. He peered into her windows, and it looks like he even sneaked around to the back of her house and let himself in at least once. This patient never complained to the police about him because he was also giving her painkillers. She's addicted to opioids, and it looks like the stalker was giving her large amounts of the drug.

"My question is whether a stalker-harasser is typically capable of violence? And by violence, I mean would you expect him to commit physical harm against the targeted person someday?"

"For starters, peeping into a person's house, for whatever reason, isn't a benign act, even if the Peeping Tom doesn't commit any other crime. And yes, stalkers are dangerous. They're manipulative. And they could be dangerously controlling, especially if they had information of a personal nature about the target." He paused. "It's important for you to know that a high percentage of women who are stalked are eventually killed by their stalker."

"Really!"

"As for a personality profile, stalkers are often obsessive in multiple areas of their life. Especially in their romantic inclinations. They often believe their targets belong to them and become so convinced they'll even invent details in their head about a romantic relationship that doesn't exist."

"What should people do if they're targeted?"

"They should communicate at least once, very firmly, that they don't want to hear from them or see them. But other than that, don't respond to their communications. That would only encourage them. If they threaten you, or behave in a way you could only interpret as dangerous, such as peering into your window, or breaking into your house, you'll need to go to the police."

* * *

Emma was shaken after her telephone conference with Dr. Washington. He didn't tell her anything she hadn't suspected, but it was frightening to hear his warnings.

It was already four o'clock in the afternoon, but she wanted to drop off the tapes to the DA's office and to the sixth precinct before it got too late. None of the police officers had contacted her about their investigation at the refinery site. So, she'd prepared a request for an updated homicide report on both Todd's and Sally's murders. If the officers found anything at the refinery, it should be reported there. She also needed to file a couple of reports.

"Do you feel like taking a drive to the DA's office and the Sixth Precinct? After all you've been through, I'd understand if you didn't. But I need to file a report against Brad LeFleur, for kidnapping and Dr. Rayford for stalking. I thought you might want to file reports against Brad and his sister Holly. What do you think?"

Angela nodded. "Sure. I'd wanted to do that anyway. I'm done for the day, and I'm feeling well enough. I may not want to run a marathon, but I can file a report."

Emma and Angela drove downtown to the DA's offices together. Emma glanced into her rear-view mirror. Dr. Rayford was following her again. His silver Ferrari was several cars back.

She dropped off the copies of the tapes at the DA's offices and headed toward the Sixth Precinct on Royal Street. As she was parking, she saw Dr. Rayford pull in and park in an empty spot about twenty feet away.

She and Angela walked through the double glass doors of the precinct just as Ren was walking out.

"You're looking so much better, Angela. I can't believe it's only been a day since the assault." Ren didn't make eye contact with Emma.

"Thanks. I don't have a concussion, so everything's okay."

"Angela and I are dropping off some evidence, and we need to give our statements to the police. Are you going home?"

"Yeah. But we need to talk."

"Angela, would you tell the intake officer why we're here so he can assign desk officers to take our statements? I'll be right with you."

Ren pulled Emma closer and spoke in a softer voice. "Look. I'm upset with you, and we need to talk about that. But I think we should table it until we have some time. It's silly not to speak to each other."

Emma nodded. "I agree." She smiled. She was so relieved Ren finally said something. Someone needed to break the ice.

Ren sighed. "Okay. Thought I'd let you know that we reviewed all active homicide cases today, and one of the detectives reported that new evidence was found in both the Todd Wilcox and Sally Wilcox cases. Those are yours, right?"

Emma nodded. "I've got Sally's case. Not Todd's. After I finish what I've got to do here, I'll get copies of the updated reports. Thanks for the heads up."

"No prob. One more thing. The officers who showed up at the LeFleur's house did an inspection of the place after you left for the hospital. They found a lot of medicine, all in Holly LeFleur's name. And they found her medicine schedule on Brad's computer. Seems he liked to make spreadsheets."

"Wow. Holly lied about everything. Do you recall the name of the medicine she was taking?"

"There were a bunch of bottles. I remember one was carbamazepine. Someone said it's for mood disorders."

She squeezed his arm. "Thanks." She nodded toward the window at the front of the station. "Take a look out there." She frowned. "That's the silver car I told you about. The one I think is following me around."

Emma let her hand stay on Ren's arm for a few seconds longer than necessary, testing the waters, pleased he didn't jerk it away.

"Do you know who the driver is?"

"Dr. Douglas Rayford. He was Jeremy's psychologist for a while and Sally's too. I'm starting to think he's involved in her murder."

"What? You should've told me about this sooner."

"I'm just now putting the pieces together."

"When you make your report, don't forget to let them know that Dr.

Rayford is parked across the street. They might want to talk to him, especially if you file the stalking report today."

"I think there may be more in store for Dr. Rayford than a misdemeanor charge." She squeezed his arm again. "I know you worry about me, but I think it's almost over."

"I'll stay here in the lobby to watch Rayford's car while you talk to the officers. If he starts to leave, I'll find some excuse to go talk to him. I can't believe he followed you to a police station. That was stupid."

"Dr. Rayford thinks he's above reproach. He apparently believes his own spin."

She noticed a desk officer walking toward her. "I'll be right back."

Within fifteen minutes, Emma and Angela were back in the lobby. Emma peered out of the large picture window, checking to see whether Dr. Rayford was still parked across the street.

"An officer is going out to speak to him. Angela, we need to stay here a while longer. If we leave now, he'll just follow us."

Angela nodded. "It's like watching a TV show."

Ren swiped the hair out of his eyes. "I'm going out there. I don't want him to leave."

"No, wait. You might scare him off. I'll go. I can engage him in a little banter. His ego won't be able to resist."

"Okay. But I'm coming out there if anything weird happens."

Emma approached Rayford's car, noticing that an NOPD officer was simultaneously exiting the station's side door. When they reached the car, the uniformed officer made a rolling window gesture with his hand.

"Hand me your driver's license, and step out of the car."

"What is this all about? I haven't done anything. I even paid the meter. I can stay here for another hour if I want to."

"A complaint has been filed against you by this young woman," The officer nodded his head toward Emma. "Other complaints have been filed, too, for stalking and sexual harassment."

Dr. Rayford sneered. "She's paranoid and delusional. You should be questioning her, not me."

CHAPTER FORTY-ONE

"Would you step out of the car, please?"

"I will not. I've done nothing wrong."

"Step out of the car, sir, or I'll be forced to draw my weapon."

Dr. Rayford huffed. Then shoved his car door open and stood, scowling, in front of Emma and the officer.

"Turn around and put your hands on the car." The officer fastened handcuffs around Dr. Rayford's wrists, then read him the Miranda Rights.

"You are under arrest for stalking and threatening Ms. Thornton. We also have evidence implicating you in another case. You're going to be with us for a while."

Dr. Rayford was led toward the police station.

Emma walked back to the lobby where Ren and Angela were waiting.

"Did you see that? Rayford was arrested. Other complaints had been filed against him, too. I guess there's a limit to how many times you can blame your accuser. It's a shame it took so long."

Chapter Forty-Two

Emma threw the updated reports on her bed. She was tempted to start reading them, but it was dinner time. The boys and Ren would be hungry.

She put a pot of water on the stove for pasta and started peeling a couple pounds of shrimp. The aroma of shrimp sauteing in olive oil and herbs soon filled the house. She poured herself a glass of wine.

Dr. Rayford would try to post bond to get out of jail as soon as he could. But she suspected that the police would hold him under the stalking charge while they conducted an investigation on the new evidence they'd found. She was anxious to review the reports.

Emma placed the shrimp and pasta on the table and called Ren and the twins. Billy and Bobby avoided eye contact as they trudged down the stairs and walked into the room. Emma's eyes narrowed.

"I can tell something's up. What happened?"

"Do you want to tell your mom, or should I?" Ren's voice was low, but he smiled at Bobby. Emma's heart began to beat faster. What had happened this time? Her mind clicked through the possibilities as she passed the bowl of pasta to Ren.

Bobby shrugged. "I'll tell her." His face turned a deep shade of red.

"Um. Today, Ren passed me when I was walking home, and..." He hesitated, glancing up at Emma. "I was, uh, I was smoking a cigarette." He hung his head. "I'm sorry, Mom."

Emma sighed. "I see." She paused. "Has smoking become a habit?"

He shrugged. "I don't know."

Emma frowned. "How many packs do you buy a week?"

"I bought a pack a couple of weeks ago. I don't really smoke that much."

Emma's face flushed. "Bobby. I've explained this to you before. The more you smoke, the more you'll want to smoke. You already know the hazards. Why are you doing this?"

Bobby shrugged and looked down at his hands.

Emma shifted her gaze to Billy. "How about you? Have you started smoking, too?"

"Not really."

Emma shook her head and closed her eyes for a moment. "So, is that a 'yes?'"

"Sometimes. I smoke sometimes. But not a lot."

"So, stop, right now. There's a zero-tolerance policy when it comes to smoking in this house. Your restriction, the one you're on for running around with James Skinner and Terry Mitchell and for drinking beer and smoking cigarettes, just got longer. Do you get that?"

Billy frowned. "That's not fair!"

"We'll never be able to do anything." Bobby's cheeks reddened. "How long do we have to be punished?"

"It depends on how well you comply with the 'no smoking' rule and everything else I've asked you to do. Like your homework and cleaning up after yourselves." Emma looked at Bobby and then Billy. "Once you're finished with your dinner, go back to your rooms to finish up your homework. We'll have dessert a little later. I'll call you down for that."

"I'm done." Bobby shoved his chair back from the table.

"Me too." Billy threw his napkin on the table.

Emma looked at Ren as the boys walked up to their room.

"What have I done wrong? I've always told them how awful smoking is, and how difficult it is to quit. It took me the better part of two years to stop. Are they doing this because I smoked?" She paused. "This is my fault, isn't it?"

"You're upset for good reason, but the more upset you get, the more likely the kids will dig their heels in and do exactly what they want to do. All kids rebel. Your kids are no different."

"But I smoked, and their dad had an addiction problem. I don't want them to take the same path. I don't understand why they'd be so drawn to something that's so bad for them."

Ren nodded. "Like a moth to the flame." He smiled. "Why did you start smoking when you were younger?"

"I guess I thought it was cool. A cool kid sort of thing to do."

"Right. And a little rebellion against your mom?"

"I don't know. Maybe. I can't protect them from everything, and almost nothing's in my control anymore. I feel as if I've lost them."

"You'll never lose your boys. You just have to help them over the hills for a few more years." Ren kissed her on her forehead. "This is a hill, Emma, and a small one at that."

* * *

Ren and the boys had gone to bed, but Emma stayed up late to go over the supplemental reports. She spread everything out on the coffee table, separating the reports into two piles, one for Sally's case, and one for Todd's.

Sally and Todd's preliminary homicide and autopsy reports each listed a knife as the murder weapon. But the knives had always been missing. Then her eyes traveled to the bottom of the page, to the supplemental section of the reports.

Two knives were discovered by officers as they were searching the grounds of the abandoned refinery after Emma's kidnapping. One of the knives appeared to have been taken from the same knife block that was on Sally's kitchen counter. And it was identical to the knife found in Sally's hand. One of the knives had been wrapped in a bloody plaid shirt, the other in a faded black hoodie.

The knives were buried together. Blood spatter was found on the shirt and hoodie. And all of the evidence, the shirts, and the knives, were to be sent to the forensic team for examination and more testing.

Separate addendum reports, dated April 21, 1997, were attached to the back of the supplemental report. Fingerprints matching Holly LeFleur's were found on one knife. Brad LeFleur's fingerprints were on the other.

The knife found in Sally's hand had been examined previously by Dr. Stephen Jacobs, who found trace evidence of blood on the blade belonging to a 'close relative.' The knife was sent off a second time for an analysis by the forensic serology unit. Hair and blood found on both the plaid shirt and the black hoodie were also submitted for forensic analysis.

The forensic team performed sibling DNA testing on Sally's knife and discovered that the blood on the blade was from a female, with a '99.5% probability of being a sibling.' Emma closed her eyes. She recalled a tiny cut on Holly's hand the first time they met that was beginning to heal. She didn't think anything of it at the time. But now she realized that Sally had probably nicked Holly's hand in an attempt to defend herself.

A sibling DNA test was also performed on the hair and blood found on both shirts. The hairs found on the plaid shirt belonged to a male sibling of Sally's. The blood on the shirt was a match for Todd Wilcox. The hairs found on the black hoodie belonged to a 'female sibling of Sally Wilcox.' The blood on the hoodie was Sally's.

Emma stared at the report for several seconds. The LeFleurs, who weren't the brightest of criminals, had made her job so much simpler. Especially Brad's decision to bury the evidence instead of throwing it into the river. The evidence found at the refinery clearly supported everything Emma had overheard in the trunk when she was kidnapped. Holly had killed Sally, as she suspected, and Brad had killed Todd.

But what about Dr. Rayford? She was confused that there was no physical evidence of Dr. Rayford's participation in either murder. She rubbed her forehead. She had been certain of his guilt.

But one thing was clear. The evidence against Jeremy was diminishing daily. The knives and shirts found at the refinery would easily raise a reasonable doubt about his guilt. If she could get Becky to testify, there was an explanation for the tennis ball found at the scene. Brad, Holly, Becky, and Jeremy all wore Converse All Stars, which weakened the charges against Jeremy. And finally, none of Jeremy's fingerprints were found on the murder weapons. And if his fingerprints could be found in the house, Becky would be able to explain that.

But no one knew where the LeFleurs had gone. They could have escaped to another state, or even to another country. They had to be found.

Chapter Forty-Three

The next day Emma slumped in her office chair as she opened her mail. She'd stayed up too late reviewing reports the night before and needed another coffee. She looked up when she heard rapping on her door.

"Come in."

The door opened, and Holly LeFleur stood in the entrance.

Emma jumped up from her chair, unable to speak for several seconds. "This is a surprise. I thought you and your brother would be out of the country by now." Emma could hardly hear her own voice. Her heart beat so rapidly it hurt, and her hands began to shake.

"Brad doesn't know I'm here. He was still asleep when I took the car." Holly's voice quavered.

"Take another step, and I'm calling the police." Emma's eyes quickly scanned the desk for her cell phone, but didn't see it. She began to feel dizzy.

Holly stepped inside Emma's office, closing the door behind her, clutching and unclutching the zipper of her shoulder bag. She sat down in the chair across from the desk, her hands visibly shaking as she pushed a strand of hair from her eyes, looping it behind her ear.

Holly's unsteadiness calmed Emma. She could handle anything if she didn't lose her composure. Emma picked up her desk phone's receiver, and sat back down, keeping an eye on Holly.

"I wouldn't do that if I were you." Holly nodded toward the phone. She unzipped her purse and fumbled with something inside. "I just need to tell you something." She swallowed, making a loud noise, as if all saliva had dried up in her mouth and throat. Her eyes seemed glazed.

Emma's heartbeat slowed as she stared at Holly's purse. Was she rummaging around for a gun? She took a deep breath. Her head was clearing.

"Why are you here?" Emma said, pleased that she sounded calmer than she felt.

"I told you. I just wanted to talk to you." Holly's mouth twitched.

"I'm a little confused. The last time I saw you, you and your brother had just thrown me in the back of your car. And that was after one of you hit me on the head and knocked me out. I don't think things would have ended well for me if I hadn't escaped. There should be an arrest warrant out for you and Brad soon. They may have already issued it."

Emma was trying to speak loudly so people walking down the hallway could overhear their conversation. She noticed that Holly was dressed in jeans and a black sweater, very similar to what Becky and Jeremy might wear. Except for her tiny pearl necklace. Her signature touch.

Holly hung her head. "I'm sorry that happened. But I really didn't want to hurt you or anyone else."

Emma raised her eyebrows. "That's a little hard to believe. You could have killed Angela when you hit her on the head. You weren't coerced into doing that. Brad was as shocked as I was. You executed it pretty well, too. Angela was out for hours. I don't think you're the damsel in distress you pretend to be." Emma paused. "And I don't like the way you threatened me just now. But, giving you the benefit of the doubt, why are you really here today?"

Holly began wringing her hands. "I thought I could live with myself and everything we'd done. But I can't. I can't sleep at night. I can't eat. My hands shake almost all the time."

Emma almost laughed. "I don't buy that. Why are you here instead of at the police station if you want to confess?"

"You're Jeremy's lawyer. I thought you could help me set the record straight. I'd like to be able to tell the police what happened the night Sally was killed. And," she paused. "I'd like to avoid jail time. So, if I confess about what Brad and I did to you and give the police information about Sally's murder, I was hoping that you could help me get all of my charges reduced? That way, Jeremy could go free, too."

Emma squinted at Holly. "That's interesting. You say you've had a change of heart, but what you're really interested in is a compromise. A deal. Your testimony for your freedom."

"I think that's a pretty even exchange."

"I can't help you. I represent Jeremy. I can't represent you, or work out a deal for you, and I won't drop my charges against you. And, if you really wanted to help out, you would have come to see me earlier. It's been more than a month since Sally was murdered."

"I was afraid. And I didn't know what I'd do if Brad was arrested. He makes all of the money. He pays for everything. I couldn't make it without him." Tears ran down her face.

"I'm sure the prospect of jail frightens you. But I think something else has happened." Emma glared at Holly. "What has scared you so badly?"

Holly looked down at her hands which were still clutching her purse.

Emma tracked Holly's gaze.

"Were you threatened? Threatened by someone who knew you were at Sally's house the night she was killed? Or are you trying to cut a deal before the police figure out everything you've done? Before they discover your role in Sally's murder? And maybe in Todd's, too."

Holly didn't look up.

Nearly everything Holly had told Emma since their first meeting had been a lie. She was good at it.

"You're a primary suspect in Sally's case now. Did you kill your sister?"

Holly shook her head. "No. But I know who did."

Emma narrowed her eyes. "And who was that?"

"If I say anything about that, I'd have to have a promise that I won't be prosecuted."

"You know I can't do that. You should be speaking to the DA's office if that's what you want, but something tells me they won't want to cut a deal with you either. Let's start with a simpler question. Why were you at Sally's house the night she was killed?"

Holly met Emma's gaze, then hesitated before she spoke.

"Brad knew that Sally's will and trust were kept in one of her desk drawers. He wanted me to find them and any other real estate or financial documents. He wanted to know how much she'd paid for the house on the West Bank, and he wanted to see who inherited what."

"Why did he need to know that? I don't understand. None of that would come into play unless Sally died." Emma frowned. "Did Brad plan to kill Sally so he could take over the estate?"

Holly hung her head. "He said he needed to know these things so he could make some plans." She shrugged. "I'm not sure what the plans were."

And there was another lie. Holly didn't even blink.

"Let's stick to what actually happened that night for now. Why did you go to Sally's house after dark instead of in the daylight hours when she was at work?"

"We knew about the cameras that surrounded the house, and we thought it would be easier to break in at night. And people are a problem on that street. There's always a gardener or a neighbor out working in their yard. They always want to talk. We wanted to avoid that."

"When you got there, what did you do?"

"I grabbed the key from under the doormat and let myself in. Then I turned off all of the electricity at the fuse box under that calendar in the kitchen and walked over to Sally's desk. It's next to that crazy bird, so the bird started whooping." Holly's entire body seemed to be shaking.

"Whooping?"

"He says 'you who' if he knows someone. He'd seen me several times and recognized me, so he started making a racket as soon as I walked in. I was afraid he'd wake up Sally, so I walked back into the kitchen, hoping he'd calm down. As soon as I got there, this old guy opens the back door and comes in. I almost screamed."

"How did you know he was old?"

"He walked like an old guy. And I saw his glasses." She swallowed again. "I didn't want to say anything to him 'cause I didn't want to wake up Sally. But about that time, Sally started climbing down the stairs. And I kinda panicked." Her breathing was shaky, sporadic.

"What did that man do when Sally walked down the stairs?"

"He ducked behind the kitchen island. I think Sally heard something because she walked into the kitchen and grabbed a knife. That's when he stood up and stabbed her in the back."

"In the back?" The autopsy report said that all of Sally's wounds were in the abdominal area.

She nodded. "Yes. I ran over to her to try to help, but he stabbed her again and again. I thought he was going to stab me too, so I ran to the front door and started to open it when he grabbed me and shoved me against the wall. He said he'd kill me and everyone in my family if I said anything about seeing him there. I jerked back real hard and ran for the door."

"Could you see whether Sally was moving at that time?"

"I don't think so. I'm pretty sure she died right after that first stab."

"Do you know the name of the person who stabbed Sally?"

"I didn't then, but I do now."

"Who was it?"

Holly sighed. "Dr. Douglas Rayford. One day, he almost ran me over in a grocery store parking lot. I yelled at him, and he stopped the car and got out. Someone coming out of the store knew him and called out to him to see if they could help. That day he told me that he was watching everything my brother and I were doing. And he still is."

It was difficult to sift through Holly's lies, but some of what she was saying sounded like the truth.

"When did this happen? Was it before or after Sally's murder?"

"After."

Emma paused. "You should know that I overheard you and Brad talking when I was in the trunk of your car, and I reported what I heard to the police. I know that Brad killed Todd. And I know that you and Brad buried knives at the old abandoned refinery on River Road."

Holly folded her arms across her chest. Her mouth twitched. She waited a few seconds before answering.

"We buried the knife Brad used when he stabbed Todd. And we wrapped

Brad's shirt around it. We also buried the knife Dr. Rayford used to kill Sally. Rayford gave it to me that night and told me to 'get rid of it.'"

Emma sat up straight in her chair. That was a lie. She shook her head.

"That doesn't make much sense to me, Holly. Why would he ask you to get rid of the knife? He could have easily dumped it in the river himself. Dr. Rayford wouldn't trust someone else to get rid of a murder weapon. I think you were the one that murdered Sally, not Dr. Rayford. And that's why you buried the knife."

Holly tilted her head and pulled out a gun from her opened purse. "I didn't want to do this, but I don't seem to have a choice. You know too much."

There was a soft rapping, and Emma's office door opened. Angela stood in the doorway. Holly's back faced Angela.

Holly glared at Emma and made a motion with her fingers across her neck. The meaning was clear. Emma was to get rid of Angela. Holly's gun was leveled at Emma's chest.

"Hi, Angela. I can't talk with you right now because I'm grading mid-semester exams. Can you come back later?"

Angela raised her eyebrows. "No problem. I'll come back tomorrow." She walked away, leaving the door open.

Emma hoped Angela had read the signals correctly. There were no mid-semester exams in clinic. There were no exams at all. Students were graded on their participation in their assigned cases.

Emma sat down. "Are you sure you want to do this? If what you told me is true, you might not even get arrested, especially if you help the police convict Dr. Rayford, or your brother."

Holly stood up. "That's enough chit-chat. I was hoping things would work out between us, but now I see they can't. I wanted to see what you know, and, like I said, you know too much. We're going to get in your car, and we're going to drive back to that refinery. I'll finish the job we started a couple of days ago." She motioned with her gun for Emma to stand up.

"Why don't you want to go to the police station and give them your statement? You may be given some leniency."

"No, Ms. Thornton. It's time to go."

Just then, Emma's office door burst open. A police officer and campus security guard stood in the entrance, their guns drawn and aimed at Holly.

"Put the weapon down. Now." With his gun still raised, the officer took a step toward Holly.

She laid the gun on Emma's desk.

The officer kept his gun aimed at Holly's head and handcuffed her. Then he grabbed his Miranda card.

"You're under arrest...."

Chapter Forty-Four

Emma sat down, waiting for the pre-trial conference call from Judge Quigley's clerk. It was April 25, the day they were scheduled to pick a trial date in Jeremy's case. But she and Angela had prepared and filed a Motion to Dismiss, citing all of the new evidence the forensic team had discovered—the fingerprints on the knives, the DNA analysis of the shirts—everything and anything that would point to Jeremy's innocence. But she didn't think the judge would hear motions until the day of trial.

The phone rang. She picked it up and waited for the Judge and the ADA to be added to the call. A couple of seconds later, Judge Quigley asked everyone to identify themselves.

"I've read the motion to dismiss filed by counsel for Jeremy Wilcox. I don't have a response from the Assistant District Attorney. Ms. Manor, to you have an objection to the motion?"

Emma caught her breath when she heard Stephanie Manor say, "No, your honor. I will agree to a dismissal of this case."

The judge gave Emma instructions about the preparation of the order and for Jeremy's continued placement at Charity. And that was it.

Emma picked up the telephone to call Katherine Green, still in shock at the turn of events.

* * *

Emma and Ren finished up the dishes while Billy and Bobby watched "South Park." The boys loved the show. She'd told them they were finally old enough to watch it, but the truth was, they'd worn her down. She was tired of arguing with them. There were bigger problems to tend to.

"I haven't smelled cigarette smoke on the boys at all for the past two days. Do you think they've stopped sneaking smokes?"

"I wouldn't count on that, but I haven't noticed anything suspicious yet." Ren wiped his hands on a kitchen towel.

Emma shrugged. "If they're still smoking, I'll be able to tell sooner or later. I'm not going to obsess about it." She smiled. "Promise."

"Glad to hear it." Ren draped the towel over the oven handle. "Want to go sit on the balcony?" He grabbed a beer.

"Absolutely."

Emma poured herself a glass of wine and joined Ren. She pulled her favorite wicker chair closer to the railings so she'd have a view of the entire street. It was her favorite time of day. The sun was setting, and the sky had a purplish-pink cast. Their apartment was directly in front of the Episcopal Cathedral, which stood silhouetted against the mauve sky, gargoyles keeping watch. The weather was perfect. Cool breezes gently blew up from the river. Traffic from below the balcony whooshed by, mimicking sounds of the surf and lulling Emma into a sleepy trance.

"I love it here. We're going to miss this when we move."

"Yeah. But it'll be good to have a bigger space."

Emma nodded.

"What's going on in that head of yours? I can tell you're thinking."

Emma smiled. "There was a pre-trial conference in Jeremy's case today to pick a trial date. But I'd filed a motion to dismiss, and, believe it or not, the ADA agreed to dismiss the case. I was shocked, but our motion set out new evidence, and it all exculpates Jeremy."

Ren nodded. "I heard about that new evidence."

Emma raised her eyebrows. "Really?"

"Yeah. From what I understand, Holly and Brad were both arrested, and they ratted each other out. Holly signed an affidavit saying that Brad killed Todd, and Brad said Holly killed Sally. I think they got it all on tape down at the station, too. And not too long after he was arrested the other day, Dr.

Rayford reported that he saw Holly stab Sally." He stopped when he noticed Emma's astonished face. "Isn't that what you're talking about?"

Emma sat back in her chair. "No. I didn't know any of that. No wonder Stephanie dismissed the case."

"Were you surprised?"

Emma nodded. "Yeah. I just assumed she was basing her decision on our motion. But she didn't have a choice after Holly's arrest and after she confessed to police officers. Plus, the evidence we cited incriminated the LeFleur siblings, too. No one else."

Ren turned his chair so he could face Emma. "So Dr. Rayford didn't play any part in Sally's death?"

Emma shook her head. "Doesn't look like it."

Ren frowned. "But he's a stalker, even though he's still denying that. And he admitted that he was at Sally's house the night of the murder."

Emma nodded. "Dr. Rayford isn't capable of admitting he's done anything wrong, especially about his creepier habits. But even though we've got him on tape lurking around Sally's house the night she was killed and then following Holly inside, he didn't kill anyone, He just watched. But he didn't help Sally that night, and he didn't report the crime for more than a month."

Ren shook his head. "Could he be charged with aiding and abetting the murder?"

"No. He didn't have an obligation to help. But he had an obligation to report her murder, and he waited until it looked like he might be charged with Sally's murder before he said anything. I'm sure he didn't want the cops to know he was there that night.

"He might be fined for waiting to report what he saw, but I doubt it. And he could serve some time for stalking. I could be mistaken, but I'd bet he'll only get a fine for that, too."

"He's already posted bond. So, he's out."

Emma nodded. "I need to follow up and file a motion for a protective order or a restraining order against him. That way, I'll have something to use against him if I need it."

Ren nodded. "That guy's sick. Get that restraining order as soon as you can."

"The dismissal of Jeremy was the best news of the day. The judge said he'd order Jeremy to continue his treatment at Charity until he can safely be released, and then Katherine will find a good group home for him. Second best thing of the day was discovering that the LeFleur siblings are going to testify against each other. So, that's it. Case closed."

Ren smiled. "Congratulations."

"I was convinced of Holly's devotion to Brad when I first met them. But it wasn't devotion, it was dependency. She didn't think she could survive without him. And, contrary to what she said, Brad was the stable one. At least he seems more stable than Holly. She's compulsive, rash, even manic. And manipulative.

"I suspect Brad was driven by greed. He wanted to control Sally's estate, and he didn't want to fight Todd over it, so he killed him. But Holly was driven by something else. Fear maybe. And jealousy, too." Emma shook her head. "None of that really matters anymore. The evidence supported their arrest and Jeremy's dismissal."

"What about Todd's case?"

"One of the knives had traces of Todd's blood on it. That same knife had Brad's fingerprints on the handle and the blade. They also found Todd's blood on the shirt that was wrapped around the knife. The shirt belonged to Brad. He had his initials on the inside of the collar for the laundry."

"That should be enough to indict him."

"That's right."

Emma's cell phone interrupted them. She ran back to her bedroom to pick up her phone.

"This is Stephanie Manor. I'd like to speak to Emma Thornton."

"Hi, Stephanie."

"Sorry to call you on your personal line, but I prepared the order dismissing the case against Jeremy tonight. The judge should have it tomorrow. I'll bring it by the court to get it signed. I'll send you a copy. You don't need to appear."

"Thanks, but the judge told me to prepare the order. So, I'd better do that.

I'll see you tomorrow."

ADA Manor snorted. "I'm just trying to save you some time. I'm not going to lie to you about something like this. I could get disbarred. And I see Judge Quigley in court all of the time. I can't afford to lose his trust. I might stretch things a little, Ms. Thornton, but I'm not going to commit fraud. You can come if you want to, but it's really unnecessary."

"Of course. Thanks." Emma hung up the phone and walked back to the balcony.

"I can relax tonight."

"I think you should relax every night. But, what's up? Who was that on the phone?"

"The ADA. She's running the order of dismissal through to the judge tomorrow."

"Wonderful. Now we can concentrate on the move." Ren grinned.

"I'm going to ignore you said that. But you did say we needed to talk about how upset you were with me. Although, I seem to recall you've expressed yourself pretty well already."

"Yeah." Ren took a deep breath. "We don't really need to talk about it all again, but I meant it when I said you need to go see someone about your reckless behavior."

"What you said earlier is that you think I'm trying to prove something. That I don't feel I'm good enough." She shrugged. "Maybe. But some things are just in my DNA. Passed down from my parents to me and from their parents to them. I'm not sure what to do about this legacy of mine. Everyone has something—don't they? Some nagging problem that gives them grief, or something that makes them feel insecure. I don't want Billy and Bobby to feel the way I do. I want these problems—this insecurity—to stop with me. But my kids are having the same problems I had. They're making the same mistakes I made. I don't know what to do about it."

"I'm no expert, but I think we'll all be okay if we all just talk to each other. Stay close. Make sure the kids know they're not alone. We're all we've got."

Emma nodded. "I know. Sally was alone, making decisions by herself about Jeremy. Dr. Rayford only made her feel worse. Her decision to leave her kids was a terrible mistake, but she thought she was doing the right thing. If she'd paid attention, she would have realized that they loved her anyway. They broke into her house to write her little notes. I'm sure stealing her painkillers was a way to get her attention."

"What's going to happen to Jeremy and Becky?"

"Thanks to Sally, he and Becky have a house. And, like I said, I'm going to work with Katherine Green and Roger Lewis. Katherine will work on the housing issues, and Roger will help them manage the money Sally left them. He volunteered to do that without charge. When Jeremy gets out of Charity, he'll probably go to a group home for a while. We'll have to play a lot of this by ear. It depends on how Jeremy does at Charity, if he is willing to comply and take his medicine.

"And Becky's over eighteen, so she wouldn't have a legal problem moving into the house Sally left them. The Shepherd's permission isn't necessary, but Katherine and I will speak to them about it. They never adopted Becky and aren't her official guardians. Becky said she's done with her 'Girl Friday' role at their house and is ready to leave. And there is no reason she shouldn't. In a couple of years, Katherine thinks we can look into moving Jeremy into the house with Becky. But we'll take a look at that then. Of course, a caregiver can always be appointed for him, too.

"So, they should be okay. Sally left them enough money for Becky to go to college and to pay for Jeremy's caregiver. Becky wants to enroll at St. Stanislaus for the fall semester." She shrugged. "We'll have to see what happens."

"And you're going to go talk to someone? And by someone, I mean a therapist."

"Sure. I've already got someone in mind."

Ren reached over and squeezed Emma's hand. "Good."

Emma nodded. "All I know to do is to keep moving forward. I think it's important to keep putting one foot in front of the other." She paused. "I really try hard, Ren."

"I know. Life's a struggle. But you've found someone you can struggle with. I'm not going anywhere."

A Note from the Author

The Legacy is a story about a young man with a serious mental illness who has been charged with the murder of his mother. It is not a true story. But it is based on true-to-life circumstances. While researching *The Legacy*, I discovered that across the country, there are more mentally ill people in jails and prisons than there are in hospitals. In 2004, there were 51,458 prisoners in Louisiana in jails and in state prisons. Of that number, 8,233 were mentally ill, but only 1,807 patients had been admitted to state or private psychiatric units. That year, sixteen percent of the prison population was seriously mentally ill.

I taught for a few years at a law school in New Orleans, and was the Director of the school's homeless clinic. During that time, I was asked by the school's death penalty clinic to interview a young man at a prison who had been sentenced to death for killing two convenience store clerks. They were interested in uncovering facts which could be used to mitigate his sentence. When I spoke to him that day, he had no memory of the crime. The young man and I sat in the same the same prison cell for more than an hour. He swung his feet, which were covered with pink fuzzy slippers, while he told me the horror stories of his childhood. I was impressed by his gentle and articulate delivery. Several months after our conversation he was diagnosed with schizophrenia, and was transferred to a state mental hospital. But he was lucid the day we spoke. His thinking was clear and even though he didn't remember his crime, he understood why he was on death row.

Several of the law clinics' homeless clients had also been diagnosed with schizophrenia. They preferred living on the streets, and refused to enter available shelters. After I retired, I did voluntary work with Atlanta Legal Aid, and learned how difficult it can be for a seriously mentally ill person to find adequate housing. *The Legacy* is inspired by the personal struggles of people I've met through the years, and is my attempt to tell—through fiction—their collective story.

References:

1. https://mentalillnesspolicy.org/ngri/jails-vs-hospitals.html
2. Haney, Craig, "Madness" and Penal Confinement: Some Observations on Mental Illness and Prison Pain," Punishment & Society, Vol. 19(3), 2017, 310-326.
3. James, Doris, and Glaze, Lauren, "Mental Health Problems of Prison and Jail Inmates," Bureau of Justice Statistics Special Report, revised, December 14, 2006.
4. Am J Public Health. 2014 March; 104(3): 442-447, Fatos Kaba, MA, Andrea Lewis, Ph.D., and Homer Venters, MD, MS, "Solitary Confinement and Risk of Self-Harm Among Jail Inmates."
5. Poythress, Norman, Edens, John, and Watkins, Monica, "The Relationship Between Psychopathic Personality Features and Malingering Symptoms of Major Mental Illness," Law and Human Behavior, Vol. 25, No. 6, December, 2001.
6. Wagner, Richard, and McKinney, Michael, "The Third Floor, Charity Hospital New Orleans Psyche Ward," Jean Lafitte Press (November 24, 2021.)

Acknowledgements

New Orleans continues to be my muse. Filled with as much beauty as decadence and decay, it's a perfect city for murder.

I would like to thank the following individuals and beta readers for their help and guidance in reviewing the book: Mally Becker, who not only read my book, but offered thoughtful commentary. *The Legacy* is a much better book because of Mally's insightful critique. Thanks also to Carolyn Jarboe, Rip Sartain, and Pat Pennington King for their thoughtful pre-publication reads.

Several others have also read *The Legacy* prior to its publication and have offered kind praise and suggestions. I'd like to thank authors Ellen Byron, Roger Johns, Valerie Brooks, Lawrence Keltner, Mally Becker, Lori Robbins, and Cathi Stoler for their time and their willingness to read and comment on this work. Their kind and encouraging words are so appreciated, and their talent and dedication to their craft will always be an inspiration.

Thanks again to the women in my writing group, fabulous writers, all: Dawn Abeita, Nicole Foerschler Horn, and Dawn Major. Their insight is invaluable. A special thanks goes to Dawn Abeita for her generosity, friendship, and her thoughtful critique and commentary on the book.

I'd also like to thank Dr. Howard Drutman, a forensic psychologist, and my neighbor, for generously taking an entire afternoon to explain the intricacies of certain serious mental illnesses in layman's terms. He is a kind and patient man.

I'm grateful to Harriette Sackler and the team at Level Best Books, including Shawn Reilly Simmons and Verena Rose, for guiding me through the publishing process for one more book. I am very lucky to be involved with this group. A special thanks goes to Harriette for her patience and expertise through the years, both of which I relied on heavily during the editing of *The Legacy*. Harriette, who is now retired, will be sorely missed.

Finally, I'd like to thank Leigh Revely Kellogg and her family for permitting me to refer to some of the remarkable beauty of her childhood home—a home that will always contribute to the elegance and unique spirit of New Orleans.

About the Author

C.L. (Cynthia) Tolbert's Thornton Mystery series incorporates her love of traditional mysteries and includes elements of the places and people she's encountered throughout her thirty-five-year law practice. Her experiences as an attorney, especially during the years she taught at Loyola Law School and directed its homeless clinic, continue to inspire her stories today.

Licensed in Georgia, Louisiana, and Mississippi, C.L. Tolbert's roots are in the deep south, though her stories are universal, with characters ranging from a young deaf man accused of murdering his girlfriend in rural Georgia, to a young homeless woman charged with killing the leader of a suspicious cult in New Orleans.

In 2010 C.L. won the Georgia State Bar Association's fiction writing contest, and, in 2020, following her retirement, developed the winning short story into the first novel of the Thornton Mystery Series, *Out From Silence*, featuring Emma Thornton. In 2021 C.L. published a follow up novel, *The Redemption*, a mystery set in New Orleans, which *Kirkus Reviews* called an "engaging and unpredictable whodunit." In 2022, the third book in the series, *Sanctuary*, was published. *Kirkus Reviews* featured *Sanctuary* in the April, 2023 edition of *Kirkus Reviews Magazine*, calling it, "A well-plotted nail biter with believable and sympathetic characters." C.L.'s love of New Orleans and murder mysteries continues in *The Legacy*, the fourth book in the Thornton Mystery series.

C.L. is a recent transplant to Austin, Texas, where she lives with her husband and schnauzer, Yoda. She has two children and three grandchildren.

SOCIAL MEDIA HANDLES:
www.facebook.com/cltolbertwriter
www.instagram.com/cltolbertwriter

AUTHOR WEBSITE:
www.cltolbert.com

Also by C. L. Tolbert

Out From Silence

The Redemption

Sanctuary

Printed in the USA
CPSIA information can be obtained
at www.ICGtesting.com
LVHW092347280924
792407LV00005B/904